His words were soft, like silk.

Polly gulped as his hand came to rest on the back of her neck, making her temperature rise. How could she feel so innocent and inexperienced? Yet when she was around this man, that was exactly the way she felt.

Polly realized that as much as she might enjoy Joshua's advances, she couldn't permit this to happen. "Joshua, I don't want you to think that just because we're friends, or because we went to the dance…"

"Do I frighten you, Princess?"

"No, of course not."

"You said you aren't a virgin. How long has it been since you've had a man?"

"Well, I… It's been a while. But I haven't minded at all. I'm really not a very passionate person." She nervously brushed back a curl that floated on her cheek.

"If that's so, then surely there would be no harm in allowing one kiss…."

DeLoras Scott was raised in Sutter's Mill, California—an area steeped in history. At one time it was gold country, and the legacy of wagon trains, cowboys and miners has remained. It's no wonder she enjoys writing about a chapter of history referred to as the Old West.

Recent titles by the same author:

GARTERS AND SPURS
SPRINGTOWN
ROGUE'S HONOUR

TIMELESS

DeLoras Scott

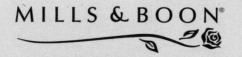

MILLS & BOON®

First published in Great Britain 2001
Harlequin Mills & Boon Limited,
Eton House, 18-24 Paradise Road, Richmond, Surrey TW9 1SR

© DeLoras Scott 1994

ISBN 0 263 82339 3

Set in Times Roman 10½ on 11½ pt.
04-0201-82530

Printed and bound in Spain
by Litografia Rosés S.A., Barcelona

Prologue

The Mojave Desert had nothing to offer but bare, rocky mountains, sand plains and salt flats where only burroweed and creosote bush could survive. The only evidence of man were the small clouds of dust churned up by the wheels of a prison wagon and the deep ruts it left behind. The lumbering vehicle looked like an enclosed cell with two barred windows on each side for air.

The four guards following the wagon on horseback were spread out. They had their hats pulled low to protect their eyes from the sun, and they remained slumped in their saddles, trying not to stir the heat.

The fifteen-year-old driver occasionally checked to make sure the mules were still headed toward the distant cliffs. The rest of the time he kept his eyes closed and periodically drifted off to sleep.

With the outside temperature well over a hundred degrees, the interior of the wagon was sweltering. Five of the seven men inside sat drenched in sweat and were forced to smell the stench of being contained for three days of travel. The heat was too suffocating to move. The other two men had slid to the floor, either passed out or dead.

The driver suddenly brought the wagon to a halt.

"Buck, what the hell are you stoppin' for?" the scar-faced man demanded. Clancy brought his horse alongside.

Buck tried not to show the panic he was suddenly feeling as he pointed ahead. "There's a sandstorm makin' straight for us."

Clancy saw the dark gray cloud stretched across the horizon. Gale-force winds were sweeping the desert floor. Soon it would close out everything, including the sky. "Put the whip across them mules' hides!"

"The wagon's too heavy. I can't outrun the storm!"

The other three guards rode up. "What're we gonna do?" Loge asked worriedly.

"Hell, can't you ever think for yourselves?" Clancy scanned the area. "Head for that outcrop of rocks we passed some quarter of a mile back. When you get there, throw your dusters over your heads so you won't suffocate. And make damn sure you hold on to them horses' reins and use your bandannas to cover their noses! It's gonna take all of us to carry the gold out of here."

The men kicked their mounts into a hard gallop.

"What about me?" Buck asked frantically.

"You're on your own, boy."

"You can't just leave! I'll die!" Determined to take Clancy's horse, Buck made a desperate dive from the wagon seat.

Clancy was too fast. He drew his gun and shot the boy in midair. After a quick glance to see how long he had before the driving hell descended, he reined his horse about.

Clancy laughed at the men inside the wagon who were frantically reaching out between the steel window bars and begging to be released. "Josh! Are you still alive? Can you hear me?"

"I hear you," a deep voice replied from inside.

"I guess I'm not going to have to kill you after all. I'll just let the sandstorm do the job for me. It seems more fitting. When I come back to collect the gold, you'll have already joined the devil."

Joshua shoved a couple of men from the window. "You're not going to put your hands on a single bar."

"Oh, yeah? And who's gonna stop—" Clancy's words were cut short and his eyes bulged. He grabbed for the knife embedded in his throat. His hand fell away and his eyes glassed over as he slid from his saddle and landed in a heap on the ground.

"Like I said," Joshua muttered, "you don't get the gold, either." He returned to the wooden bench.

Within minutes, the prisoners began to feel the first stinging sensation of blowing sand coming through the windows. They all knew that unless the devil intervened, they would soon be dead.

The panicked mules snorted and tossed their heads. The leader suddenly thrust its weight against the leather trappings. The others did the same, straining to free the wagon wheels wedged in the salt and sand. Finally the wheels moved, and with each rotation the team gathered momentum. The ball-eyed animals turned their tails to the wind. Gathering speed, they headed wildly away from the storm, taking the prison wagon with them.

An hour later, the sky was clear and the scorching sun once again shone down on the desert floor. Except for a dead mule's hide and some wood from an overturned wagon peeking out from beneath the thick covering of sand, everything looked the same as it had for centuries. The heat waves rising from the ground distorted the tall figure of the lone survivor as he walked toward the mountains in the distance. The offerings had been made to the gods, and the land was at peace once again.

Chapter One

Columbia, California, 1857

In the early morning hours, the town slept, and only the few muffled sounds coming from nearby saloons disturbed the silence. The night sky was already being brushed with gray, and houses and buildings would soon be showing their faces. But as yet, there was no one about to see the one-horse buggy moving down Washington Street. Though the vehicle was of a dilapidated nature, its well-greased wheels maintained the silence. And with the scarred leather top brought forward and the back curtain down, the driver remained well hidden in the shadows.

Dressed in dark blue so she'd be less apt to be seen, Polly O'Neil clutched the reins tightly in her hands. She hadn't planned on having to sneak out of town, but she hadn't planned on dangling from a hangman's rope, either. Contrary to what Henry Adam was telling everyone, she was innocent. She had not murdered his sickly son, Lester! Never again would she show her face in Columbia. It was better to be around people who appreciated her better qualities than those who looked for faults.

Not until she had crossed the Stanislaus River on Parrott's Ferry did Polly start to believe her escape had been successful. Nevertheless, when she reached the other bank, she headed north instead of west. Jake Hunter had told her that Parrott's road would lead straight to Angels Camp, but it was too well traveled for her liking. She wanted to be completely sure that she was rid of Henry Adam.

According to what she had been told, Sacramento was only 119 miles away. So what harm would it do to take a little detour? And it wasn't as if she didn't know the area. True, she'd only made the trip once—almost a year ago. And yes, they had gotten lost, but that wouldn't happen again. This time she was better prepared.

This time, she knew the sun set in the west.

At three that afternoon, Polly finally brought the horse to a halt under an old oak tree. She couldn't travel a single mile farther. She was hot, exhausted and famished.

She winced as she stepped to the ground. Every bone in her body was stiff. But at least she was being covered with blessed shade.

She glanced around at her surroundings. There was nothing but hills, dry grass, brush and trees. At the rate the horse moved, it was going to take a year to reach her destination. She doubted that they had even averaged two miles to the hour. Admittedly, the lack of a trail to follow, combined with not having driven a wagon in years, didn't help matters.

Polly unfastened the rest of the buttons of her velvet jacket. She should never have worn such a heavy suit, but white or any other light color would have drawn attention. Still, she hadn't passed a soul when she left town, and all day she had suffered the consequences of being overly cautious.

She slid the jacket off her shoulders. Feeling the cool shade on her bare skin was like touching a bit of heaven.

She had left in such haste that she hadn't stopped to think about a change of clothes. She couldn't possibly make the entire trip wearing the heavy velvet suit. One more hour of traveling under the hot sun and she would melt like butter. She needed a cooler dress. But there was a problem. Jake had tied her trunk to the boot at the back of the chaise. If she untied it, she would never be able to put it back. It was far too heavy.

Too tired to try to work out her dilemma, Polly proceeded to strip down to her percale pantalets and camisole. Making sure nothing dragged across the ground, she placed her clothes on the buggy seat. She felt a pleasing breeze that, until now, she hadn't even realized existed. She was tempted to remove her camisole and corset, as well. After all, she hadn't seen a soul since leaving the ferry early that morning. But she was no longer a dance hall girl. She was a lady, and a lady would never do such a thing. She had already pushed the boundaries by being half-naked.

Releasing one yawn after another, she proceeded to spread her bedroll on the ground and place the basket of food on top. But before she could do any more, she had to take care of the horse.

Polly frowned. Besides her clothes and lack of directions, there was another little matter that she had failed to take into consideration. She knew nothing about the beasts.

After a careful study of the contraption that attached the two poles to the gelding, Polly determined she could remove the harness-like thing—but then what? Would she remember how to put it back on? And how was she supposed to lift the two front poles and hold on to the horse at the same time? Better yet, what would keep the horse from running away? On the other hand, what if she left the vehicle attached? It would certainly solve her problem.

Having decided that the wisest choice would be to do nothing, Polly led the roan to the edge of the grassy meadow. She had been told to give the gelding feed, but that could wait. Ahead of him was all the grass he could want. And he couldn't be tired. He hadn't even managed a trot.

Five minutes later Polly lay on her bedroll, sound asleep.

Other than crawling under the blanket sometime during the night, Polly slept straight through until the following morning.

She sat up and stretched. Her full lips spread into a smile as she watched the sun's rays sparkle on the dew, still clinging to the tall blades of grass. The air smelled clean, the birds were in fine voice, and other than a bit of stiffness from sleeping on the ground, she felt wonderful.

Polly reached over, grabbed the basket and placed it beside her so she could indulge in a morning repast. She broke off a chunk of bread, took a bite and glanced toward the meadow where she'd left the horse. Surely he couldn't have gone far.

She sliced off a piece of cheese, then stuck it in her mouth as she continued her perusal of the meadow. Several times she had to lean back or forth to see the other side of one of the trees scattered about.

Another bite of bread followed before she slowly stood. The horse and chaise were nowhere in sight.

"Well, if you ain't the most fetchin' thing I've seen this morning."

Polly spun around. Luck certainly wasn't with her on this trip. Not five feet away, Sam Logan sat astride his buckskin horse. She had been concerned that Lester's father might follow her, but not once had she considered the possibility of Sam doing the same thing. She should have left town the day she'd found out the no-account gambler had returned.

"You followed me!" she accused, as angry at herself as she was with him. "You might as well keep going."

"Of course I followed you." Sam gave her a lecherous grin and dismounted. "Since you sneaked out of town, I guess you really did have somethin' to do with Lester Adam's death."

"If you were any kind of a gentleman, you'd turn your head at seeing me dressed so improperly."

"My, my, my. Haven't we become uppity." He reached out, jerked her to him, and gave her a bruising kiss before turning her loose. "If you're not nice to me I may be forced to turn you over to some sheriff for murder."

Polly wiped her mouth with the back of her hand. "Lester got into one of his coughing fits and up and died. But go ahead. Turn me over to a sheriff. At least then I'll be rid of you. I haven't forgotten that you left me for another woman. And if you're planning to step back into my life and carry on from where we left off, you'd best do some rethinking. I told you in Columbia that I wanted nothing more to do with you."

"Now that's no way to talk. I returned to Columbia just to get you."

Polly didn't believe him for a minute. Disgusted at the way he kept ogling her, she marched toward the meadow to retrieve her horse. A moment later she hopped back and plopped down on the bedroll. She should have known better than to go anywhere without her boots. "I told you to get out of here, Sam!"

"I hear tell that you got yourself some money while I was gone. We can be partners." He climbed back into the saddle. "And just to show you things are going to be different this time, I'll fetch your horse. Where did you tie him?"

Polly pointed to the meadow. "Over there." She pulled on a boot.

"I don't see no horse."

"He won't be hard to find. There's a chaise attached to him."

"Didn't you unhitch and hobble him?" The look on Polly's face was all the answer he needed. "I'll be damned. You didn't, did you? Hell, he could be twenty miles from here by now."

"Are you or aren't you going after him?"

"Of course I am. You know I would do just about anything to make you happy."

Polly grunted. "Of course, until you found another woman to take my place."

"Now there you go misjudging me. I'm a changed man, honey, and I know you still have that special feeling for me."

"Don't count on it."

Sam scratched the back of his head. "Now that I think about it, I'll bet you left Columbia because you couldn't convince the saloon girls that you'd got yourself a stash."

He chuckled with satisfaction upon seeing Polly's mouth tighten. "That's it! You tried showing off and it didn't work. Don't worry, sweetheart, I believe you, and that's all that matters. I'm the man who's going to double your money. From here on, you can stake my poker games. We'll split fifty-fifty." He rested his hands on the saddle horn. "By the way, just how much money have you got?"

"Enough to take care of seven generations."

"Sure you do, just like I'm fixin' to become president." Sam knew he'd eventually find out the truth. "Just make sure there's plenty available when I sit down at a card table."

Polly watched him ride off. He was so cocksure of himself. If it was within her power, she'd gladly put a rope around his neck and leave him hanging from this very oak tree.

Seeing her basket was open, she snatched up the lid and replaced it. Still not satisfied, she rolled up her bed and stacked it on top of the basket. She wasn't about to share her food.

Polly brushed the rear of her pantalets, then took a quick look to see if anything else needed dusting off. Satisfied, she raised her hand and shaded her eyes from the sun. Sam was already approaching the other side of the meadow. She leaned against the tree trunk and watched him ride on.

Returning to Columbia had been just one of many mistakes she'd made lately. Henry Adam standing in the middle of the road yelling she had murdered his son had been her welcome back to Columbia.

Sam had been right. For nearly two years she'd made a living by working in a saloon, and she couldn't wait to return to Columbia and show off to the other girls. She wanted them to see that she'd become somebody. She had even taken each one a gift. But neither her fancy clothes nor the presents had convinced them she was any different. As far as they were concerned, Polly O'Neil talked and acted the same as she always had, and would never be anything but a dance hall girl. They had even laughed and taunted her, but she didn't give any of them the satisfaction of knowing it hurt.

However, the humiliation turned out to be an advantage. Because of it, she now knew what she had to do. By the time she was finished, no one would ever accuse her of being in that profession again.

As if Henry and the girls hadn't been bad enough, Sam had also returned to Columbia. Why couldn't he have made his appearance after she had left instead of arriving at the same time? And of all people, why did he have to be the only one who believed she really did have money?

Sam. The man who had talked her into leaving her aunt's farm for adventure in the gold country. She had been so enamored that she would have killed for him. Being young and inexperienced, she had thought he was the most wonderful person who had ever stepped into her life.

Traveling from one mining town to another soon became tiresome. But like a fool, she had thought she was someone special because Sam always had her stand behind his chair for good luck. More than one man had tried to get her to leave Sam, but their words fell on deaf ears.

Looking back, it was hard to believe she even forgave Sam for the times he would get drunk and beat her. She kept telling herself that because Sam loved her, things would eventually get better.

Polly smirked. When they arrived in Columbia, everything had changed, but not the way she'd expected. After a week of losing, Sam up and left town with another woman. Polly had wept for weeks. And if someone mentioned his name, the crying started again.

Polly moved away from a circling bee. With Sam being gone so long, time had become her ally. She was forced to take a good look at the gambler. It wasn't hard to see that the only person Sam Logan cared about was himself. With that realization her attitude changed. Never again would she allow some man to lord it over her.

Sam came back into view, leading her horse. Polly shook her head in amazement. How could she have ever thought she loved him. He wasn't even close to being as good-looking as Chance Doyer; his brown hair was thinning, and he was short. Shorter than she'd remembered. Or maybe she'd grown taller.

"The damn horse had the chaise wedged in a thicket," Sam complained as soon as he was within hearing distance. "I had a hell of a time gettin' it loose. It's a wonder he didn't kill himself. You never were very smart, Polly."

"Don't start belittling me, Sam. It won't work anymore.'' Polly stepped forward and looked in the buggy. ''Where are my clothes?''

''How should I know?''

''I left them on the seat.''

''Well, they sure as hell ain't there now.''

''They couldn't have just vanished!''

Sam shrugged his shoulders. ''They must've fallen off while the critter wandered about. Who sold you that nag, anyways? He should have been put out of his misery years ago.''

''You know I never learned to drive or ride a horse proper. I made darn sure I got one that wouldn't try to run away with me.'' Why was she even bothering to explain?

Polly glanced where her trunk used to be. Even the boot was missing. ''What did he do? Drag the chaise against everything he could find? Even my trunk is gone. I have no clothes!''

''What difference does it make? I've seen you in less. I gotta say, Polly, at your age, you're still one fine figure of a woman.''

Polly's hands balled into fists. ''You make me sound like an old woman,'' she accused. ''I'm only twenty. But then you always were good at pointing out others' faults.'' She squared her shoulders. ''Well, take a good look, Sam, because this is the most you're ever going to see again. I'm not about to travel in my undergarments. Now you get busy and find my trunk and clothes!''

''Think again. I rode all over looking for that bag of bones. I don't intend to turn around and go lookin' for your clothes, too. And don't try sayin' it's all my fault, sweetheart. You're the one who didn't take the time to hobble the critter.''

''Things aren't so different after all, are they, Sam?''

''What do you mean by that?''

''You're not using your head. You should be nice to

me.'' She deliberately softened her voice. ''There's no way you can get hold of my money, and you know it. What do you plan to do? Follow me around forever? Eventually we'll join others, and getting away from you won't be a problem. If I wanted, I could even hire someone to put a bullet in your back.''

Polly was delighted at seeing the side of his mouth twitch. A nervous habit he'd always had. ''So if you want to be in my good graces, you'd best change your attitude. If you aren't going to fetch my clothes, I suggest you find trousers and a shirt for me to wear.''

''Now, that I'm willing to do.'' Sam didn't like the way the useless woman was giving orders, as if she were somebody.

Polly began loading her things back into the buggy. Obviously her threat had worked. She knew that until Sam had his hands on her money, he'd stick as close as flypaper, and maybe she could use that to her advantage. She knew nothing about traveling across country, so let Sam care for the horses and whatever else needed to be done. Then when she arrived in Sacramento, she'd get rid of him once and for all.

Sam handed Polly the trousers and shirt he'd pulled from his saddlebags.

Even though Sam was a small man, Polly still had to roll up the pant legs and tie a rope around the waist to keep them from falling off. The hips fit fine. The shoulder seam on the shirt hung way down her arms but, all in all, Polly was satisfied. When she had become wealthy, she had sworn she'd never see another day without being dressed to the nines from the time she left her bedroom. Yet here she was, looking like a waif.

Thirty minutes later, Polly again had the horse pulling the chaise across the land, but this time Sam rode alongside. He'd offered to drive, but she had refused. When he didn't insist, Polly smiled with satisfaction. For a change, the shoe was on the other foot. She was giving the orders and he was obeying them. She liked it that way.

The next three days of travel went surprisingly smooth. Not once did Polly have to fight Sam to keep him out of her bedroll. It was hard to believe that, to the best of his ability, he was actually trying to play the part of a gentleman. Even so, his self-admiration made it impossible for him to understand—or believe—that she wanted nothing more to do with him.

"Are we still headed north?" Polly asked the morning of the fourth day.

Sam turned in the saddle and looked at the petite woman. "You mean you don't know?"

"Well...I never said I did. But I think it's time we headed west."

"You think?" Sam's voice boomed. "You're the one who is supposed to know where she's goin'!"

"I do. All we have to do is follow the sun."

"Dammit, Polly, you're lost, and my supplies are startin' to run low!"

"I'm not lost! I'm going to Sacramento." Polly was feeling the familiar tug of fear. Not because of what Sam had said, but because everything was becoming too familiar. She'd become lost the last time she made this trip. She tried to shrug off her growing concern, but the fringes of fear clung tenaciously.

"To hell you're not!" Sam nervously glanced around at the terrain. "With all these pines we been seein', we're definitely in the Sierra foothills. But where in the foothills?" What bothered him most was that he couldn't remember seeing any trails. "Turn that crow-bait nag to the left."

Polly did as she was told.

"Better turn him more than that," Sam snapped. "You've gone way too far north, so we gotta head southwest." He had been a damn fool. He was the only one who had believed Polly had really come into money. What if he was wrong? And when she said rich, just how much was she talking about? A hundred would be a fortune to her. Why was he wasting his time on something that probably didn't even exist?

To add to Sam's aggravation, Polly insisted on sleeping late of a morning and stopping early at night. She said she got too tired to travel any longer. And then there was her horse, who seemed to have difficulty just picking up a foot and moving it forward. At this rate, they'd never reach Sacramento.

Sam yanked his hat off, wiped his forehead with the sleeve of his shirt, then jammed the hat back on. He'd already had his fill of kowtowing and listening to Polly whine about bugs, dirt, or anything else she could think of. And what about his personal needs? Being around Polly was quickly becoming more than he could handle, and the witch wouldn't even let him satisfy himself.

Though a little thing, Polly had the kind of curves that were made for a man to slide his hands over. He wanted to run his fingers through that thick, curly auburn hair that hung in an unruly mess around a face that was as clear and smooth as a lake at dusk. The combination would draw any man's attention. Even dressed as she was, she was prettier than when he'd first seen her three years ago. When he'd stopped at her aunt's farm for water and seen Polly digging potatoes, he knew he had to have her.

Enough was enough. He'd already made up his mind that if they didn't come upon a town by tomorrow, he was riding on. Polly would have to make do on her own. On the other hand, if she begged him to stay and was generous

with her lovemakin', he might consider remaining a bit
longer. But that wasn't likely to happen.

During their short time together, Sam had discovered that
Polly no longer hung on his every word, or wanted nothing
more in life than to make him happy. In her place was as
stubborn a woman as he'd ever had the misfortune to meet.

It was nearing noon the following day when Sam decided
the time had come to head in a different direction. On every
hill they'd topped, he had looked over the land for signs
of a town. He not only didn't see one, he didn't even see
any people! But he'd already decided he wasn't going to
leave until after he'd forced Polly to strip and pleasure him.
It was time to show her just who was boss. After what he'd
been through these past few days—plus having to leave
without any extra dollars in his pocket—she owed it to him.

Seeing what appeared to be large, overhanging boulders
ahead, Sam decided that was where he'd have it out with
Polly. At least there would be shade.

However, as they descended a hill, they came onto a
well-traveled road. Sam's plans and sour disposition
changed immediately. He flexed his fingers, and for the first
time in days, he smiled. There had to be a town ahead. And
if there was a town, there had to be a bar and a poker game.

Polly licked her dry lips. She was so tense she felt as if
she were sitting on porcupine quills. Her breathing became
shallow and rapid. Though she couldn't pick out any particular thing, the area was too familiar for comfort.

She kept looking…looking for something.

Then she saw what she had probably been searching for
all along.

The sign Welcome To Springtown.

An uncontrollable shudder shook Polly's body. She
yanked back on the reins, bringing the gelding to a halt.
She already knew every detail of the town that was

stretched out ahead of her. But it couldn't be! She had seen it all reduced to ashes.

Seeing Sam continuing on, she tried to yell a warning. But the words became trapped in her throat as her attention focused on the barking black-and-white dog that was running toward her. The last time she had seen the dog, he was dead!

Terrified, Polly jerked backward, but the seat prevented her from going anywhere. She yanked at the reins, desperately trying to turn the horse and chaise in the opposite direction. She had to get away! The hardmouthed horse paid no heed. He was too busy trying to avoid the dog that now nipped at his fetlocks. The horse suddenly lunged forward.

Polly's shrill scream sounded far away. She couldn't go back to Springtown! She leaped from the chaise onto the ground. Quickly she scrambled to her feet and started running, ignoring the pain in her ankle.

Then she heard the dog barking. He was coming after her! It was so difficult to breathe. Terrified, she started to look over her shoulder, but she tripped on something and pitched forward onto the ground. Then everything went mercifully black.

As Polly came out of her swoon, she was disoriented. Thinking it was Sam lifting her into his arms, she looked up. Suddenly she was staring at the face of a complete stranger.

He started walking, and Polly panicked. She couldn't let him take her into Springtown. She screamed, kicked and flayed him with her fists. To her relief, he lowered her to the ground.

Polly quickly backed away from the tall, dark man. When she was satisfied he wasn't going to grab her, she turned a quick circle to establish her position. But there was no welcoming sign, no town, and no Sam. "It can't be," she whispered. "I couldn't have imagined it!"

"Are you all right, madam?"

The man's question brought Polly back to the present. "Madam? How dare you! I'm no madam!" She turned on the man, prepared to give him a piece of her mind. Instead, she clamped her mouth shut and took several more steps backward. With one sweeping glance, she noted the vivid red scar on his right cheek. He was dressed in black, from the top of his hat to the toe of his boots. Even his hair and his horse were black. His lips suddenly twisted into a slow smile, and Polly could see that the devil danced in his black eyes.

"I made the comment purely out of respect for such a lovely lady. I assume you're all right."

"I'm not looking for nice words. I want to know where you came from." Polly was having difficulty trying to maintain even a degree of sanity. She eyed her horse and buggy. What were they doing here? The horse had been headed for town when she jumped.

Polly knew she should be grateful for the man's concern, but she couldn't shed the fear that still clung like the legs of a grasshopper. She wanted desperately to climb onto the chaise and leave, but to do so would require passing right by the stranger. She took a deep breath to fortify her determination, then stated, "You haven't answered my question."

"What question was that?"

"How did you get here?"

"I was riding this way when I saw you fall from your buggy. Did you hit a hole or something?" He walked over and began checking the wheels.

"I don't believe you!" Polly persisted. "Where is Sam Logan?" She began edging her way to the far side of the conveyance.

"If you're talking about the man on the buckskin, I saw him ride over that far hill."

Polly's nerves were too raw for a try at diplomacy. She placed her hands on her hips and stared him straight in the eye. "You're lying. I know you're lying. I saw Sam enter Springtown. Now all of a sudden, everything has disappeared. The dog, the town, Sam, and now you've come out of nowhere."

"I have no idea what you're talking about."

"You came out of Springtown!" Polly accused. To her horror, he extended his hand. She jumped away.

"Please, let me help you into the chaise. I'll drive."

"I don't want you to drive me anywhere! Now get out of my way so I can leave."

"Nonsense. Apparently your fall has caused you to hallucinate."

As if he had cast a spell, Polly suddenly became very still. Though her mind told her to keep her distance, her body didn't seem to want to listen. She allowed the tall man to take her hand and assist her up to the passenger's side of the buggy. After tying his horse to the back, he climbed onto the seat beside her. She watched his strong, capable hands grasp the reins. With the ease of a man accustomed to handling horses, he actually put the nag into a trot. Even the horse obeyed him!

Dark and brooding was the only description Polly could think of. And though he was lanky, she could clearly remember feeling hard muscle when he had lifted her in his arms.

"Where are you taking me?" Polly asked.

"I assumed you would want to go to the nearest town. That would be Murphys. It's only about five miles from here."

"How did you know about Murphys if you were traveling?"

"Well, I wasn't exactly traveling. I'm from around here."

From Springtown to Murphys was also five miles, which gave her all the more reason to believe he'd come from Springtown. Polly clasped a hand over her mouth to keep from screaming. There hadn't been anyone in sight when she and Sam arrived at Springtown. She wanted to ask more questions, but what was the use? He wouldn't even acknowledge where he came from!

Because she was having difficulty thinking, Polly squeezed her eyes shut, then opened them. It didn't help. Perhaps the stranger was right after all. Perhaps she had hurt her head when she fell. There wasn't any possible way she could have seen Springtown. It no longer existed.

"You must have had a rough trip. I'm sure someone as lovely as you prefers pretty dresses to men's clothing."

"Ye…yes, I do."

"Did you lose your trunk on the way?"

She had no trouble remembering that incident. She reached up and shoved her unruly hair from her face. "Yes, I lost all my clothes, but I'll have more made when I reach Murphys."

"Where are you traveling to?"

"Sacramento," she blurted out. "I have friends there," she said in a softer voice. "I'll catch a stage." She was certainly being unnecessarily informative.

Polly said little during the rest of the trip. Her companion talked about the area, but she paid little attention to what he was saying. He had a deep, pleasing voice that was quickly lulling her concerns. In fact, she was already feeling much better. And she was rid of Sam. Not only that, but she also had another man taking her to town! From Murphys, she'd catch a stagecoach to Sacramento. Lester's father would never have followed her this far.

* * *

When the man brought the horse to a stop in front of the Murphy Hotel, Polly could hardly believe how quickly the time had passed.

The gentleman climbed off, then went around and helped Polly down. "Is there anything else I can do for you? Do you need money?"

"No, I'll be fine. Thank you for your assistance."

"Are you feeling all right after your fall?"

"I'm fine."

"You might want to see a doctor. Nevertheless, if you don't need me I shall be on my way. Perhaps we will meet again."

"Yes, perhaps." Polly watched him untie his horse, then mount up. He tipped his hat and headed down the street.

The boy moving forward to take care of Polly's vehicle momentarily caught her attention. She smiled at him before looking in the direction the stranger had gone. He had to have turned the corner while she was observing the boy, because he wasn't anywhere in sight. How fortunate for her that he had been near when Sam Logan had left her stranded in the middle of nowhere. She hadn't even thought to ask the gentleman's name.

Chapter Two

Auburn, California
One Year Later

"Well, what do you think, Sable?"

The tall, black woman pulled her shawl tighter about her shoulders as she glanced around the barren parlor. "It's not as big as Mr. and Mrs. Doyer's house in Sacramento."

"Of course it isn't," Polly replied in a huff. "They have more servants and already have one child and another on the way." She glanced at the marble fireplace, easily envisioning the warmth it would give during the winter.

"How many rooms are there?"

"I believe the agent said twelve."

"I don't know why we couldn't live in Sacramento." Sable's voice echoed through the empty rooms. "That there's the state capital and you mark my word, Mr. Doyer's gonna make something of himself in this state."

"I'd rather be somebody in a small town than a nobody in a big town. And I didn't force you to come along, so stop complaining." Polly shifted her gaze from the torn floral wallpaper to Sable. "You might as well get used to the house. I've already bought it."

"You bought this place?" Sable shook her head. "I knew I should've been here. Whatever you paid, you got took, girl. It smells damp and moldy. And look at them rat turds on the floor. The termites are probably already at work."

Sable left the parlor and walked down the hall. "I wonder how much it's gonna take to make this place livable?" she said, loud enough to be sure Polly heard her.

Polly moved to the large bay window and looked out. Strange she hadn't noticed that there was nothing but weeds for a yard. At least she hadn't been so addle brained that she'd forgotten to ask the agent the two most important questions when buying a house. Were there ghosts and had anyone died in the house? When the agent had replied, "No," she went on to explain that a person could never be too careful. She had ignored the suspicious look he had given her. But after her experiences in Springtown, she knew the importance of making such inquiries.

Sable acted more like her mother than a companion-housekeeper. Nevertheless, Polly wasn't about to admit to the nosy woman that she'd purchased the house without looking inside. The place was big and impressive, which was exactly what she had been looking for.

Polly heard the stairs creak as Sable went up them. She straightened her shoulders and fingered the diamond necklace circling her neck. She was somebody now, and rich, rich, rich. She especially liked the last part. But now she needed a big house to proclaim her new station in life. She hadn't spent over six months working with a tutoress to turn around and live in some shack! After all that work, she wasn't about to sit back on her heels and wait for the world to come to her. She was going to meet it more than halfway.

"Miss Polly?" Sable called from upstairs. "Did you say the salesman told you twelve rooms?"

Polly pursed her lips, trying to remember just what the man had said. "Something like that. What difference does it make?"

"You can't be expectin' me to take care of a place this big all by myself!"

"Why must you yell, Sable? Come down here and we'll discuss it. A few minutes ago you were complaining about the house being too small."

"It appeared that way from the outside. I'm gonna look at the rest of the rooms."

Realizing how quickly the morning was passing, Polly moved to the dining room. The wagons would be arriving anytime and she had to decide where to place the various pieces of the furniture she'd bought from Mr. Breuner's store in Sacramento. So far, she didn't even know which bedroom she wanted.

After taking stock of the first floor, Polly went to the second floor. She made a mental note to have someone fix the stairs. They squeaked loudly enough to wake the dead. *Oh, I didn't mean that!* she thought. *I should never think such things!*

"Miss Polly?"

"Oh, what is it, Sable?"

"That man that sold you this house might've said there was twelve rooms, but I count thirteen."

"But...but that can't be. It's bad luck. I'll count for myself."

By the time Polly had a fairly good idea as to where she wanted the furniture placed, she was already regretting her hasty purchase. She should never have bought the house. The inside was a disaster. In some places it appeared that rats had virtually eaten their way through the walls. But that wasn't all of it. The wallpaper was torn, the wooden banister wobbled, and the pine flooring was warped in places, just to mention a few things. More importantly, there were indeed thirteen rooms.

"We can't live here," she announced to Sable as they finished their inspection. "Not with the house in this condition. We'll have to remain at the Orleans Hotel until this place has been properly renovated."

"That's fine with me, but you once told me you didn't like hotels 'cause they reminded you of the past."

"Oh, I was just talking. Pay no attention."

"What about the furniture?"

"I guess we'll have to pile it in as few rooms as possible, then cover everything with dust sheets. I saw an ad in the *Placer Herald* newspaper this morning, placed by Reed and French builders and carpenters. I suppose I should get in touch with them."

"This time you get all the right information before you go paying anything. And ask around to make sure they know what they're doing."

Polly's blue eyes flashed a warning at her companion. "I've heard enough for today. Maybe I didn't make a wise buy, but it's done and we have to live with it."

Sable started back down the stairs. "I know we gotta live here 'cause no one else would be foolish enough to buy this place from you."

Polly gritted her teeth. The woman never let up. She should have fired Sable months ago because of her loose tongue. But of course she wouldn't. Oddly enough, they got along well together.

"You know, Sable, I'm going to like living in Auburn." Polly strolled into the sitting room. "We're low enough in the foothills that we seldom get snow, yet high enough to miss the hot summers. I found the heat in Sacramento to be insufferable."

Hearing noises outside, Polly hurried to the front door

and swung it open. "The furniture has arrived," she announced gleefully.

"Them rats is also gonna be just as happy to see furniture as you are," Sable muttered as she followed Polly. "They can chew holes in the upholstery. And don't you be forgettin' to hire me some help," she called after Polly. "I told you, this house is too big for me to take care of alone!"

"I heard you, now hush. We have work to do."

Three days later, Polly waited impatiently in the sitting room for the man from Reed and French to finish his figuring. Her right hand rested on the handle of her umbrella, which stood as a cane. The other hand toyed with the red and white fold of her skirt. It seemed to be taking the gentleman forever to tally the cost of repairs. Though she resented having to spend more money on the place, there really was no alternative. If she tried selling it, she would never get back what she'd paid—assuming someone would even want it.

"Excuse me."

Polly looked toward the doorway. Her face lit up with pleasure when a tall man stepped into the room, his hat clutched in one hand. He had the looks and a smile that would beguile any woman. "What may I do for you?" she asked. He reminded her a great deal of the man who had driven her to Murphys a year ago. But of course that was impossible. Still, she felt he should have a scar on his right cheek.

"The name is McCreed, ma'am. Joshua McCreed. A black lady at the hotel I am staying at told me to hurry on over when she found out I was looking for work. She said you needed someone to make repairs on your house. I'm good at that sort of thing, and my fee would be a lot less than a contractor's."

Polly's eyes narrowed. "Have we met before?"

"It's doubtful. I wouldn't likely forget meeting a beautiful lady such as yourself."

"Are you from Auburn?"

"I've been drifting—following the Mother Lode and hoping to pick up a little gold dust. But I found myself low on money and decided to stop in town and see if I could get work."

"How do you know you can do it? You haven't even taken a look around." Polly wondered what was keeping the gentleman from Reed and French. He should be downstairs by now.

"There isn't anything I can't do when it comes to building and repairs. I'd be a good investment. A contractor could take you for a lot of money and not even do a proper job."

Polly thought he was beginning to sound like Sable. But what he said did make sense.

"And they would have to charge extra for material so they could make a profit off everything. I don't have to look around to know I can do the job without the extra cost. You can pay me a flat rate per hour. Then if you don't like my work you won't have money tied up in me."

"You do have a valid point, Mr. McCreed. When could you start?"

"As soon as I have the materials needed. A line of credit at Baker's would do just fine."

Polly wasn't sure whether he was all gab or if he truly did know what he was talking about. However, if he proved to be incapable of doing the work, she could always fire him. "Very well, we have a deal. I'll attend to the account on my way back to the hotel. There is a lot of work that needs to be done."

"In that case, I'll stay in the carriage house until the job is finished." He left the room.

He acts more like the employer than hired help, Polly

thought. However, she rather liked his logic and authoritarian attitude. He was obviously his own man. Of course she would have to make it clear that she was the one who gave the orders. And if he was as good as he claimed, her house problems would soon be solved.

Polly thought about Sable constantly telling her to ask questions. Admittedly, the one reason she had hired Mr. McCreed was his reasoning about saving money. Perhaps she shouldn't have been so hasty, but what was done was done.

"I have your estimate, Miss O'Neil."

Polly jerked around and stared at the red-faced man. His words seemed to grate on her nerves after listening to Joshua's deep voice. What was the matter with her? She couldn't even remember this gentleman's name. "Thank you." She took a quick look at the paper. "I'll give it my consideration."

As soon as the man had departed, Polly took one last look around the room. Once the house was in a proper state, the people of Auburn would realize how wealthy she was. Then they'd start inviting her to affairs and asking her over for tea. It was just a matter of time.

After locking the heavy front door, Polly walked down the stone pathway toward the fancy black carriage with red stripes and a high-stepping horse. A new acquisition that had cost her a considerable amount of money, and of which she was quite proud. No one else in Auburn had a barouche carriage. The green uniform the driver wore matched the cushiony interior.

The driver came about and helped her up onto the steel step. As soon as she was comfortably settled, he closed the small door, then took his place in front. "Take me to the lumberyard, Thomas. Then I'll want to go to the best mercantile store in town."

Polly opened the ruffled red-and-white umbrella and held

it over her head. "Oh, Beelzebub! I forgot to give Mr. McCreed a key. How can he start working if he can't even get into the house?"

"Did you say something, ma'am?"

"No, Thomas." There was nothing she could do about the key now. Mr. McCreed had already left. "Just continue on." She would return after she'd taken care of her business. She suddenly thought about her furniture. How did she know the stranger wouldn't steal a piece at a time and resell it? This could end up costing a considerable amount of money!

Though tempted to forgo the entire matter and direct her driver back to the hotel, Polly remained silent. She knew she couldn't back down on a verbal contract. When Mr. McCreed was around, everything had seemed plausible. Now she was already questioning her assessment of him.

Nearly two hours had passed by the time Polly returned to the house. The disadvantage to living at the outskirts of town was the time it took to get Thomas and the carriage ready and travel the distance. The advantage was the three acres that came with the house. She wasn't side by side to someone else's place like the homes were in town.

As soon as Thomas brought the carriage to a halt, she turned and took her first honest appraisal of the place. It was a monstrous disaster, cold and ominous in appearance. Even the turret looked as if it should be surrounded by clouds. Perhaps after it was painted, everything would look brighter.

Polly turned away. How could she have failed to notice this before? She had actually envisioned it as being a grand house where people gladly came to visit. And why did she continue to use bad judgment? Maybe if she would stop allowing her imagination to run amok things would turn out differently.

Not until Polly was about to put the key in the lock did

she notice the door was ajar. But she had locked it! It
squeaked as she cautiously pushed it open. "Hello?" she
called. "Is anyone in here?" The silence was overwhelming. With considerable trepidation, she forced herself to go
inside.

By the time she'd reached the sitting room, Polly realized
she was tiptoeing. She cleared her throat. At least with the
furniture stacked in some of the rooms, her voice didn't
echo. The place was still more like a morgue than home!
"Is anyone in here?" she called again.

After a quick inspection of the house, Polly ended back
at the front door. The place was deserted. She stuck her
key in the lock, then wiggled the handle to see if it worked
properly.

"Is something wrong?"

Polly was sure she had to have jumped a foot straight
up in the air. Realizing Joshua was standing behind her
didn't alleviate a thing. "Next time be so kind as to give
me a warning!" She removed the key and handed it to him.
"You will need this. Something is apparently wrong with
the lock. The door was open when I returned—and it also
squeaks."

"I'll fix it first thing." A smiled played at the corners
of his lips. "We certainly wouldn't want anyone taking off
with your furnishings."

"No, we wouldn't. I've established a line of credit at the
stores. I shall watch the account closely to be sure you do
not purchase anything that isn't needed for repairs."

Still amused, Joshua nodded.

"Have you decided where you will start first?" She suddenly noticed he had changed to a white shirt. The sleeves
were rolled up, showing strong forearms and bronzed skin.

"Yes. If you haven't anything urgent to do, why don't
I show you?" He held the door open for her.

Polly automatically glanced over her shoulder to reassure

herself that Thomas hadn't driven off. A silly thing to do, considering Thomas had to be every bit of sixty and wouldn't stand a chance against Joshua's superior strength.

Determined not to make a fool of herself, Polly squared her shoulders and went back inside. She passed so close to the tall man that she could smell the pleasing odor of tonic water.

After closing the door, Joshua led the way into the parlor. When he came to a halt, she almost ran into him.

"I assume you're eager to move in as quickly as possible."

"Yes," Polly agreed. The sunlight coming through the window made his hair shine like polished onyx. She suddenly realized she hadn't been listening to him. "I'm sorry, what did you say?"

"I was talking about getting rid of the rat holes, and putting the house in good enough order for you to move in."

"I don't just want the holes taken care of, Mr. McCreed. I want this house in perfect condition. That includes the walls, the floors, the cupboards, and anything else that needs to be taken care of. And before I move in, I also want the place painted both inside and out. If you feel that this may be too big a job—"

"Not at all." Joshua chuckled. "It just puts more money in my pocket."

"There's another thing I want done."

"What's that?"

"I want an extra room added to the house."

"Don't tell me you're superstitious."

"I don't know what you're talking about."

"It never occurred to you that there are thirteen rooms?"

"Of course not. And what difference would that make?" Polly glanced at her lapel watch. "I really must be going. I have other engagements."

"Although I am apparently barking up the wrong tree about superstition, I still want you to know you have nothing to fear. I'll protect you."

"Ha!" Polly headed for the door. "And just who will protect me from you?" Joshua was following behind her, and she didn't fail to hear his chuckle.

"Perhaps I should start the extra room first."

"Yes, perhaps that would be a good idea."

"On the other hand, it wouldn't have to be finished to already be another room."

Polly stepped out onto the large circular porch. "I suppose you're right." She turned to tell him to build the room first. She hadn't realized he was so close until she came against a hard chest. The contact was equivalent to being struck by lightning. She immediately stepped away. "I will be by daily to check on your progress."

"But of course."

"What do you want from me?" Polly suddenly asked.

"Work."

"I don't know that I believe you. Are you thinking to get me into your bed? If so, you'd best think again."

Joshua pulled a tobacco pouch and papers from his shirt pocket, and proceeded to roll a cigarette. "You don't hedge around, do you? Are you always so outspoken about such matters?"

Polly felt her cheeks flush with embarrassment. A lady would never have asked such a thing. They weren't that brash. "I apologize. What I said was completely uncalled-for."

"No need to apologize. You are a very pretty woman, and you do possess the most beautiful hair I think I have ever seen. It reminds me of cinnamon."

Her face gleaming from the compliment, Polly reached up and patted the cascade of curls at the back of her head.

"I especially like that hat you're wearing—and that is a charming town dress."

"Oh, really?" Polly purred.

Joshua sat on the glider swing and stretched his legs. "However, red is not your color."

Polly spun about and stared at him. "I beg your pardon?"

Joshua grinned. "You needn't get your Irish ire up, Miss O'Neil. You're a very beautiful woman, and there are plenty of other colors that would be far more complimentary."

"How dare you say such a thing to me! I'll have you know I personally picked out the material for this suit. What I wear or don't wear is none of your business. Make sure you stay busy working instead of spending your time sitting around." Piqued, she left the porch and headed for the carriage.

"Miss O'Neil," Joshua called.

Polly stopped and turned.

"I can wait. You are indeed a rare beauty that any man would be proud to escort around town on his arm. But I don't want just your body, I want your soul."

Not waiting for Thomas's assistance, Polly climbed into the carriage and slammed the door shut. She kept her back rigid and eyes straight ahead. Her soul indeed! Whoever heard of such a thing?

Thomas flicked the reins over the horse's shiny rump, and Polly glanced toward the porch. The swing was moving, but Mr. McCreed had apparently gone inside the house. She put the matter aside with sudden good humor. The gentleman certainly did have a way with words. He had criticized her dress, then he'd turned right around and told her she was beautiful. She wasn't sure whether she should feel angry or flattered.

* * *

Polly forgot all about the mysterious Mr. McCreed when she entered the hotel lobby and saw the attractive older gentleman sitting on one of the plush red seats, reading the *Placer Herald* newspaper. She had noticed him on more than one occasion. His name was Malcolm Sawyer, and he owned a prosperous mine some thirty miles out of town. He preferred staying at the hotel, where he had all the conveniences. At least that was what the desk clerk had said when she'd inquired.

On top of Malcolm's silver-streaked hair sat a gray derby. He had on an expensive gray sack coat and a red velvet waistcoat with a diamond pin stuck in the center of a black silk cravat. She was quite taken with his gentlemanly appearance, but unfortunately he never seemed to notice her. Though he had to be somewhere in his early fifties, he was exactly what she was looking for in a husband. There was no doubt in her mind that, whomever she chose to marry, she would eventually grow to care for him. Of course there would never be any possibility of love. The only man she would ever love was married to another, so she had no choice but to settle for second-best.

As she passed the prominent Mr. Sawyer, Polly was about to drop her red handkerchief when she remembered Joshua saying red was an unbecoming color. Could he be right? Maybe it made her look like a dance hall girl. She walked right past the gentleman. She wanted to look her best when she awakened Mr. Sawyer to the reality of her existence.

Seated in the hotel dining room that night, Polly again saw the illustrious Mr. Sawyer. As the maître d' proceeded to escort him to a table, it became apparent that they would pass right by her.

Quickly sliding her lace handkerchief from her sleeve, Polly conveniently allowed it to float to the floor. A thrill shot up her spine at seeing Mr. Sawyer's gaze go directly to it. But suddenly, the handkerchief was being dangled directly in front of her eyes. She looked up to discover Joshua McCreed standing beside her table.

"Dammit! In case you're interested," she whispered, "you just ruined my plan! What are you doing here?" She snatched the lovely piece of material from his hand as Mr. Sawyer passed on by.

"A man has to eat." Joshua pulled a chair out and joined her. "For such a little thing, you certainly know how to get to the point. You're going to have to learn to curb that tongue if you're planning on joining the ladies of society."

Polly knew she had to learn to watch what came out of her mouth during a flare of temper. Still, he didn't have to point it out to her. She could remember Mrs. Parker in Sacramento also telling her to watch her tongue. "You act as if you're an authority on etiquette, yet you don't even have the manners to ask if you can join me."

"That's because I knew the answer would be no, and I never have liked eating alone."

"May I take your order," a waitress asked.

Joshua flashed a devastating smile at the woman, and Polly watched the waitress's face soften with pleasure. Polly had to admit that Joshua's smile was most effective.

After giving his order, Joshua returned his attention to Polly. "Now, what was this plan that you accused me of ruining?"

"That's none of your business." She glanced impatiently toward the kitchen. "I hope they're not going to hold up my meal until yours is ready."

"Surely you didn't drop your handkerchief to draw the portly Mr. Sawyer's attention?"

Polly's blue eyes flashed. "What's so funny about that?"

Leaning back in his chair, he studied her for several minutes. It seemed strange, but it was apparent that she had no idea how beautiful she was. "Mr. Sawyer is married, princess."

"How do you know?"

"We have talked on several occasions. He asked me to work at his ranch."

"Why didn't you?"

"I don't particularly like the man. However, Mr. Sawyer did tell me he'd been married for twenty years."

Polly toyed with her fork. "Then why is he staying in town?"

"He doesn't like living at the ranch anymore."

"Why isn't his wife here?"

"She likes the ranch. They're at an impasse."

Polly raised her chin defiantly. "Then that's *her* problem. I've decided I want him."

Totally amused, Joshua shook his head. "You mean you'd deliberately steal another woman's husband?"

"Perhaps. I would treat him better than she does."

Joshua leaned forward and rested his elbows on the table. "And just what do you plan to do with Mr. Sawyer? He wouldn't be nearly as good in bed as I am."

"Is that all men think about? I'm thinking about husband material, and after twenty years of marriage, he's certainly trained. He appears to be of a gentlemanly nature, which is exactly what I am looking for in a spouse."

"You're looking for? You mean you're husband shopping?" This time he couldn't contain his laughter.

Polly glanced nervously around the dining room. "Shh!" she ordered. "People are looking!" She was grateful that the waitress arrived with their meal.

Not until Polly had devoured several bites of the delicious lima beans did her temper subside enough to say, "I have every intention of marrying and raising a family. What is so amusing about searching for the right man?"

Joshua didn't bother to try to hide his amusement. "To

begin with," he commented as he cut his steak, "once it was discovered you had deliberately taken another woman's husband, you would never be socially accepted. Besides, you have got too much fire in you to settle for a man who would do nothing but keep you sitting at home."

He took a bite of his steak, then took his time chewing it. "How old are you, princess? Eighteen? Twenty? You'd be much happier with a man who can keep ahead of you, and show you how to purr like a kitten."

"My purring days are over, Mr. McCreed."

"I happen to think they haven't even begun."

Polly stirred her gravy into her mashed potatoes, deliberately ignoring his comment. "Did you get anything done on the house today?"

"Nope. If you'll remember, you just hired me. I did purchase lumber and supplies. They'll be delivered tomorrow."

Polly tried to concentrate on her meal. She refused to converse anymore with him, knowing that to do so would only encourage his attention. She didn't want him assuming he was welcome to eat with her each night.

The minute Joshua swallowed his last bite of food, he placed his napkin on the table, shoved his chair back and stood. "Thank you for allowing me to share dinner, princess. By the way, that green dress is very becoming. Makes your cheeks rosy."

Dumbfounded, Polly stared at his broad back as he walked away. Joshua McCreed was the only man she'd run up against that she couldn't seem to second-guess. What came out of his mouth was never quite what she expected. Then she realized he'd left her with the bill for both meals!

"Excuse me, my dear, but you dropped your napkin."

Polly turned and saw Mr. Sawyer. "How foolish of me. Thank you very much."

"Since you are alone, perhaps you would allow me to buy you a cup of coffee?"

"How nice of you to offer, but I'm quite tired and eager to go to my rooms. Perhaps another time."

Polly stood. Damn Joshua. He'd ruined everything. Mr. Sawyer didn't even look attractive now. But she smiled sweetly, just as Mrs. Parker had taught her, then left the dining room.

Though she didn't want to pay attention to anything Joshua had to say, he had been right about one thing. She had no business breaking up a marriage.

Holding on to the wooden banister, she started up the stairs to the second floor. What difference did it make that she had lost interest in Mr. Sawyer? There were plenty of men about, and all of them eager to claim a woman. She'd just have to find a man a bit younger, not married and equally suited to her needs.

As she reached the top landing, Polly suddenly realized that something interesting had happened tonight. She no longer felt strange in the outspoken Joshua McCreed's company. Was that good or bad?

Chapter Three

"How's Mr. McCreed comin' along with the house?" Sable asked as she finished buttoning the back of Polly's dress.

"I wouldn't know." Polly ran her hand over her breasts to smooth the multicolored striped material. "I haven't seen him since we shared a table in the hotel dining room last week." She turned from side to side to check her appearance in the full-length mirror.

"How do you know he's doin' a proper job? How do you know he isn't buyin' stuff then reselling it and puttin' the money in his pockets."

"Since you seem to know so much about that sort of thing, perhaps you should be the one to keep an eye on him. Besides, I have other things I can be doing instead of dogging the man."

"Like what? You told me that there isn't anything more important than gettin' a place of your own and bein' settled in. If I go over there, that man's not gonna take orders from me."

"That's foolish. He takes orders from me." Polly picked up the gray hat and ran her finger over the delicate fabric roses.

"I think you're wrong. From what you've said about him, it appears to me that he lets you say what you have to say, then goes ahead and does what he wants."

"If you feel that way, why did you send him to the house?"

"What you talking about?"

Polly looked at the woman suspiciously. "According to Mr. McCreed, you were the one who sent him to the house looking for work."

"I never done no such thing! I don't even know what the man looks like."

"Well, I'll be! Are you sure?"

"Of course I'm sure."

Polly tossed the hat onto the bed. "Grab your shawl and come along, Sable. We're going to confront Mr. McCreed and find out just what he's up to." Without waiting, Polly marched out of the hotel room.

When they arrived at the house, Polly was furious to see the front door once again standing open. There weren't even any sounds of labor coming from inside.

Polly entered, with Sable right behind her.

"The man has no respect for property," Polly complained angrily as she started peeking in each room. "At least not my property! And just where is he? Hiding?"

"Mr. McCreed?" Polly paused, listening for an answer. "Anyone could have walked into this house and taken off with everything I own! Mr. McCreed!" she yelled. "No wonder he wanted to be paid by the hour. That way he can sit around and do nothing!"

"Look here, Miss Polly," Sable said when they'd returned to the sitting room. "No rat holes! He's been busy."

Polly spun around and took a step forward. The floor suddenly gave way, and her right leg went straight down through the boards, pitching her forward. Her hands burned as they slapped the floor. But it was her hands and knee that allowed her to hold herself up.

"Miss Polly! Are you all right?"

"Of course I'm not all right." Polly tried pulling her leg out, but the sharp edges of the splintered wood dug into her flesh. "Sable, come here and see if you can do something to help me out of this mess."

"If I get too close, I might fall in."

"Get over here, now!"

Sable cautiously made her way to Polly's side.

"Maybe if you put your arms under mine, you could pull me out." Polly tried raising up on her knee, but it was too painful. "I've changed my mind. Instead of trying to help, go get Thomas. He can at least fetch someone."

Sable had no sooner left the room than Polly heard a loud bang. "Sable?" she called.

"Thomas is not out front, Miss Polly," Sable said as she hurried back into the room.

"But I told him to wait!"

"That isn't all. The front door slammed shut and I can't get it open. What are we gonna do now, Miss Polly?"

Hearing the quiver in Sable's voice, Polly felt guilty about barking at her. "Now just calm down, Sable," Polly said soothingly. "Everything is going to be fine. How could the front door have locked? Oh well, it doesn't matter. Try the back door. Maybe Mr. McCreed is in the carriage house. That's where he's staying while he works on the house."

"I'll go look. Miss Polly, doesn't it seem awful cold in here to you? I don't know how that can be with it so hot outside."

Polly realized Sable was right. She nervously glanced toward the windows. At least there was a degree of comfort at seeing sunlight shining through the glass. "Sable, you call for Mr. McCreed from the doorway, and if he doesn't

answer, you get right back here. I don't want to be alone
any longer than necessary.'' She watched Sable turn to
leave. ''Oh, and hold the door this time so that it doesn't
shut on you.''

Polly closed her eyes and let her chin rest against her
chest. Though she couldn't tell Sable her concerns, she was
inclined to think there were demons at work here. Of course
that was nonsense. Still, she had to bite her bottom lip to
keep from calling Sable back into the room.

Polly had no trouble recognizing the old fear that was
already creeping up her spine. Cold rooms made her think
of ghosts and Springtown. Both of which she had hoped
never to have to deal with again.

At least ten minutes passed without a sound from Sable.
Polly forced herself to take several deep breaths. She was
sure her lungs hadn't functioned from the time Sable had
left. What could the confounded woman possibly be doing
that would take so long?

Polly stayed as still as possible, listening for any strange
noises. She hadn't realized that the house creaked. It
creaked a lot! She'd been afraid of demons since she was
a child living with her grandmother in West Virginia. The
wrinkled old woman was always warning her of the evil
that lurked in the night. Then when her grandmother died
and she went to live with her aunt, it was the same thing.
Aunt Agnes would say, ''It's never wise to leave the house
at night because you never know what is waiting for you
outside.'' It was no wonder her thoughts tended to turn in
that direction.

Polly again tried to shift her position, but a painful stab
settled her back down. Being uncomfortable didn't help
matters. And if a ghost— She refused to think about it.

Polly jerked her head up and listened. Were those footsteps she'd heard? She wanted to call out and ask who was
there, but her mouth had become too dry. It couldn't be

Sable. She didn't walk that heavily. The footsteps grew louder. Someone was coming down the hallway—in her direction.

Teetering on the edge of hysteria, Polly was prepared to yank her leg out of the hole, no matter what the consequences.

"Miss O'Neil? What room are you in?"

Polly could think of nothing more wonderful than the sound of Mr. McCreed's deep voice.

"She's in the sitting room," Polly heard Sable reply.

Just thinking about how close she'd come to tearing a gash in her leg made Polly feel queasy. Would she ever learn to keep a control on her imagination? Why did she allow herself to become so emotional? She should have learned her lesson in Springtown—or maybe she was like that because of Springtown.

Polly was overcome with relief when Joshua stepped into the room. His large frame momentarily filled the doorway, blocking Sable, who shuffled in behind him. Polly was about to ask Sable why she looked so peaked, but Joshua spoke up.

"Miss O'Neil," he said, shaking his head, "how am I ever going to get this place patched up if you make more holes?"

"This isn't funny, Mr. McCreed. You probably made the hole in the floor so you'd have more work to charge me for."

"Now, now, you accuse me falsely. I'll pull you out."

Polly's face turned ashen. "No! There are several pieces of wood pressed against my leg. I've tried moving, but they cut into my flesh."

Joshua knelt beside her. He tried to move her many petticoats and skirt aside to see the problem, but they kept getting in the way. "Please forgive me," he said with a smile, "but I'll have to reach under your clothing to feel what kind of a situation we're faced with."

"But…" she protested.

"How am I going to know how to get you free?"

Polly gulped. "Very well, but don't you dare let your hand linger."

Joshua chuckled. "I'll try to be as quick as possible."

Polly suddenly wondered if he knew her past profession. Perhaps it was his ornery expression she'd seen on more than one occasion. She felt his hand brush her leg, and was shocked at the sensation it caused. It had been a long time since she'd shared a man's pleasure.

Joshua straightened up, sat back on his heels and slowly shook his head. "That wood is as solid as the day it was put in here. I don't understand how your foot could have gone through it."

"Can you get me out?"

Joshua thought a moment. "If I try breaking the wood to make a bigger hole, your leg would get cut even worse."

"What do you mean worse? Am I cut?"

"You can't feel it?"

"No. Just a burning sensation."

"Good. That means the cuts aren't very deep, though I can't understand how you kept from—well, it doesn't matter." He stood.

"What did you start to say?"

"I was only going to say that you're a lucky woman. You should have one deep gash from your ankle all the way to your hip."

"Mr. McCreed, you're going to have to think of something soon. I can't stay in this position forever."

Joshua beckoned Sable forward with his finger. "You're going to have to get Miss O'Neil's clothes off."

"What?" Polly screeched. "She'll do no such thing!"

"I have to see what I'm doing. Or perhaps you can come up with a better idea as to how I'm going to free you."

Polly turned her head and stared at the booted feet positioned near her hand. "I probably can," she lied. Her mind was blank. "However, you tell me your idea first."

"I can't use a saw because there isn't enough room."

"Right. I thought about that, too."

"And if I try breaking off the wood, you could be badly injured."

"Would you just answer the question?"

"I'm going to make another hole and saw toward the one you're caught in. The point being, no matter what option I choose, I still can't see without you removing your dress. I'm willing to listen to any other suggestions you may have."

Polly knew her fate was sealed. "Come over here, Sable, and get this dress off," she finally conceded.

"It's going to take the two of us to accomplish it," Joshua stated casually.

"Why?" Polly demanded.

"Because one of us has to hold you up while the other attends to the clothing. Considering how much you have on, I seriously doubt that Sable can take care of it by herself. Besides, it will temporarily take the pressure off your arms."

Polly was actually experiencing embarrassment as the pair set about unbuttoning her dress. Whoever heard of having to be undressed while on hands and knee? Joshua certainly wasn't inhibited with embarrassment. He acted as if this were a task he did daily!

Polly felt the material around her bodice become slack. Surely he didn't intend to undress her all the way to her bare skin?

"All right, Sable," Joshua said, "let's push as much as

we can past her waist. Then I'll lift her and you'll have to
pull everything over her head.''

Polly was mortified. Her backside suddenly became cool,
and material went flying over her head, making her feel as
if she had just been shoved into a tunnel. Then a strong
arm wrapped around her waist and her hands were lifted
just a fraction off the floor, relieving the strain.

At last the clothes were off, and Polly was left with only
her undergarments. In the process of undressing, her hair
had come loose from its confinement and now hung in her
face. She had to look a sight. What good was all of Mrs.
Parker's tutoring if this was the end result? Joshua would
never be able to think of her as a lady again. Polly swallowed a giggle. And what about the seamstress, Miss Baxter? She would have fainted dead away if she had witnessed
all of this.

''Put your hands back down, Polly.''

Reluctantly she did as she was told.

''Sable, go see if you can find pillows, blankets, or anything else for Miss O'Neil to lie on so she can take the
weight off her arms.''

Joshua looked down at the beauty and smiled. With her
thick auburn hair hanging loose and a figure that any
woman would be proud to possess, Polly O'Neil presented
a very tempting picture. ''I'll go get the tools I'll need.''

Polly realized that Joshua had qualities she definitely
liked. Besides seeing to her comfort, he hadn't made a single snide remark about her unfortunate circumstances.
More importantly, she delighted in being treated like a lady.

By the time Sable had the blankets and pillows stuffed
under her so she could relax, Polly was exhausted. She
closed her eyes, perfectly willing to take a nap.

''Miss Polly, I have to tell you something before Mr.
Joshua returns,'' Sable whispered.

Polly opened one eye and found Sable's face right in front of hers. "This had better be important."

"The back door was locked. I tried every which way I could to get it open, but it wouldn't budge. Then just when I'd given up, the doorknob turned and Mr. Joshua walked right in. It wasn't natural, Miss Polly."

"Don't be silly. He probably already had a key in the lock."

"I didn't see no key."

"He could have put it in his pocket."

"I would have heard the lock turn."

"You were too busy worrying to hear it!"

"It's not natural. Maybe he's the devil."

"That's not so. Touch him. Believe me, he's as real as you and I. Shh. I hear him returning."

"All right, ladies, let's get this over with." Joshua placed the tools he'd collected on the floor.

"How long do you think this is going to take?" Polly asked.

"Are you in a hurry to go somewhere?" Using a brace and bit, he began drilling a hole in the floor nearly a foot away from where Polly was stuck.

Seeing how Sable had plastered herself against the wall, Polly suddenly remembered the reason for being here. "Mr. McCreed, as soon as you get me out of this predicament, you're fired!"

Wringing her hands, Sable inched away from the wall. "Miss Polly, I don't think this is the right time to be sayin' such things."

"I don't sneak around or lie like some people I've had the misfortune to meet." Polly's blue eyes flashed with indignation. "Even if it means having to find someone else to get me loose."

Joshua stopped the drilling and looked up. "Apparently you are talking about me. Have I done something wrong?"

Polly carefully adjusted one of the pillows to make herself more comfortable. "Since Sable has never laid eyes on you until today, it's not very likely she sent you to me for a job."

Joshua rolled off his knees and sat on the floor. "Can you blame me? I needed work. I also knew I could save you money and you'd end up with a better quality of work." He smiled. "You wouldn't have even talked to me if I hadn't mentioned Sable."

"How did you know her name or that the house needed repairs?" Polly asked suspiciously.

Joshua chuckled. "I saw the two of you at the hotel, and the man at the desk likes to gossip."

Polly knew that to be the truth. The same man had told her about Mr. Sawyer. She shifted her gaze back to Sable. At least some coloring had returned to her face. Strange, even the chill had left the room.

"When I get you out of the hole, I'll show you the repairs I've already made. Then perhaps you'll decide to keep me on. Come here, Sable, and stand on this plank to be sure it doesn't move while I saw the wood."

Sable hurried forward, but her furrowed brow made it clear that it wasn't something she wanted to do.

Polly held her hands over her ears upon hearing the grating noise as Joshua began working the saw toward her. Mr. McCreed's leanness was deceiving. His neck was thick and strong, and she could hardly help but notice the way his muscled arms pressed against the plain blue-green material of his shirt. She noticed the way his raven-colored hair curled up at the ends, and wondered what it would feel like to run her fingers through it. He badly needed a haircut, yet it certainly didn't detract from his undeniable masculinity. And even though he must have been working earlier, he smelled clean!

Polly was shocked at the lusty feelings he seemed to

ignite. She'd thought such feelings were buried forever. However, she wasn't about to let a simple spark turn into a roaring inferno. Besides, he was definitely not the type of man she wanted to marry. He had no money. And he was dangerous. She didn't know why or how, but he exuded it. Combine that with his devilish sense of humor and Joshua McCreed would be a temptation to any woman.

Polly closed her eyes and wondered what Joshua thought about her. She was practically naked! He had to have had a wicked notion or two.

A tap on the shoulder made Polly open her eyes and remove her fingers from her ears. Sable motioned her head toward Joshua.

"I've made three different cuts in the plank," Joshua informed her. "Now I'm going to break the two pieces of wood out. It's the only way I can get enough room to free you. I'll be as careful as I can, but I can't guarantee it's not going to hurt. So I want you to tell me if you feel pain."

Polly nodded and squeezed her eyes shut. She hated pain!

After what seemed like only minutes, Polly felt herself being lifted. Her eyes flew open. At last! She was free of the hole. She especially delighted in the feel of being cradled in Joshua's arms. She liked it *too* much.

Joshua carried Polly into the parlor, and placed her on one of the covered chairs. Sable came rushing into the room.

"I brought your clothes, Miss Polly. Now you get them on right now!"

Joshua winked at Polly. "What a shame. You look mighty tasty just the way you are."

Polly couldn't contain a smile.

Joshua stepped away. "While you're dressing, I'll fetch some whiskey to put on that cut. It would be a crime to have such a beautiful leg damaged."

Polly's moment of undeniable pleasure was shattered when Sable spoke up.

"You shouldn't let him talk to you like that," Sable grumbled. "He'll be gettin' ideas." She pulled the first petticoat over Polly's head. "Stand up so I can tie the string around your waist."

Polly looked down at her injury. The pantalet leg was pulled up, her stocking destroyed, and she had a cut on the calf. There was no pain, but it looked terrible.

"You gonna stand or not? That Mr. McCreed will be back any minute and you sure as the devil want to be properly covered by then. As for tending to your leg, I'd best do that. He shouldn't be touchin' you there."

Polly stood. "How come you're so bossy about everything, but when it comes to doing something about it you lose your nerve?"

"That's not so. I just know when to be quiet and when to speak up, which is more than you can say."

"Very well, then you tell Mr. McCreed you'll tend to the cut."

Sable helped with the second petticoat. "That's not right. After all, he works for you, not me."

Polly rolled her eyes. Sable had an answer for everything. It occurred to Polly that when she was a dance hall girl, she'd been virtually free of responsibilities. Now that she was rich, it seemed as if she were always having to handle everything.

Polly was fully dressed and waiting when Joshua returned. Seeing Sable hesitate about taking the bottle of whiskey, Polly released a sigh of resignation. She held her hand out and he handed her the bottle. "I think it would be advisable for you to leave the room and allow Sable to take care of the wound, Mr. McCreed. When she's finished, she can take that tour of inspection with you. She is a much better judge of such matters than I am."

"Me?" Sable looked pleadingly at Polly. "I don't know nothin' about house repairs."

Polly wanted to wring the woman's neck. "Let's get the leg attended to, Sable."

As Joshua left the room, Polly pulled up her skirts. But Sable just stood with her nose scrunched up and staring at the wound. Her temper already on a short fuse, Polly snatched the bottle from Sable and poured the whiskey onto the injured area. The burning sensation caused her to suck in her breath, but a minute later the pain had passed. She dropped her skirt and stood.

After checking all the rooms, Polly was amazed at how much Joshua had accomplished. All the rat holes had been repaired and the wood replaced. The house was already starting to look livable. He had even begun painting and replacing wallpaper. Soon he'd be ready to start on the new room.

"I must admit, Mr. McCreed," Polly said as they descended the stairs, "I have been unjustly critical of you. You have indeed done marvelous work. Are you comfortable in the carriage house?"

"Yes, I'm fine. Do you still want to fire me?"

Polly looked toward the bottom of the stairs and saw Sable nodding her head yes. "I was upset when I said that. Of course I don't want to fire you. You do excellent work, and I would be hard put to replace you." There, Polly thought, that should teach Sable to tend to her own business.

Polly felt a sudden shove against her back. She would have fallen down the stairs had Joshua not been in front of her. Even so, she landed hard against his back. It was amazing that they both didn't topple to the bottom.

As soon as Polly regained her footing, she jerked around to see who had done the pushing. There was no one there.

"Did you trip on the stair?" Joshua asked. He reached for her hand to lead her the rest of the way down.

"Someone pushed me from behind!" Polly declared.

Sable backed toward the wall. "There's bad things goin' on in this house. I can feel it in my bones."

Joshua shook his head. "I think it was just a breeze. I left some of the windows open upstairs."

"Maybe so." When they reached the bottom floor, Polly expelled a sigh of relief. Again she turned and looked up. Deciding Joshua was probably right, she headed for the door, then stopped abruptly. "My goodness. I forgot that Thomas left us stranded!"

Joshua looked questioningly at her. "I'm sure I heard him drive up some time ago."

"The front door is locked," Sable spoke up. "I couldn't go get help for Miss Polly earlier."

"It isn't locked, you just have to know how to open it." He grasped the knob with his big hand, then lifted and turned. The door swung open.

"See?" Polly chided Sable. "You were worried over nothing."

Sable hurried outside mumbling, "Never had trouble openin' it before."

Thomas was indeed waiting.

"Where did you go?" Polly demanded when she stood before the older man. "I gave you orders to wait!"

"But the maid came out of the house and said I was to drive into town and pick up your new chapeau."

Polly stared at him angrily. "Have you been drinking, Thomas? You know I haven't hired anyone." She turned to say goodbye to Joshua, but he was nowhere in sight. He apparently thought their discussion was over.

She looked back at Thomas, then Sable. Only three people worked for her, and it was beginning to look as though there wasn't a sound one in the group.

Polly climbed into the coach. Before settling back in the soft leather seat, she glanced up at the windows on the second floor. For some reason, she had expected to see someone up there. "Take me back to the hotel, Thomas."

As soon as the carriage was gone, Joshua moved to the bottom of the stairs. Falling into a hole of good wood and not getting hurt was humanly impossible.

His face drawn and his eyes shiny black stones, Joshua stared up at the landing. Slowly a woman's body began taking form in the void space, and her laughter floated through the house. "Now don't be angry with me, Joshua. You know how much I care for you."

Joshua stared at the lovely creature, but his cold expression didn't change. "When Polly's foot went through the floor, I suspected you were up to your old tricks."

The slender woman flipped her thick strands of blond hair from her shoulder and descended the stairs to where Joshua stood. "I know you're glad to see me. You could never forget the wild and wonderful times we have shared." She wrapped a long, slender arm around his neck, and slid her other hand down his front. She laughed when he pushed her hand away.

"Go away, Frenchy. I'm tired of you following me."

"I'm your woman. My place is by your side."

"I told you from the beginning that there could never be anything between us. I know you well, and I know what you are capable of in a fit of jealousy. I warn you, Frenchy, leave the woman alone."

"Not that I wouldn't like to change it, but I'm aware that you only think of me as a woman to soothe your needs. But what are friends for if not to keep each other happy? And I've kept you *very* happy on a good many occasions."

She danced into the parlor and started lifting the dust covers from the furniture. "I didn't harm your lady friend.

I could though. She is terribly frightened of ghosts. All I would have to do is suddenly appear and she would be gone. Now come here, and let me show you how useful I can be.''

''I'm not interested. Find yourself another man.''

''No man can satisfy me the way you do.'' Frenchy arched a fine eyebrow. ''You're acting very strange, Joshua.''

''What do you mean by that?''

''You're not acting like your old self. Do I detect a touch of caring for your little playmate? I know how important she is to your future, but you *have* been altering her mind, and that wasn't part of the bargain. What do you think is going to happen when Miss Polly finds out who and what you are?''

''You're making something out of nothing. I don't care what happens as long as I make her so in love she would even be willing to die for me.''

''You are such a cold person, but I wouldn't have you any other way. But be careful, Joshua. You've never known love. It can sneak up behind you before you even know what's happening, and men like you ususally fall the hardest. I'll wait around. I'm curious to see what happens. My guess is that once you've finished with the redhead you'll be wanting me again.''

Frenchy disappeared, but Joshua could still hear her laughing. She'd dearly love to see him get his comeuppance, but it wasn't going to happen. It was true, he was starting to have some feelings for Polly, but not the kind Frenchy was talking about. He had spoken the truth when he'd said she needed looking after. Polly was inept at everything, especially her ability to judge men.

Chapter Four

The jingle of the bell hanging over the door caused the small, elderly lady to look up. She smiled and straightened her apron as the attractive redhead stepped into the bakery shop. "Miss O'Neil," she acknowledged. "I had hoped you wouldn't forget this was Wednesday." She moved from behind the counter. "I have your sugar cookie set aside."

"You know me too well, Mrs. Fritz."

"You've been coming in every Wednesday for over a month now."

Polly raised her chin and inhaled deeply. "Mmm. It always smells so good in here." She handed the gray-headed shop owner three cents, then carefully placed the cookie in her reticule.

"Mrs. Chapman ordered too many scones, and they're still hot. I thought I might be able to talk you into joining me for tea."

"Well, I—"

"I'll be so disappointed if you refuse. I hate having tea alone."

Polly really didn't want to dally, but Mrs. Fritz was such

a sweet soul that she couldn't very well refuse. "I can't stay long, I have other business to attend to."

"As do I, but a little break won't hurt either of us. Elizabeth will take care of the customers. God bless her. I don't know how I would manage without her. She comes every morning at three-thirty to bake the bread, rolls and doughnuts, then stays until three in the afternoon. At my age, the work is just too much of a strain."

Inez Fritz's living quarters were located in back of the bakery. Polly sat at the round table and waited for her hostess to return with the tea. Her gaze quickly scanned the small, crowded room. The furniture was adequate but worn. Every bit of available space had something to occupy it, whether it was handicrafts or pictures.

"Here we go," Mrs. Fritz said as she returned, carrying a silver tray.

Polly had offered to help, but the frail woman had insisted on doing it by herself.

Beaming with pride, Mrs. Fritz placed the tray on the table. Her best cozy covered a china teapot, and she had brought two matching cups and saucers.

"I was born and raised in England, and I don't believe I could ever give up my afternoon tea." Mrs. Fritz sat across from her guest.

"I've wondered about your accent. I've heard England is such a lovely place. You must have hated leaving."

Polly was quite proud of herself. She was acting the perfect lady.

The elderly woman poured the tea. "Oh my, I forgot. Do you take sugar?"

"No, no. This is fine," Polly commented after accepting a cup and saucer. She sipped the surprisingly strong brew and immediately regretted having refused a sweetener.

"Yes, leaving England was difficult. But my husband, Otto, was such a wonderful man. You see, he had a breathing difficulty, and we had hoped the air here would cure him. He died shortly after we arrived in California.'' She brushed away the tear that had trickled down a cheek that was as clear as porcelain. ''Seeing you always brings to mind when I was young. That was such a wonderful time. The memories will always be there. Tell me, child, do you have family living near?''

''No, they're all dead.''

''How sad for you to not have anyone.''

''I don't feel sad. I have good friends.'' She forced herself to take another sip of the bitter tea.

''Do your friends live in Auburn?''

''No, Sacramento. However, once I get settled in my house, I'm sure I will make new acquaintances.''

''I'm sure you will. You're such a sweet girl, and so pretty. Enjoy it while you can, my dear, because when you get old it's only the memories that keep you going.''

''Do you have children?''

''Two sons. I don't know what I would do without their love and support.''

As soon as Polly had made her excuses and left, Mrs. Fritz called, ''You can come out now.''

Two men stepped from behind the worn curtain that closed off a bedroom.

The older woman's entire countenance changed. She stood straight and gingerly began placing the china back onto the tray. ''I had hoped you boys would hear us coming and would have the sense to hide. Well, did you get a good look at her?''

''She's very pretty,'' the handsome blonde replied. ''Quite the lady, isn't she? I especially liked her diamond necklace.'' Berk rubbed his hands together. ''I'm going to enjoy bedding this one.''

''Make sure you don't bloody well foul it up like before,'' Daniel barked. The bull of a man with shaggy brown hair and a bulbous nose stepped from behind his brother. ''This time, leave the jewels and money alone. Damn if that woman doesn't look familiar, but I can't place where I would have been to see the likes of her.''

''You've probably seen her riding around in that fancy carriage,'' the old woman commented.

''Maybe.''

''You make sure you stay away from her,'' Berk warned. ''With your looks you'll scare her off.''

''Now boys, quit your spitting at each other.''

''Mums, was our father's name really Otto?'' Berk asked.

Inez Fritz slammed the tray back down onto the table, causing the lid to the teapot to fall to the floor. ''Why was I cursed with such sons? If only you had Daniel's brains, or Daniel had your looks. Of course Otto wasn't your father's name, just as Fritz isn't our last name. How many times must I tell you I have no idea who your father was? I had many lovers back then. Instead of thinking about who your father was, you should be grateful that we escaped the hangman and made it to America! Remember, without me you boys would have nothing.''

Berk looked down at the plank floor. ''I'm sorry, Mums.''

Inez went to her son and hugged him tightly. In her own way, she loved Berk. He was without a doubt her favorite. Perhaps it was because he was always getting into some kind of trouble, and inevitably, she was the one who ended up getting him out of it.

''Now that you've seen the girl, we have to make plans.''

Daniel leaned his shoulder against the doorjamb. ''What needs discussing is Berk's temper. Especially when a tart doesn't give him what he wants. If he can keep his hands off this one—as well as her jewelry and money—''

"Don't be so hard on him, Daniel. He did just fine with the slut in San Francisco. Her money is what gave us this bakery and a few other pleasures."

"And he killed her," Daniel reminded his mother.

"What difference does it make? The way she flaunted her money was indecent. She needed punishing. Berk, I want you and Daniel to take the stage to Sacramento in the morning. It leaves at eight. Daniel, don't come back until you have him outfitted in the best of clothing."

Daniel had to look away to keep from laughing. He'd just remembered where he'd seen the red-haired beauty before and he was enjoying himself. His mother had always held on to money tenaciously, and that included what he and Berk had coming. It felt good to see her throw some of it away on a foolish cause. She'd be talking differently if she knew about Miss Polly O'Neil's friendship with her gambler friend. He'd just wait a bit before letting the other two in on his secret.

"How come we have to go all the way to Sacramento?" Berk asked.

"Because we don't want anyone to get suspicious! In a couple of months there is to be a ball at the Empire Hotel and I want you to be there. Oh, and Daniel, Berk will need one of those fancy evening suits. When all that's taken care of, get right back here. Until the dance, I want Berk visible in the Orleans Hotel lobby, smiling and tipping his hat to Polly O'Neil every time she passes by. You know what I'm talking about, Berk.

"I have gone to a considerable amount of trouble—plus paying money out of my pocket—to find out the woman has more wealth than any of us could ever imagine. She makes the woman in San Francisco look like a pauper. If we do this right, boys, we will soon have a new member in our family. Then we can all sit back and do as we please for the rest of our lives."

Inez ran a stubby fingertip across Berk's chin. "This is the opportunity we have been waiting for. The twenty dollars for both of you to go to Sacramento and back is just the beginning of the money we're going to have to spend to pull this off. I have saved for just such an opportunity. If you do anything to mess this up, Berk, I promise it will be the last thing you do in your short life. Do you understand?"

Berk gave his mother a cocky grin. "Don't worry about a thing. Before long, you will have a new daughter-in-law."

Inez smiled sweetly and patted her son's hand.

Polly placed her needlework on the side table and stared into space. Being a lady left a lot to be desired. She was bored, bored, bored! Maybe it wouldn't be so bad when she had moved into her house instead of being relegated to a suite of rooms.

She glanced toward the door. The traveling seamstress should have already arrived. At least the fittings would break up the day. Sable wasn't even around to talk to. She had probably gone to get some more of Smith & Co.'s new remedy. She was convinced that by taking it, she would live forever. Polly questioned that the elixir took care of rheumatism, as well as impurities of the blood, as it claimed. It was more likely that it contained liquor, and *that* was what made Sable feel so good.

Polly went to the window and looked down at the street below. As usual, it was busy with what seemed like an endless array of wagons and people on horseback.

As she watched a man ride down the street on a high-stepping sorrel, an idea began to formulate. What if she learned to ride a horse properly? No, no. It was a foolhardy notion. She hated horses.

She pulled back the lace curtain. On the other hand,

maybe her fears and distrust would vanish once she knew how to handle the beasts. And one big advantage would be no longer having to rely on Thomas. Hearing a knock on the door, Polly went to answer it. Miss Isabel Baxter, the seamstress, stood patiently waiting on the other side. To Polly, Isabel seemed such a prim creature. Even the wire-rimmed glasses that rested on a narrow, hooked nose added to a stern appearance. And no matter what the weather, she always wore high-necked dresses. She kept her hair pulled back so tight it had to give her headaches. But Polly knew her to be a gentle, thoughtful woman. And what the woman could do with a needle was indeed amazing.

"I want six new dresses," Polly said excitedly, "and a ball gown so beautiful that the women for miles around will die of jealousy." Though she hadn't told a soul, Polly had decided to take Malcolm Sawyer up on an invitation to the dance. As of late, they had been having friendly conversations in the lobby, and she could hardly refuse such a tempting invitation. Of course with him being a married man, they wouldn't dare arrive together.

Isabel smiled, showing even white teeth. "You must be planning to go to the ball at the Empire Hotel. How exciting."

Polly glanced toward the open window. "But before you make any of the other clothes, I want you to make me a pair of britches."

"What?" the seamstress gasped.

Polly had made up her mind to learn to ride. It was better than sitting in the room twiddling her thumbs. She smiled reassuringly and led the spinster into the room. "A very good friend of mine said that the most comfortable way to ride a horse was astride instead of sidesaddle. There was a time when she and I both had to wear men's britches, and it did indeed make moving about easier."

"I don't understand what you're saying. Are the trousers for riding or walking?"

"For riding. I would never walk about town without wearing a dress."

"Why pants? I have a customer who wears what looks like a skirt, but it's split in the center like men's pants. Perhaps something of *that* nature would suit your purpose."

"Yes. That's perfect. And I'd like a colorful vest to wear over a white painter's shirt."

Isabel laughed. "You're beginning to sound more like a gambler."

"Perhaps I'll set a fashion trend."

"Perhaps you will. Well, we might as well get started. I can see there is a lot of work to be done."

"As soon as Sable returns, I'll have her get you a room here in the hotel until you're finished. Oh, and I don't want any red material. Only flattering colors."

"I'll need to measure you. And I have several new designs that came straight from Paris."

While Miss Baxter fetched a pencil and various other items from her reticule, Polly thought about how pleased Malcolm was going to be when he saw her in an exquisite new ball gown. As of late, he had been taking every opportunity to speak to her. However, Joshua had made her feel guilty, so she had tried to ignore the gentleman. But surely even Joshua couldn't fault her for not refusing an invitation to a fancy ball!

For the next week, Polly contemplated her situation. She wanted to purchase a horse, but because she knew nothing about them, it would be easy for a horse trader to take advantage of her. As for someone to teach her to ride, she knew of only one person to ask. Joshua McCreed. Strange how she sometimes had the feeling that he beckoned her to him.

Another week passed without Polly having made any decisions. She hadn't even gone to the house because she found Joshua to be too intimidating. But the desire to learn to ride had continued to grow until it had become an obsession. She was even to the point of dreaming about it.

The following morning, Sable helped Polly into the new white summer dress with yards of material and lace. A matching umbrella and a white straw hat completed her outfit.

"You're not gettin' all dressed up for that Mr. McCreed, are you?" Sable asked suspiciously.

"How could you even think of such a thing?" Polly took one last look in the mirror.

"Because you said we're goin' to the house!"

Polly headed for the door. "You forget that, on the way, other people will see us. Nevertheless, there is something I want from Mr. McCreed."

Sable raised her eyebrows as she hurried after her mistress. "What could you want from a man like that?"

Polly stopped dead in her tracks and turned to face the slender woman. "What is it you don't like about Mr. McCreed?"

"In the first place, he don't seem like a man who uses his hands to make a livin'. He don't even have calluses. And it's plain to tell he's educated. So why would he want to work on your house? And I gets scared when he looks at me."

"Why?"

"Maybe it's 'cause he's too nice, too fine lookin' and too everything. It makes me think he isn't what he seems. I don't trust him, and I'd be right pleased if you was to get rid of him."

Sable's words feathered Polly's insecurities about the man. Then she thought of all the money he was saving her. She immediately brushed off her moment of indecision. "It isn't as if we will be living with the man, Sable. Even you said you couldn't believe what excellent work he'd done and how quickly he'd accomplished it. When everything is finished, he'll leave.''

''Are you sure?''

Polly continued on down the hall to the stairs. ''There won't be any reason for him to remain.''

When they arrived at the house, Polly was amazed to see the outside had been painted sparkling white. It looked so different. It looked beautiful!

Her gaze traveled to the front door. Again it was standing open. Didn't anyone ever listen to what she said about keeping it closed? Joshua's frame suddenly filled the doorway, and she forgot her peevishness. The sculptured lines of his face, the black hair and dark eyes fringed with thick lashes, were enough to light up any woman's desire. She had to remind herself that sex wasn't what she was looking for.

''You look as if you were expecting me,'' Polly said as she walked up.

''No, just hoping.'' Joshua stepped back so Polly and Sable could enter the house. ''You ladies look very pretty today.''

''Don't go thinkin' she's dressed for the likes of you,'' Sable spoke up.

Joshua smiled. ''How lucky Miss Polly is to have you to watch after her, Sable. I'll bet there isn't much that misses your eyes.''

''That's right,'' Sable assured him.

''Come along, ladies, and let me show you what I have been doing. I believe you'll be pleased. As I see it, there is no reason why you can't move in anytime you like.''

They all stepped into the parlor.

''The new room is already started, so one could no

longer say there are thirteen rooms,'' Joshua muttered. ''Don't you agree, Sable?''

''Well...I reckon that's right.''

Polly was particularly pleased with the block-printed wallpaper that had been hung in the dining room. It was almost the exact pattern she had envisioned in her mind.

After inspecting the rooms downstairs, the threesome moved to the next floor.

As the rooms were inspected, Polly became amazed at the amount of work Joshua had done in so short a time. No one would ever be able to guess the condition of the place before Joshua took over. The house looked new. If the servants' quarters were in equally good condition, there was indeed no reason for them not to move in.

When they returned to the main floor, Polly was eager to compliment Joshua on the fine work he had done. But her smile faded when she looked into Joshua's intense dark eyes. He was watching—no, studying—her. Everything seemed to disappear, except those penetrating eyes.

The spell was broken when Joshua asked, ''Do you agree with me about moving in?''

Polly blinked. For a brief moment, she had felt possessed. ''Yes, I see no reason not to. I'm up to my ears in boredom at that hotel.''

''Once you're moved, that will all change. There are a lot of interesting places to see nearby, and you and Sable could ride out and take a look.''

''You won't be gettin' me on no horse,'' Sable stated emphatically.

''How do you know there are interesting things to see?'' Polly questioned. ''I believe you said you had just arrived in Auburn when I hired you.''

''I've done a lot of traveling in this area.'' He followed Polly back into the dining room and watched her run her hand across the wallpaper. ''So what do you think about moving in? Of course you will be wanting to hire more help. This house is too big for just one small woman to keep up.''

Sable smiled and reassessed her opinion of the fine gentleman.

Polly walked out into the hall. ''Where is the new room you're building?''

''At the back of the house. Have you decided what you're going to use it for?''

''No, but I'm sure you have a suggestion.''

''As a matter of fact, I do.''

''By all means, let's hear it.''

''Make it Sable's room. As the housekeeper, it would allow her to keep an eye on things.''

Sable nodded her approval. ''He's absolutely right. And I wouldn't have to be climbing all them stairs every time I turned around.''

Polly refused to acknowledge the validity of the idea. ''We'll see.'' Still excited about her beautiful house, she could no longer hold back a smile. ''If I can find movers today, I'll be back early in the morning to supervise the furniture placement.''

A loud bang on the floor above Polly's head made her look up. ''What was that? Why…is that female laughter I hear?'' She looked accusingly at Joshua. ''Have you been keeping a woman?''

''Perhaps the laughter came from someone passing outside,'' Joshua offered. ''The breeze that comes through the open windows makes all kinds of strange noises. As for a woman hiding, that's not likely. You've just been in every room. As for the other noise, one of my tools must have fallen to the floor. Are you always this jumpy?''

''Of course not.'' Polly smoothed out one of the white gloves she wore. The house was well off to itself and it wasn't likely someone would be passing by. "How much longer is it going to take to finish the new room?"

"Two weeks at the most."

Polly took money from her reticule and handed it to him. "This is part of what I owe you. I'm sure your funds are getting uncomfortably low. We'll probably see you in the morning."

Joshua nodded. "Bye, Sable."

Sable giggled but made no reply.

Polly stopped on the porch and looked at the yard, which needed a considerable amount of weeding. Even the picket fence would have to be repaired and painted. What could she have possibly been looking at if she didn't see all this when she had bought the house? She couldn't even remember there being a picket fence. She continued on to the carriage.

"Thomas, after taking me back to the hotel," she said when she was seated, "I want you to fetch some sturdy men to help move the furniture. They are to be here no later than seven in the morning."

"Yes, ma'am." Thomas climbed to his seat.

Polly looked at the house. She wasn't surprised to see that Joshua had gone back inside. The man never waited around. Perhaps he had gone to his lady friend.

"Wait, Thomas! Don't start the horse." Polly exited the carriage. If Mr. McCreed was using her time to dally with a woman, she was going to catch him red-handed. "Drive off, and don't come back for ten minutes. Sable, you go with him."

"But Miss Polly—"

"I don't want to hear it. Just do as I say."

Once Polly was back inside the house, she stood silently and listened. She thought she heard voices coming from the second floor, but she couldn't be sure. If she went up the squeaking stairs, Joshua and his friend would hear her approach. She really should remember to have Joshua repair them. There! That was definitely a woman's laughter!

Angry, Polly started climbing the stairs, not caring if her footsteps would warn them of her arrival. And if they were making love, they wouldn't hear her anyway.

To Polly's aggravation, she found no one. Even the attic was empty. Her exasperation growing at not being able to catch Joshua in a lie, she went back downstairs and out the back door. Perhaps the laughter had drifted in from the carriage house.

That effort also proved futile. The only living thing inside was Joshua's horse. Just where had Joshua gone? She started to walk around the brick building, but gave up the effort when her skirt kept getting tangled in the weeds.

Her determination turning to anger, she was about to yell for the mysterious man when, to her embarrassment, she saw him leave the outhouse. Feeling guilty as sin, she tried to duck around the side without being seen, but she'd waited too long.

"Was there something else you wanted to talk about?" Joshua called as he walked toward her.

Polly had to think of something quickly, or he'd know she had been snooping. His slow smile didn't help matters. "Yes, there was something else I wanted to talk to you about. Riding…riding was what I wanted to discuss."

"Riding? I assume you mean a horse."

"Of course that's what I mean!" Still not convinced he didn't have a woman, she kept glancing around to see if anyone tried to sneak away.

Joshua took her by the elbow and proceeded to guide her back to the house. "Just what about riding did you want to discuss?"

"I've made up my mind to learn to do it properly." Polly lifted her skirt to avoid another thistle. "I must admit, sitting on top of a horse doesn't particularly please me. However, it seems to me that I could get around easier and I wouldn't have to wait on Thomas.''

''And who is going to teach you all this?''

''Well, I thought…'' She couldn't ask. It wasn't the right time. ''I'll have to hire someone. Of course I can't do anything until I find a horse.''

Joshua nodded. ''Sounds like a good idea to me. By the way, what is happening with your married gentleman, Mr. Sawyer?''

''I took your advice and have been looking elsewhere for a man,'' Polly lied. She was eager to tell him about her invitation to the ball, but thought better of it. Joshua wouldn't understand how much going to the festivity meant to her.

''As I was saying,'' Polly continued, ''first I need to purchase a proper horse. One that likes me. But I've heard talk about hoodwinkers. Not knowing anything about the beasts, I could be taken advantage of. I thought perhaps you might be willing to help me locate a proper animal. I'd pay extra. You do know about horses, don't you?''

Joshua stared into the large blue eyes that seemed to dominate Polly's face. He liked it when she would accidentally let her guard down. Her lusty, airy quality was surprisingly mixed with a strong dose of naiveté. ''I've been known to sell a horse or two.'' He smiled. ''I'll look around and see if I can't come up with something suitable.''

''That would be wonderful.'' Polly took a deep breath. ''I also thought you might be the one to teach me to ride.''

Joshua rubbed the side of his clean-shaven chin. ''That's something you don't learn overnight. I planned on taking off as soon as I had the extra room finished.''

For some reason, Polly was under the impression that he wasn't about to go anywhere unless she forced him to leave. ''Surely it couldn't take too long if we worked daily at it.''

"I don't know." Joshua leaned forward and opened the front door. "Where is your carriage?"

"I sent Thomas on an errand."

"Sable, too?"

"Yes! I mean it was Sable that's taking care of the errand, but Thomas had to drive her. Are you going to agree to teach me?"

"I have to admit that I'm surprised you would even ask. You realize it would mean me staying longer."

"I know that."

"Let's lay our cards on the table, Miss O'Neil. I have nowhere I'm in a hurry to get to. But I can't say that teaching you to ride has any appeal."

He turned and looked down at her. "Just a few minutes ago you were convinced I was keeping a woman here. I denied it, but you didn't believe me. Just to get things straight between us, what is it about me that bothers you, Miss O'Neil?"

Polly's cheeks became hot. She was indeed guilty on every count. "I don't know what you're talking about."

"You're lying. Why all of a sudden would you want me to stay?"

"I told you. I know no one else to ask," Polly explained, avoiding Joshua's black, penetrating gaze. "But it's not so important that I'm going to beg."

"No, I never thought you would. Very well, I'll stay and teach you to ride, but on one condition."

"What's that?" Polly asked suspiciously.

"We start acting like friends instead of enemies." Joshua saw Thomas stop the carriage out front. "And to begin with, we stop the lying. I was talking to Malcolm Sawyer just this morning. He was quite proud that you had accepted his invitation to the ball."

"Oh!" Polly tossed her hands in the air. "I swear, there isn't a man who can be trusted! He was supposed to keep it secret so no one would look down on me, and the first thing he does is blab his mouth. Did he also tell you we're not arriving together?'' Polly lifted her skirt, then let it fall back down so it hung properly.

''Not all men are like that,'' Joshua countered. ''I think you have me all wrong. I'm not one who can throw stones. I simply gave you a word of advice. What you chose to do with it was your business. But be careful you don't give the old man a heart attack. I'm sure he hasn't been with someone as beautiful in a long time.''

''You really think I'm beautiful?''

''I guarantee it.''

Polly giggled. ''You do have a way with women, Mr. McCreed.''

''That I do, Miss O'Neil. Now if you plan to have workers here come morning, you'd best be on your way.''

''And you'll teach me how to ride?''

''Do you plan on telling me everything straight out without lying?''

Polly nodded.

''I consider that a promise. I always hold someone to their promise.''

As Polly hurried to the carriage, Joshua closed the door and looked down the hall. ''Frenchy!'' he barked, his face cast in granite. ''There's no use hiding.''

Frenchy materialized only a few feet away. ''Now, Joshua, don't be angry. I was only playing with her. She's such a fool to believe you actually planned to leave after finishing the room. Please, Joshua, leave her alone. I'll take care of you.''

''I've had enough of you following me everywhere I go. It's over. I've told you to leave before, but you'd best listen this time. If you try anything again, I will curse you through eternity. Now get out of here, and don't come back.''

''You're falling in love with that bitch!'' Frenchy

gasped. "I've never seen you act this way toward any woman. I won't let that useless baggage take you away from me! You're going to regret this, Joshua."

"Not nearly as much as you if you spoil my plans."

"Listen to me, Joshua," Frenchy pleaded. "You can't keep controlling her mind. One day she will have to know the truth and when that happens, she'll cast you aside!"

"Leave," he stated in a cold, shattering voice.

Frenchy stepped away, not daring to encourage his wrath. "I thought I would feel some sort of satisfaction at seeing a woman make a fool of you, but I don't." She tried banging her fist on the table, but her hand went right through it. "Next thing you know that whore will have you on your knees begging her not to leave you."

"Don't get carried away with yourself, Frenchy. We both know that day will never happen. And stop calling her your pet names."

"See? You are getting soft on her!" She brushed away the tears that had started running down her cheeks. "If you need me, you have but to call my name." She disappeared.

Joshua rubbed his chin. Maybe Frenchy had a point. Perhaps he was softening up. He was actually starting to care about people, but he refused to believe he was harboring any *special* feeling toward Miss Polly O'Neil. And certainly not feelings of love! He would never allow that to happen. He had special plans for that lady.

Chapter Five

"I've only seen the woman twice, and I didn't get a chance to talk to her either time," Berk complained.

Inez looked toward Daniel. "Is he telling the truth?"

Daniel nodded.

"And now you say she's moving?" Inez asked Berk.

"That's what the man at the registration desk told me." Berk plopped down on the divan. "It looks like all that money we spent on clothes has gone to waste. And I was really looking forward to bedding that one."

"You'll still have her. That girl's giving me more trouble than I'd expected."

Daniel shoved his brother out of the way. "It appears we'll have to wait until the dance."

"No, there is another way. Berk, I want you in the bakery tomorrow afternoon. If Miss O'Neil doesn't show up for her sugar cookie, we'll try again the following Wednesday, and so on until I'm able to introduce you.

"Daniel, Elizabeth was ten minutes late coming to work this morning. Make sure she is docked an hour's wage. Tell her that if this happens again, it will be a half day's pay and so on, until she learns to be thankful for her job. And stay out of her pants. You won't be any good to us if her husband kills you.''

Daniel shifted his eyes to Berk. Without a doubt, his dear brother had been the one to supply their mother with that piece of information. He'd learned a long time ago that Berk was about as trustworthy as a lizard. One day he'd get even for the things Berk had pulled over the years.

Polly sat in the middle of her bed surveying her room. She laughed with delight. Finally she would be sleeping in her new canopy bed. It was a wonderful piece of work, made of boldly carved mahogany. The beautiful hanging bed curtains were rich, crimson silk. And there were new, clean sheets, and a feather bed that she could sink into. The well-oiled armoire, dressing table and commode added to the warmth of the room, and the lamplight made the wood glisten. Even her white nightgown was new.

The rooms downstairs were now decorated with wonderful sideboards, tables and furniture pieces covered with crimson and gold damask, or silk, brocades and soft velvets. She'd even remembered the peacock feathers for good luck, and Battenberg lace for shelves. The floors had been covered with reeds, and then newspapers. Beautiful rugs were on top of this insulation, adding to the warm glow of the house.

Her furniture. Her bedroom. Her house! It all seemed too grand to be true. Though she was tired after having spent the day supervising the furniture arrangement, her excitement hadn't diminished at seeing all the rooms come alive. Of course there was still a lot of unpacking and putting away to be done, but the larger pieces of furniture were now in place.

Polly lay back on the soft, fluffy pillows. None of this would have ever happened if she weren't wealthy. What a lovely word that was. "Wealthy," she whispered. It still seemed too good to be true.

Polly leaned toward the lamp on the bedside table and turned it down. A giggle burst forth as she slid between crisp sheets that still smelled of sunshine after being hung outside.

She was no sooner settled than she felt a breeze across her face. She opened her eyes and glanced toward the window. With the room cast in darkness, she couldn't tell if the window was open or closed. Had the curtains been put up, she might have been able to see them fluttering.

She rolled onto her side. What difference did it make? She was comfortable. She was not going to delve into the possibility of Beelzebub roaming through her house.

She plopped onto her back and stared into the black void of her room. Surely when she married and had a man living with her, those fears would go away. She probably wouldn't even have time to contemplate evil spirits.

The sound of hammering finally forced Polly awake. Irritated at not being able to catch any more sleep, she reached over and pulled the cord that rang a bell in the kitchen. Who would have the nerve to be up this early in the morning? She rubbed her eyes.

After what seemed like an hour, Sable finally knocked on the bedroom door and poked her head in. "Was that you ringing?"

"Of course it was me ringing. Do you know of anyone else staying up here? Now go stop that infernal pounding, then come back and help me with my toilet." Polly poured water from the pitcher into a large ceramic bowl, then splashed her face with the cool liquid.

"But that hammerin' is Mr. Joshua workin' on my room."

"Mr. Joshua?" Polly dried her face. "Since when did you start calling him by his first name?"

"Since we had breakfast together this mornin'. He said it would be all right."

"You certainly had a quick change of attitude. I thought you didn't like him."

Sable scurried over to help Polly remove her nightgown. "I've decided differently. Like you said, I wasn't bein' fair. Will you be wantin' breakfast?"

"You know I don't eat breakfast. Am I going to have to listen to that pounding every morning? Fetch me the riding clothes Miss Baxter made, then you can tend to my hair."

Sable shuffled over to the armoire. "Why would you want to wear them things? You haven't got no horse."

"Not right now, but I will by the end of the day."

"But there's all the unpackin' that still needs to be done. And if you take Mr. Joshua away, that means he won't be working on my room."

"I see no reason why you can't continue to sleep up-stairs. At least until the new room is finished. It's not as if you don't have a roof over your head. Now hurry. I can't stand listening to that noise any longer than necessary. I don't even get up this early! Never mind. As soon as I'm dressed, I'll tell him."

The moment Polly was ready to go downstairs, the hammering stopped. She narrowed her eyes. "I swear, he knows I'm coming after him."

"How's that possible?" Sable asked.

"I haven't a clue. But I'm convinced he can read my thoughts!"

Polly marched along the hall then came to a halt at the top of the stairs. It was her favorite part of the house. The circular staircase made her feel like a queen. She always made a point of holding her head high and descending with the flowing grace that Mrs. Baxter had taught her.

Once she reached the landing, Polly hurried down another hall, past the dining room, kitchen and storage. As she stepped out the back door, she looked to her left where the new room was being constructed. Joshua was nowhere in sight.

She was about to follow the new path that went from the house across the weed-infested yard and to the carriage house, when she saw Joshua heading her way. A heavy beam rested on his broad shoulder, but that wasn't what drew her attention. He wasn't wearing a shirt and his trousers were riding on narrow hips just below his navel. The short dark hairs on his chest narrowed to a vee when they reached his flat, corded stomach.

The view definitely stirred wanton feelings, something she absolutely didn't need. And she was supposed to be immune to desire! Especially since she would never love any man the way she loved Chance Doyer. And besides, according to Mrs. Parker, proper ladies didn't experience such feelings.

"Good morning, Miss O'Neil. You're looking pleasurably fit. That's a mighty fine looking vest."

"I couldn't sleep with all that banging!" Polly snapped at him. "And how dare you go about half-naked!"

Joshua dropped the beam by the outer frame he was working on. "It's hot work, and I'm afraid I've gotten used to being alone." He picked up the shirt he'd left in the open window frame.

Polly looked away while he tucked his shirt into his trousers, to give herself a chance to recoup her emotions and get a handle on the desire that surged through her. But the damage had been done. She wouldn't soon forget seeing his marvelous torso. Would the rest of him be equally appealing? "From now on, you won't start work until…at least ten o'clock."

"It'll take longer to complete this room."

Polly was dying to ask why he didn't wear long under-garments, but she didn't dare.

"I'm curious. Why do you have that diamond necklace on all the time?"

Polly's hand went to her throat. "It brings me good luck. I've never taken it off since…since the first day I put it on."

"Aren't you afraid someone will try taking it away from you?"

"Are you—"

"No, to whatever you started to ask. I have no interest in jewelry. But this is rough country and times are hard. There are a lot of men who wouldn't resist the temptation to take it from you."

"If you're trying to scare me, it won't work. I've nothing to worry about. I've worn it for over two years, and never have I been in danger." Polly looked down at the ground and began drawing lines in the dirt with the toe of her boot. "Mr. McCreed, I want to get my horse today."

"I don't know if that's possible."

Polly thought about Sable having said that he listens then goes ahead and does what he pleases. "Just what do you mean by that?"

"It's not always easy to locate just the right horse. We may even end up having to go out of town."

Polly hadn't thought about that. She glanced toward the back door. Sable was right. There was a lot of unpacking to be done. However, with the three extra women she intended to hire, they should be able to handle everything by themselves, and she wanted a horse! "Then if it's going to take awhile, I suppose we should get busy. Have Thomas bring the carriage around."

"There isn't any need for you to go along. When I find the right horse, I'll tell you."

"How will I know if it likes me?"

Joshua shook his head. "Buying a horse has to do with the condition and disposition of the animal. It has nothing to do with whether he does or does not like you."

"Of course it does. I wouldn't buy one I didn't like."

"You're not a horse." Joshua moved forward to get the bandanna he'd left on a post, and Polly jumped away. The heel of her boot landed on a piece of wood, causing her to lose her balance. Joshua was immediately by her side, preventing her from falling.

"Are you all right?" he asked.

"I'm fine." As soon as Polly was steady on her feet, she cautiously moved away. Feeling the warmth of his arm about her waist didn't help the smoldering coals that now needed very little to become a raging fire.

"*We* will look for a horse together," Polly persisted, simply because he obviously didn't want her along. Maybe he planned to buy a horse cheap, then turn around and charge her a higher price.

"Very well," Joshua conceded. "Thomas is still asleep. I'll go fetch him. While we're about, you can purchase a sidesaddle."

"I've made up my mind to ride astride. Tell Thomas I shall expect him within thirty minutes."

Though Thomas pulled the carriage around on time, it was an additional five minutes before Polly strolled out of the house.

Joshua climbed from the seat and opened the door for her. The redhead had used her time to change into an apricot-colored town dress that tended to accent her lovely bosom and tiny waist. The slight breeze kicked up the dust and swirled it like a caress around her ankles. A most pleasing sight to a man with weary eyes.

Polly O'Neil was nothing like Joshua had anticipated. He had thought he could wrap her around his finger like

the other women he'd known, but she'd proved him wrong.
He should have known that winning her love wouldn't
come easily. But he had all the time in the world, as long
as he could keep other men away from her door.

Joshua helped Polly into the carriage. "Should I sit up
front with Thomas?" he asked congenially.

Polly was taken aback by the question. "Why would you
do that?"

"I am, after all, an employee."

Seeing his ornery grin, Polly replied, "I agree. You
should sit up front."

Polly was surprised when, still grinning, Joshua secured
the door, then climbed up on the seat next to Thomas. She'd
expected him to come back with some sort of snide remark.
In all truthfulness, there was no reason why he couldn't
have raised the back of the extra seat and sat across from
her. But for some reason, she felt the need to give him his
comeuppance.

Polly was quickly tiring of the way Joshua always
seemed to be humoring or tolerating her. As if he were
superior. There was no question that he was his own man,
which made her feel all the more insecure. Well, maybe he
was used to getting his way, but not this time.

As Joshua turned to look at a house they were passing,
the sunlight hit the seemingly carved line of his profile.
Polly sucked in her breath. She could clearly see an old,
faded scar on his right cheek. Memories began flashing
through her mind. The tall dark stranger hovering over her,
then picking her up in his arms. The terror she'd felt,
though she still couldn't remember what had frightened her
so. Had he been the reason? She curled her hands into fists.
She could already feel perspiration breaking out on her face
and body.

Polly wanted to leap out of the carriage when Joshua

suddenly snapped his head around. Did he know what she was remembering?

"Are you all right?"

Polly saw his lips move but couldn't hear what he was saying.

"Stop the horses, Thomas!" Joshua ordered. Without waiting, he climbed over the high back of the seat. Polly's face had become a white mask. The closer he came, the harder she pushed against the back of her seat.

Knowing to touch her would cause hysteria, Joshua raised the back of the small seat and sat across from her. "Just drive around," he ordered Thomas.

He leaned forward. "Listen to me, Polly," he said in a deep, calming voice. "What are you remembering?"

Her body rigid, Polly tried to speak, but couldn't.

"Relax. You can talk. You remember who I am, don't you?"

Polly nodded, her big eyes getting wider with each passing minute.

Joshua chuckled and leaned back, giving the impression of being relaxed. "And I'll bet you're wondering why I never mentioned it." He pulled paper and a cloth pouch from his pocket, then began rolling a cigarette. "I could see you didn't recognize me that day I came to you for work. Just like now, when we first met, you were scared out of your wits. Remember, I found you on the ground. From the way you had acted, one would have thought I was the devil. So rather than have you become frightened again, I chose not to remind you of the past."

"You followed me!" Polly whispered. "How did you know where to find me?"

"I didn't. Again, our meeting was purely coincidental." He took a long drag on his cigarette. Her face was starting to soften.

Polly could clearly remember him leaving her in front of

the Murphy Hotel—just before he'd ridden away. Even then, Joshua had treated her like a lady. But something had scared her badly, and if it wasn't him, then what?

As her fear slowly subsided, Polly felt more and more like a fool.

"Maybe we should look for a horse tomorrow."

"No," she quickly replied. "I've been spending too much time in the house lately." She eased her hands open. "You never had any inkling I was in Auburn? That's a foolish question. It's been a long time since we last saw each other. You could hardly have been following me all that time."

Joshua remained silent.

"If there is ever anything else I should know," Polly stated, her fear turning to anger, "I'd appreciate you coming right out and telling me."

Polly avoided his dark, penetrating eyes. She still felt that tinge of fear. Especially with him now sitting directly in front of her. It had always been there. Yet that same spark of fear was strangely exhilarating, and made him almost irresistible at times. She was even afraid to admit that on more than one occasion, she had been tempted to take a bite of the forbidden apple. That was why she tended to avoid him. Polly the dance hall girl wouldn't have hesitated. Polly the lady knew it was never wise to flirt with danger.

"Why do you want to ride astride a horse?"

Polly was startled by the question. "It's supposed to be safer and more comfortable." She didn't want to talk. She was still recovering from the horrible fear and realization she'd just experienced.

"There was a woman, whose name presently escapes me, who explored all the West, as well as traveling all through the Rocky Mountains, using a sidesaddle. She was considered an excellent horsewoman. And I guess it is more ladylike.''

There! He was doing it again. Trying to change her mind! ''I have every intention of riding astride, Mr. McCreed, and I assure you no one will have any difficulty knowing I'm a woman.''

Joshua grinned. ''I won't argue with you about that.''

Polly welcomed the compliment. If she had any brains about her, she should listen to what Joshua had to say. She could learn a lot about the way gentlemen think. When she was a dance hall girl, she understood exactly what men were up to with their fine talk. But she had come to realize that gentlemen were different. Half the time, she wasn't quite sure of their intention. How was she supposed to know when she was being insulted or when to slap their faces as Mrs. Parker had suggested?

Polly thought of Jack Douglass. The saloon owner had been a spotless dresser, and never drank or cursed. Until she had become wealthy, Jack was the closest thing to a gentleman she had ever known.

When Sam Logan had skipped out of town without her, he'd also taken all the money. The little gold dust she'd secretly kept hidden in one of her stockings was all she had to her name.

Polly absentmindedly fingered her diamond necklace and smiled. Three days after Sam had run off, Jack showed up on her doorstep. He had come to offer her work at his saloon as a dance hall girl. Even though she had been destitute, she never once thought of turning in that direction. She'd been considering housework or taking in laundry.

Right up front, she had told him that she would never become one of those women. Never again would she be obligated to go to any man's bed. That didn't dissuade the gentleman from offering a tidy sum. Enough to keep her comfortable. He told her it was her looks he was interested in. That alone would bring in customers and put a goodly sum in both their pockets. Besides, if she chose not to bed with a customer, the other girls could keep them happy. So she'd become what the ladies about town considered a whore.

The only other man she'd slept with was Lester Adam. He was young, a virgin and most importantly, rich. He was infatuated with her. When Lester asked her to go to Sacramento with him, then followed that up with a proposal of marriage, she had accepted immediately. It was the only way she'd get away from being called trash. Besides, as well as having his own money, some day he'd be the owner of his father's mine. But fate had dealt her a bad card. Lester up and died on the trail.

Polly's remembering brought forth a smile. What carefree days those had been. She could probably still outdrink most any man, including Mr. Joshua McCreed! She had thought about opening a saloon of her own when she first found out about the gold, but quickly came to realize that being respected meant more to her.

As they neared town, Joshua called, "Look there!" He had Thomas stop the carriage.

Polly saw a rider moving his horse across the land at a reckless speed.

"The Pony Express. Just think about it. Just fourteen years ago, it took a ship eight months to go around the horn from New York. Now I hear that the Pony Express is covering the two thousand mile trip from Saint Joseph, Missouri to Sacramento in just eight days." Joshua shook his head in wonderment.

Adrenaline pumped through Polly's veins as she watched the rider disappear from view. She couldn't blame the men for wanting to work for the Express. It was so exciting, and had she been a man, she would probably have been tempted to give it a try. Though the feat seemed impossible, mail was actually arriving daily in Auburn. Just three days ago she had received a letter from Amanda.

As they continued on, Polly surreptitiously studied Joshua through lowered lashes. She found it interesting how clothing tended to hide his strength. Another man could be fooled by thinking he was just tall and lanky. But why was she even bothering to think about such things?

Thomas turned the carriage onto Main Street, and Polly deliberately concentrated on the women's dresses as they went from shop to shop. It was much safer than thinking about Joshua's physical attributes.

The first place they stopped was the livery stable. The owner told them that a man had brought in a string of mustangs, but Joshua wasn't interested. And so they continued on from one place to the next. Polly saw quite a few animals she liked, but Joshua was never satisfied.

Three hours later, they were headed for the town of Ophir, about four miles from Auburn. Someone had told Joshua that Ned Graham raised some fine horses, and they should look there before wasting any more time around Auburn.

The trip was a continuous up and down of rolling hills, dry grass, bush and trees. Not the least conducive to travel by buggy. Still, Thomas managed to continue on.

The river was a pretty sight as it ran swiftly through the edge of Ophir, but little had been built back up after the big fire that had desolated the town. A fate that was the plight of most mining towns.

As per Joshua's instructions, they continued on over the big hills and came into a lovely valley. Everything looked so peaceful, and it made Polly wonder if she'd made a mistake by wanting to live on the outskirts of Auburn.

Even before the carriage came to a halt, an attractive woman was already waiting in the open doorway.

"Good morning, ma'am," Joshua greeted as he tipped his hat. He jumped to the ground and walked up to the door. "My name's Joshua McCreed. I was told in town that your husband might have some horses for sale. If that's so, we'd like to take a look at what he has."

Polly didn't like the devastating smile the lovely brunette gave Joshua. Then the woman had the audacity to glance at Polly to see if she'd been watching.

"I'm Anne Graham. It's my father you want to talk to. I'm not married. Is the horse for you or your wife?"

Polly was ready to leave.

"I'm searching for my employer, Miss O'Neil."

Polly resented the way Anne Graham's brown eyes lit up with interest now that they had established that they were both free! Polly was about to tell Joshua to take her home, when a man rode up on a big chestnut horse.

"Welcome," he said as he dismounted. "Saw you headin' for the house."

Joshua went over and shook hands. "Name's Joshua McCreed. You must be Ned Graham."

"That's me. What can I do for you?"

"I'm looking to find Miss O'Neil a horse."

Ned tipped his hat to Polly. "Ma'am," he acknowledged.

"Miss O'Neil isn't much at riding, but wants to learn. So I'm trying to find a mare with spirit but doesn't spook easily, and reins well."

"How much are you willing to pay?"

"Whatever the horse is worth."

Polly stared at the daughter, who now stood by her father. The woman had hardly taken her eyes off Joshua. Polly was ready to give up on this whole venture. Learning to ride hadn't been a good idea. And who would dream that it would take this much time to find one single horse. Joshua was being too picky.

"Mr. McCreed," Polly called softly, "I've concluded that the carriage suits me fine."

Ned smiled, deepening the crow's-feet at the corner of his eyes. "Just wait a minute, ma'am. I think I might have just the horse you need. I'll be right back." He looped the chestnut's reins around the hitching post, then headed toward the big barn.

"Will you be going to the social ball, Joshua?"

Polly opened the carriage door and stepped to the ground. How dare the hussy call Joshua by his first name!

"I haven't an invitation," Joshua replied.

Anne smiled. "You don't need one."

If Polly wore false teeth, she would have surely dropped them. No invitation needed? Mr. Sawyer had certainly led her down the proverbial garden path.

Though she would have preferred breaking her umbrella over Anne's head, Polly kept it to her side. She was strangely relieved when Joshua replied, "I will probably have left town by then." But then he said, "However, if I should still be here, I hope you will do me the honor of saving a dance."

"I'll look forward to it."

Polly was about to step between the pair when she saw Ned Graham leave the barn. He was leading the most beautiful animal she had ever seen. It pranced rather than walked. Its sleek hide was near black, and the lighter mane and tail were long and seemed to float in the slight breeze. The ears were pointed forward as if it were looking at Polly. No matter what Joshua said, she was going to buy the beauty.

Ned led the horse straight to Polly. The mare stretched her head forward and, for the first time, Polly felt no fear. She gently stroked the soft velvet muzzle. "You are such a beauty," she crooned. "How old is she?"

"Three. She's still a colt, but real gentle. Her name's

Duchess. By the time she's eight or ten, she's goin' to be a mighty fine looking gray.''

"You mean she'll turn color?" Polly asked in awe.

"That's right."

"How come you haven't sold her before now?"

"I've been waiting for the right person. You have gentle eyes, ma'am, and I think you'll give her a fine home."

"Oh, I will."

"You want to give her a goin' over?" Ned asked Joshua.

Joshua smiled. "Yep, but we both know she's already sold. Miss O'Neil isn't about to leave without her."

Joshua raised the mare's feet, one at a time, checking the smell for any signs of thrush, and making sure the hooves had nice thick walls. From there he examined the legs, body and mouth. Finally he stood back and shook his head. "I can't find a thing wrong with her."

Ned laughed. "I have a reputation to keep."

Joshua grabbed a handful of mane and swung up on Duchess's back. Ned took the rope he had circled around the mare's thick, glossy neck, looped it around her muzzle, then handed the end to Joshua.

With just the slightest touch of his heels, the beautiful animal leaped into motion. Her soft gait was like being in a rocking chair, and Joshua had no trouble neck-reining her. He returned to where the others waited, then slid from her back.

"Well?" Polly asked excitedly.

"I believe you've got yourself a fine horse, Miss O'Neil."

Polly's laughter filled the quiet air. "How much, Mr. Graham? There is no sense trying to bicker price. You already know I want her. But please try to be fair."

By the time they had left the ranch with the mare tied to the back of the carriage, Polly could no longer contain herself. She let out an earsplitting screech of excitement, and followed that with laughter. ''Isn't life wonderful?'' she finally asked Joshua, who she had insisted sit with her this time. ''I have a house that's all mine, and now a beautiful horse.'' She clasped her hand over her mouth. ''I'm sorry,'' she said sincerely. ''I shouldn't have said that.''

''There's nothing wrong with being excited, and you did get a fine mare at a fair price.'' Joshua watched Polly's face come alive again.

''I did, didn't I? I've never possessed anything so beautiful.''

Joshua smiled at the way she glanced back at the horse, as if she couldn't believe it was hers. Polly was at her best when she allowed her true self to shine through, instead of acting contained and huffy. He had already deduced that the latter questionable qualities were what she considered ladylike behaviors.

Joshua's gaze drifted over the apricot-colored suit Polly wore. It blended perfectly with her coloring and hair. Interesting that she hadn't worn red since he'd made the comment about it being an uncomplimentary color. It would appear that Miss O'Neil was finally starting to listen to him.

''I have an idea that might appeal to you,'' Joshua said.

''Oh?''

''It's about the ball.'' Now he had her attention.

''What about it?''

''Why don't I escort you? That way, when you spend your time with Mr. Sawyer, no one will be suspicious that you're actually with him.''

''What a wonderful idea!''

''How stupid of me.''

Polly lifted her smooth eyebrows questioningly.

''I will probably have already left by then.''

''I didn't think about that, either.''

''Well, what harm can a bit of gossip be?''

"A lot! Mrs. Parker, that's the lady I took instructions from, warned—" Polly realized her error.

"What instructions? On how to be a lady?" Joshua looked up at a crow who flew overhead, making a lot of racket. "There is no need for you to be embarrassed around me. You wouldn't be the first person who came into money and wanted to be socially accepted."

Joshua looked ahead at the large oak trees on either side of the trail. Something or someone had disturbed the bird, and it wasn't the least bit happy about it.

"For some reason, I have a hard time picturing you being penniless."

"You're right," Joshua replied unthinkingly. He was too busy scanning the trees for any signs of trouble. "Money has never been one of my problems."

"But you said you asked for work because you were out of money."

"We can discuss it another time." Joshua stood and leaned over the seat in front of him so he could poke Thomas. "Stop the carriage," he ordered when Thomas turned his head.

Joshua already had the door open and was stepping to the ground when Polly asked, "Why are we stopping? Is something wrong with Duchess?"

"I want to check out what is going on in those trees ahead." He reached up and pulled a rifle and revolver from beneath Thomas's feet, then checked to be sure they were loaded and ready to fire.

It looked like an arsenal to Polly. She didn't even know the weapons had been placed in the carriage. "Do you think there could be bandits ahead?" she asked, suddenly wide-eyed with excitement. Nothing like this had ever happened to her before.

"That's what I'm going to find out." He shook his head and chuckled. "You amaze me at how danger never seems to enter your mind. Someday you should allow that desire for excitement its freedom. You might be surprised the joys one can discover.''

Polly leaned forward. "Are you going by yourself?"

Joshua smiled. "Are you volunteering to come along?"

"Don't be ridiculous!"

Joshua sobered. "Thomas, if you see *anything* that looks like trouble, you put the whip to those horses and get the hell out of here."

"But what about you?" Thomas asked.

"I'll worry about me."

Thomas pulled a heavy pepperbox pistol from beneath his leg. "I'll make sure nothing happens on this end," he assured Joshua.

Joshua shoved the revolver into his waistband. With his finger curled around the trigger of the Whitworth rifle and the barrel resting in the crook of his left arm, he took off walking along the dirt road.

Farther ahead in the trees, Karl continued to hold his horse's nose to keep him quiet. "Let's get the hell out of here, Loge," he said to the older man.

"Dammit, I want that horse. And take a look at that diamond necklace that woman's wearing!"

"While you're lookin', you might give some thought to that big man that's headin' straight for us. He means business."

"That's only one man. One shot will take care of him."

"Use your head, Loge. We don't need shots ringin' out that's gonna draw the sheriff to us. We got the stagecoach gold, now let's get the hell out of here."

Loge looked at his young partner. The kid was right. He climbed into the saddle. "That man ain't even gonna know how lucky he was today. Any other time I'd leave him dead."

Karl leapt onto his own mount. "I know you're plannin' on coming back, but I won't be with you."

The men turned their horses in the opposite direction of the approaching stranger.

"What do you mean you won't be with me."

"You're as cold-blooded and crazy as a man can be. You almost got us killed when we robbed the stage, and I'm not about to take the chance of it happenin' again."

"Oh, you're not, huh?" Loge pulled his pistol and shot Karl in the back. As Karl fell to the ground, Loge grabbed the other horse's reins. "Even better. Now all the gold's mine."

Loge turned the horses around just as the stranger entered the shadow of the trees. Loge suddenly became very still. Though he still couldn't get a good look at the man's face, something about him looked familiar. Something about the way he walked, or maybe— Loge stiffened. No! It couldn't be. McCreed could never have escaped that sandstorm. Hell, that had been over ten years ago!

He spurred his mount forward and drew his second pistol. As he neared the tall man, he pulled the trigger. At the same time, he felt the sickening, searing sensation of a bullet entering his side.

Loge wrapped his callused hand over the wound and continued to spur his horse down the road. He veered away from the carriage when he saw the driver holding the pepperbox.

Having decided that no others were going to attack from the trees, Thomas picked up the reins.

"What are you doing?" Polly asked angrily. With everything happening so fast, it had taken a few minutes for her to collect herself.

"Mr. McCreed told me to get you out of here if there was trouble."

"If you were going to do that, you should have slapped

those horses when you heard the first shot. And since when do you work for Mr. McCreed? Drive forward. We have to see if Mr. McCreed is all right!''

Polly strained her eyes, trying to see into the tree shadows ahead. ''Mr. McCreed?'' she continued to call, her worry starting to escalate. She had heard three shots fired. She hadn't been able to tell if the man who rode away in such a hurry had been shot. But even so, Joshua must have been the recipient of one of the bullets or he would surely have answered by now.

''Get down and search for him,'' Polly ordered when they reached the stand of trees.

Thomas's face paled. ''Me?''

''Never mind. I'll do it.'' Polly yanked her skirt around her and climbed to the ground. Her worry was only tempered from having nursed more than one bullet wound. She'd also seen men die, so there was no fear of what she might find. Nevertheless, she still grimaced when she discovered a man who had been shot in the back. She hurried forward. If she didn't reach Joshua quickly, she could be burying him come morning.

Five minutes later, Polly returned to the buggy. ''I found a dead man, and traces of blood on the ground, but I couldn't find Mr. McCreed.'' She climbed up on the seat.

''Are we going to go home now?''

Polly's blue eyes darkened with anger. ''No, we'll drive around the outside of the trees. He could have crawled away. I'm sure he's wounded,'' she said worriedly.

Forty minutes later, Polly was forced to give up the search. Joshua McCreed was nowhere to be found. She had even searched around through the trees again on foot. The area was simply too small to have missed anything. He had to have staggered off somewhere. Was he dead, or dying?

Polly glanced up at the sky. There were no longer any fretting crows. All was at peace again, except for a sadness she tried to bury deep inside with the other disappointments of life. She took a moment to fight back the tears. She had actually started to like Joshua McCreed.

''Take us home, Thomas,'' she said sadly. ''There is nothing more we can do.'' She didn't bother to hold back the tears that had been threatening for some time. None of this would have happened if she hadn't insisted on finding a horse today.

Chapter Six

Seeing the food hadn't been touched, Sable frowned at her employer. "I'm beginning to worry about you." She removed the breakfast tray from the bed. "Maybe you should take some of the new elixir I found at the Drug and Medicines Store. It's called Dr. J. Webber's Sanguifier. It'll make you want to eat."

"I'm not about to take any of your cure-alls." Polly threw off the covers. "And what are you doing up here instead of sending one of the maids?"

"I wanted a word in private."

"Then hurry up and be done with it."

"First you get up. It's not right that you spend most of your time in bed."

"I don't want to get up and I don't want to eat! I'm all alone and I—"

"I can't believe you're gonna lay there and feel sorry for yourself. You've been actin' as if you was widowed. And that's what I wanted to talk to you about. You've done nothing but stare at that horse you bought, insist furniture be moved from place to place, and snap at the servants."

"They work for me, don't they?"

"Just listen to you carry on. Don't forget, I was with

you all the time that Mrs. Parker was teachin' you to be a lady.'' Sable placed the bed tray on the small, ornately carved table by the wall and turned to her mistress. It was hard to believe that with Polly's hair in disarray and wearing a sea-green diaphanous nightgown, she could still look unapproachable. Perhaps it was the way she was sitting straight up with pillows supporting her back, and her arms crossed belligerently over her bosom.

''You can't change nothin','' Sable said. ''You went to the sheriff and reported that bandit, and told him what had happened. And he told you there were robberies goin' on all the time, but he'd ride out and see if he could find Mr. Joshua. There's nothin' more you could have done. Mr. Joshua isn't comin' back.''

''I don't need you to tell me that.'' Polly swung her legs over the edge of the bed. ''But where am I going to find someone to teach me to ride?''

''Teach you to ride? What about my bedroom? It's just sittin' out there half-done. When you gonna get someone over here to finish it? I'm gettin' mighty tired of runnin' up and down them stairs.''

''I don't want to go to the livery stable. Everyone in Auburn will laugh if they hear I hired someone to give me riding lessons.''

''I thought we was talkin' about my bedroom!''

''No, we're talking about me getting on that horse I bought! Besides, if Mr. McCreed hadn't mentioned that it could be your room, you wouldn't have even thought about it.'' Polly slid her feet into her slippers and stood.

''But he did say it, and you agreed.''

Polly rubbed her temples. ''Why must you constantly badger me?''

''If I didn't, nothin' would get done around here. What you need is a man in your life to give you some spunk. I had hoped it would be Mr. Joshua, but I reckon that's flown out the window.''

"Why should I bother looking for a man?" Polly asked sarcastically. "You're drawing enough of them to the back door." Polly picked up a brush from the dresser and began pulling the bristles through her thick hair.

Sable walked over to her mistress and sat her down at the dressing table. She took the brush and started attending to Polly's hair. "How do you expect to find that husband you been wantin' if you're gonna stay in the house all the time? You need to get out. You could go to the bakery and get a cookie from that nice old woman."

"I don't want a cookie."

Sable smoothed Polly's hair back at the sides, then began twisting it into a knot on the top of her head. She shoved in hairpins to keep it in place. "Well then, how about finding someone to finish fixing this place up?"

"Why would I want to do that?"

Sable released a frustrated sigh. "So my room will get finished," she whined.

"Honestly, Sable, once you get started on something, you never quit." Polly studied Sable's reflection in the mirror. "Sable, I don't think Mr. McCreed is dead. That's why I haven't done anything about the room."

"What makes you think he's not dead?"

"Because we never found a body!"

"That doesn't mean he'll be comin' back here." Sable went to the armoire to fetch Polly a town dress. "You must've been more smitten with him than I thought."

"Rubbish." Polly pulled the nightgown over her head. "The concern is about where we are going to find someone as good to replace him? Who will teach me to ride, and who is going to escort me to the ball?"

"Is that all you care about?"

"Of course," Polly lied.

Sable laid the pink town suit on the bed. "I got a friend named Chester, and he says he's right handy when it comes to fixin' things. Then there's Bidwell. He claims he's the best gardener in these parts."

"I'll think about it."

As soon as Sable had Polly's chemise and pantelets on, she placed the girdle around her tiny waist and began tying it. Her fingers suddenly stopped moving, and Polly became very still.

"I would swear that I heard someone hammering," Polly whispered.

Sable nodded in agreement.

"Did you tell one of your men friends that he could work on the new room?"

Sable shook her head no.

"Well, don't just stand there. Go to the window and see if you can find out what's going on."

"Not me. 'Sides, you can't see nothin' from your window."

"What is there to be afraid of?" Polly quietly chastised.

Neither woman seemed capable of moving.

"You go look," Sable whispered back. "I gave no one permission to work on *my* room."

Polly glanced toward the open window. "I'm not properly dressed." Polly began wringing her hands. "He's come back to haunt us!"

"I swear, you got me actin' as spooked as you!" Sable straightened her shoulders and snatched up another petticoat. "My whole family has talked of ghosts ever since I can remember. But you're worse than any of my kinfolk. Here, put this last skirt on so I can get you in your suit."

"Sounds like his hammering."

"Miss Polly, hammerin' is hammerin' no matter who is holdin' the handle."

A sudden hard knock on the bedroom door caused both

women's hands to shake. As the door slowly opened, they stopped breathing. When a young maid's head came into view, they both wanted to throw something at her.

"I swear, you're gonna be the death of me," Sable informed Polly. She looked at the attractive girl wearing a starched white apron over a black dress. "What are you doin' scaring the gizzards out of us?" Sable asked angrily. Seeing the confused look on the girl's face, Sable tossed her hands in the air. "All right, Ruth, what is so important that it couldn't wait till I came back downstairs?"

"There's a strange man working on the house, and Mary, the cook, said I was to come right up and tell you."

"Is he a black man?" Sable asked.

"No, ma'am."

"What does he look like?" Polly asked suspiciously.

"Oh, he's right fine looking."

"I asked what he looks like, not for your opinion!"

"He's tall, he's got black hair—"

"It *is* Joshua!" Polly exclaimed excitedly. "He's come back. I knew he wasn't dead."

Sable couldn't resist saying, "But what if he isn't real? What if he's a ghost."

Ruth giggled. "Oh, he's real, all right. He has Mary fixing him a big breakfast."

Sable headed for the door. "I'm gonna go make sure we're all talkin' 'bout the same man. Ruth, you help Miss Polly finish dressing."

Ruth stepped to the bed to pick up the next article of clothing.

"Hang that suit back up," Polly ordered the young brunette. "I'll wear the orange dress instead."

A short time later, Ruth went back downstairs.

Though anxious to see if Joshua was all right, it was another fifteen minutes before Polly left the bedroom. She had spent the time adding a touch of perfume and checking to be sure she looked perfect. Had something happened to Sable? The least she could have done was report back about the hammering.

All questions and concerns disappeared when Polly entered the kitchen. Joshua was seated at the round oak table, eating a breakfast that even included biscuits. Gathered around were the three maids, the cook, Sable and Thomas, all smiling from ear to ear, and all hanging on every word Joshua spoke between bites of food. Ruth was practically sitting on Joshua's lap! No one had heard Polly enter. But Joshua knew. He looked right at her, his face wearing an all too familiar smile.

Polly cleared her throat. The smiles disappeared and, with the exception of Joshua, everyone left the table, suddenly remembering chores that needed to be done.

"Good morning, Miss O'Neil," Joshua said congenially. "Won't you join me?"

Polly pursed her lips. He was acting as if he'd been off on a Sunday drive. "I've had my breakfast."

"But you didn't eat it. As I recall, you never do."

How did he know that? Sable or one of the others must have told him. "Where have you been? I searched everywhere. Why didn't you let me know you were all right? Do you know how worried and guilty I've felt?"

"Guilty? How interesting." Joshua spread a thick layer of strawberry jam on half a biscuit, then popped it into his mouth.

Polly yanked a chair from beneath the table and sat down. "I've had enough of this. I demand an explanation as to where you've been! It's obvious you're not suffering from a wound as I had suspected."

Joshua shoved his empty plate to the side and settled back in his chair. "I took off running to try and catch the thief that escaped. But his bullet had grazed the side of my head, and after some distance I became dizzy and passed out. Fortunately Ned Graham was on his way to see some neighbors, and had heard the shots. He found me and took me back to his place.''

''I suppose Anne Graham took care of you?'' Polly remembered how the two of them had acted when they were looking for a horse. She had thought she might have to put a rope around Joshua to get him away.

''She's mighty pretty. Don't you agree?''

''If you like the type.''

Joshua chuckled. ''The Grahams are nice people. As soon as I could ride, they let me borrow a horse to come back here. I didn't want you to be overwrought with concern.''

Polly placed her elbows on the table and leaned forward. ''Now, let me tell you what *I* think happened. You didn't give a hang about whether I was worried or not. You had a hankering to bed the woman, and the thief gave you the perfect excuse to return. Then you devised that story. Of course you couldn't stay there forever so you finally came back here. Well, I don't buy it. I wouldn't be the least bit surprised to discover you did something to make sweet Anne convinced you had been injured.''

Joshua leaned his chair back on the rear legs. ''Now do you really think I am capable of doing such a thing?''

Polly slowly nodded. ''Yes. I don't think you would back away from anything if you made your mind up to do it.'' Polly rose from her chair. ''For what it's worth, thank you for letting me know I was a fool to worry about you. You're dangerous, Joshua McCreed, and I don't need or want someone like you around. I hired you to do a job, but I want you to leave. Wait here, and I'll get the money you've got coming.''

Joshua lowered the chair back onto its four legs. ''And which job are we talking about?''

''The room, of course.''

"Once again you're making unfounded accusations. I thought we had straightened this all out before when you accused me of having a woman in the house. I knew at the time that I should never have agreed to anything other than to finish what you originally hired me for. I wouldn't have been shot at and I'd have been long gone. However, we agreed that I'd fix the house and build an extra room. I'll stay until it's finished."

Polly hated the way he already had her feeling even more guilty than before. He was right. She had no proof that her accusations had been right. It was just that she had been sick with worry, and here he sat as if he hadn't a care in the world. "It wasn't my fault that you got shot. As for our agreeing, it was also said that we wouldn't tell any lies. You're the one who broke the pact," she reminded him defensively.

Joshua turned his left side to her and pulled his black hair back to where Polly could clearly see the scab just above his ear and running the length of his head. She had been guessing, and he'd proved her wrong. She'd seen enough wounds caused by bullets to know he couldn't have made the mark himself. She felt like a no-account sidewinder. At a loss for words, she silently watched him pick his hat up from the floor where he'd apparently tossed it, and stand.

"All right!" Polly finally spit out. "I was wrong again." She looked toward the cook, who was busy kneading bread dough. She hated making apologies. "Do you think you're well enough to go back to work?"

"I think so." The side of Joshua's mouth curved into a lopsided grin. He put his hat on, never taking his eyes off the auburn-haired beauty who refused to look at him. She certainly kept him on his toes. He'd known from the beginning what he was letting himself in for. But one way or another, he'd find a way to make Polly O'Neil eager to do his bidding. It amused him to wonder what her reaction would be if she knew the truth about him. He headed for the back door.

"Joshua," Polly called.

He stopped and turned.

"What about teaching me to ride?"

"No."

"With your head hurting, it would be better if you took it easy for a few days. So why not work with me. You could sit on the corral fence. We could work on it until you get to feeling better. I promise there will be no more accusations. It will never happen again."

"You'll do everything I say?"

"Of course. This is very important to me."

"And you won't argue?"

Polly was getting excited. "Not a word."

"Promise?"

"I promise not to argue about the riding lessons."

Joshua's laughter filled the kitchen. "We'll see how good you are at keeping your word this time."

"Then the answer is yes?"

He nodded. "If you like, we can start right now."

Polly hurried forward. For some unexplainable reason, Joshua seemed to be even better looking than the last time she'd seen him. Of course that was impossible. She was just getting used to him. If she didn't give him any trouble, he'd leave her alone and she'd end up getting everything she wanted.

"I hope you continue to call me Joshua," the tall man commented as they stepped outside.

"Did I say that?" She was pleased to see they were headed toward the corral at the back of the carriage house. "Calling you by your first name isn't right. We don't know each other that well."

"And just how well acquainted do we have to be?"

"Oh, years, I would think."

"Does that mean that when you marry, you're going to call your husband by his last name for years?"

Polly giggled. "I hope not. All right, I'll call you Joshua."

Joshua was certain that by the time he got through with her, she'd be thinking of all kinds of names to call him. "That didn't take much coaxing."

"I never liked calling anyone mister."

Joshua stopped in front of the carriage house. "Go inside and get Duchess. I'll meet you at the corral."

"Zeek," Polly called through the open doors. "Take Duchess to the corral."

"I said for you to do it, not the groom."

Polly was surprised at Joshua's statement. "But that's what I pay the stable boy to do."

Joshua placed his big hands on Polly's shoulders and turned her to face him. "You said you wanted to learn to ride. No one said it was going to be easy."

"I understand that."

"Do you? Didn't you once say you were afraid of horses?"

"Yes."

"How do you expect to learn to ride if you're afraid? A horse senses fear, and I assure you she's going to see just what she can get away with."

"But I thought—"

Joshua studied the ground for a moment. "First we get rid of the fear. Perhaps you consider such work as being below you."

Polly had started to turn toward the house, but his words stopped her. "And just what was that remark supposed to mean?" she asked in a snippety tone of voice.

"I think it pretty well explained itself. After all, you can pay people to do the dirty work."

"Why, of all the—" Polly swung around and headed for the carriage house. As she entered, she smelled the pleasing blend of fresh hay, and the oil and saddle soap used to keep the tack in good condition.

"I'll get Duchess to the corral right away," the tow-headed boy said as he hurried to the last stall.

"That won't be necessary," Joshua stated, stopping the boy in his tracks. "Miss Polly will be doing that. For the time being, she is going to take care of all the horses. Your job will be to instruct her and make sure she does it properly."

Zeek's mouth dropped open as he looked from Joshua to Polly.

"Now just a minute. I never said—"

"What you said was that you would give me no arguments. Oh, and Zeek, make sure she cleans around the horses' shoes." Joshua returned his attention to Polly. "Shall we begin?"

Polly would have liked nothing more than to lash Mr. McCreed with a few well-chosen words. Instead, she shoved her hands into her skirt pockets. "And just what is the purpose of this?"

Joshua smiled. "Once you learn how to work with horses, your fear will leave. And if you're going to ride, you have to know how to take care of your mount. We'll start with the simple part. Taking Duchess out to the corral for her exercise. While she's doing that, you can attend to the other horses. After they're exercised, you can give them all a good brushing. You won't have to bother with my horse. I'm returning Ned Graham's gelding this afternoon."

With all the chores Joshua had her doing, Polly was filthy and worn-out come evening. By the time she entered her room, she had already silently cursed him a good many times. She was sure he didn't want to take the time to teach her to ride, so she had long since determined that it was all a means of getting her to change her mind. He was about to learn that she didn't give up on something that easily!

Because she hadn't eaten all day, Polly quickly devoured the food Sable brought up on a tray. That was followed by a long, hot bath. Polly scrubbed her body from head to toe to rid her skin of the horse smell. Sometime during the day, Joshua must have returned the horse to the Grahams' stead, but she hadn't even been aware that he had left or returned.

Polly was certain that it would be months before her body would stop aching. She climbed out of the tub, half dried herself, and fell onto the large canopy bed with the towel wrapped around her torso. She planned to just close her eyes for a moment, but she immediately fell asleep. She wasn't even aware of Sable returning for the tray.

The attractive black woman looked down at her mistress. Sable thought of Quency Alexander. He was pushing awfully hard to get her to marry him, but she hadn't said anything about it to Polly. She couldn't leave the girl after all this time. Polly could never make it on her own.

Sable reached across and pulled the sheet over the naked white body, then left the room. She'd tell Quency she didn't want to marry, and get rid of him once and for all. Besides, she didn't really cotton to taking care of Quency's children.

The following morning, Polly was awakened by someone shaking her arm. She opened one eye to see who the intruder was. "How many times have I told you to let me sleep, Sable," she growled.

"But—" Sable looked at Polly, who had pulled the pillow over her head. She reached out and grabbed it, but the redhead was stronger than she looked and was still holding on. There was a struggle, but Sable finally managed to get it loose.

"Now you listen to me—" Seeing the stubborn woman

grab for one of the other pillows, Sable managed to get to it first.

"I warn you, Sable, if you don't leave me alone there is going to be hell to pay!"

"You know I wouldn't bother you, but Mr. Joshua—"

Polly became still. "What about Mr. Joshua?"

"He said I was to wake you 'cause you got work to do. I don't know what he was talking about, but I believed him when he said that if you don't come right downstairs, he's comin' up to get you."

Polly rolled over onto her back and shoved her hair out of her face. "He wouldn't dare! I'd fire him!"

"All I know is he said you two had made some kind of a deal and you're gonna hold up your end."

"Deal, indeed! I'm surprised every bone in my body doesn't ache. He's making me work, not teaching me to ride. You go tell him there was nothing said about having to get up early in the morning. I'll attend to what needs to be done later. Emphasize the word *needs*." She turned onto her stomach and pulled the sheet over her head.

"I don't think I can make that man do anything he doesn't want to do. So if he comes up here, don't blame me 'cause you've got no clothes on."

The minute Polly heard the door shut, she poked her head out. Hadn't Sable said something about Joshua making her keep her end of the bargain? Though she certainly wouldn't mind having a man in her bed, that man wouldn't be Joshua, even if he did make her pulse beat rapidly. She hadn't failed to see the look of rapture on the servants' faces yesterday morning when they were talking to him. Polly jumped off the bed and hurried to the armoire. Sable was right. It would be just like Joshua to come bursting in.

Having to dress herself proved to be more difficult than Polly had remembered. But she didn't used to wear as many clothes, either. She managed the underclothing, until she came to the corset. In her haste her fingers didn't seem to want to cooperate. She finally tossed it onto the floor, giving it up as a hopeless problem. She returned to the armoire, and suddenly realized she had nothing to wear. At least not for working around horses! The clothes she wore yesterday were too unbelievably filthy to put on again.

Angry and frustrated, Polly plopped down onto the edge of the bed. Let Joshua come barging up here. She no longer cared! But that was exactly what he wanted. He was doing this to prove she couldn't handle working with the beasts, which would allow him to forget the riding lessons.

She stood. Not that she really cared, but there was one redeeming factor about all this. If he spent time with her, he wouldn't be spending time with sweet Anne!

Squaring her shoulders, she marched back to the armoire and pulled out one of her calico work dresses and a starched apron. They were far too fine to spend in horse stalls, but she'd be damned if she'd let Joshua get the better of her. And speaking of Joshua, how come he wasn't knocking on her door?

When Polly was ready to leave her room, she placed her hand on the doorknob and stopped. Was that hammering she was hearing? Damn that man! It had all been a ploy! He'd had no intention of coming after her! She yanked the door open and walked out.

Without a single pause in her step, Polly went down the stairs and the long hall, through the kitchen and out the back door. "Joshua McCreed?" she yelled as she stepped into the new room. "I demand to know what you are trying to pull."

Joshua swung down from a beam and landed on the flooring with the agility of a cat. "It's past time to clean out the stalls."

"I thought your head hurt?"

"I didn't say my head hurt, I just showed you the injury.'' He placed his hammer and nails on the floor and went out into the warm air.

Walking behind him, Polly noticed the way his worn shirt was molded to his broad, muscled back. Even his wide shoulders tapered attractively down to a firm, appealing... Joshua's chuckle caused her to stumble.

''What were you laughing at?'' she asked suspiciously. Did he know what she'd been thinking?

Joshua pulled up and waited for Polly to come alongside. ''I was thinking about how you are going to love your morning chores.''

''Are you sure that's what was running through your mind?'' She didn't like the twinkle in his eyes.

Joshua started walking again. ''Is there something else I should be thinking about?''

''No!'' Polly snapped at him.

By noon, Polly stood resting against the corral fence, once again mentally cursing Joshua in every foul way she could think of. What he was making her do had no bearing on riding. He was making a fool of her, and worse yet, she was letting him do it!

It had taken every ounce of determination to clean the wet and soiled bedding from the stalls. More than once she had savored the idea of piling some of the smelly straw in a wheelbarrow and taking it to where she could throw it in Mr. McCreed's face. She just knew her dress was soiled beyond belief. It would undoubtedly have to be thrown away with yesterday's clothing.

Besides tending to the stalls, she'd also had to water and feed the horses before letting them out to exercise.

''Are you ready to give it up?''

Polly opened her eyes as Joshua came up behind her. ''And just what is that supposed to mean?''

"I'm sure such work is offensive to your…delicate nature."

Polly shoved her hands into her apron pockets. The sun was directly in her path and she had to squint to see him. "I'll bet Anne Graham doesn't soil her hands."

"Quite the contrary. Owning a horse ranch requires everyone to pitch in and get the work done. She's quite a remarkable lady. Seeing you standing there and looking dejected, I came over to tell you that if you want to quit, I'll understand."

Hearing the respect in Joshua's voice when he spoke of Anne was the catalyst to spur Polly on. "I wouldn't think of quitting." Joshua had never talked about her that way! she thought angrily. "After all, we made a bargain that I wouldn't question anything you told me to do."

"That we did. I guess you really do want to learn about horses." Joshua smiled, tipped the brim of his hat and walked away.

Polly was tempted to grab a pitchfork and throw it at him. Instead, a rank smell turned her attention to the soiled dress she wore. Hearing Zeek whistling in the carriage house gave her an idea. Zeek was only twelve, and it was quite likely his clothes would fit her. Once again she would be back to wearing men's duds. She could never get clothes made as fast as she was destroying them. And they'd all be threadbare by the time Vera got through scrubbing them. And what about the cost? Zeek's shirt and britches was the only alternative. She pushed away from the corral fence and went back into the carriage house.

For nearly two weeks, Polly rose early in the morning and went to bed early at night. To her surprise, her distaste for having to rise with the sun quickly faded. As did the sore muscles that she had Sable rub with liniment the first few nights.

Joshua had finished Sable's room, but Polly wasn't about to let him leave. She insisted he make one of the rooms downstairs into a library, with bookshelves covering all the walls.

"Why are you havin' him do that?" Sable had asked. "You don't even know how to read."

"I can read," Polly had said in a huff. "I just can't read very well. Besides, all rich people have lots of books, but that doesn't mean they've read them all."

At the end of the second week, Polly unthinkingly slapped a horse on the rump to make him move out of her way. It wasn't until she did it to another horse that she realized her fear of the beasts had vanished. She didn't have time for it. Maybe Joshua had been right all along. Getting to know the animals had changed her entire attitude. She also discovered something else. She liked being busy instead of playing the part of wealthy Miss O'Neil who did nothing of any value. And she wasn't nearly as restless as she'd been previously.

Now that she knew her chores, things went quicker. Her extra time was spent working with Sable's friend, Bidwell, whom she'd hired as a gardener. Not too long ago, she'd had only herself to look after. Then she'd hired Sable. After that came Thomas, Joshua, two maids and a cook, and now a gardener. But like Joshua, Bidwell did know what he was talking about when it came to plants. Together, he and Polly had a good start at ridding the yard of weeds.

As far as Polly was concerned, everything in her life seemed to be coming along just fine. Before long, she'd be riding Duchess all over the place, and her days would be full. But what about finding a husband as she'd planned?

Chapter Seven

"Mums, this is boring me to pieces! Can't you see the snit isn't going to come? And if she does, it probably won't even be on the same day!"

Inez Fritz sat on the sofa, glaring over the edge of her cup at her beautifully groomed son. "It would appear you could be right for a change." She sipped her tea, then placed the delicate china cup back on its saucer. "Very well, there is no need for you to wait. But before you take off to one of those hidden card games, be sure to change your clothes. We want everything fresh for when you start courting Miss O'Neil."

"I never said anything about playing cards."

"Berk, don't try to pretend that isn't where you're headed. It doesn't suit you. Have you seen Daniel? He hasn't poked his head in since a week ago."

"He's probably been too busy rutting with some whore since you fired Elizabeth."

"The man who took her place does a much better job, and he doesn't go around whining all the time."

Before going out the door, Berk turned and looked at his mother. "And who is bedding the baker now?" He shut the door behind him before she could speak her piece.

"You worthless ingrate," Inez spat out. "One of these days you'll come to regret the way you treat your mum." She poured herself another cup of tea.

Loge Snipes kicked the ground with the toe of his boot and grimaced. His side still hurt where that damn bullet had gone clean through. It might have healed more if he'd been able to get the rest he needed. But he'd been too obsessed with finding out if Joshua McCreed was the man who had shot him.

Just thinking about the heat and the Mojave Desert made beads of sweat pop out on his upper lip. He'd relived the choking, partial suffocating, and the sand filling his pores over and over again in nightmares that had spanned the years.

The sandstorm had ruined everything. From the beginning, he had planned to kill Clancy and the other two guards. He wanted the gold all to himself.

As it turned out, that hadn't been necessary. The storm killed one guard and Loge had shot the other one between the eyes. But he couldn't find Clancy or the prison wagon. Blistered from the sun and lacking water and food, he had barely made it to a settler's place alive.

Loge could remember every ache and misery he suffered for the next four years as he searched the desert for the gold. He'd found what was left of Clancy the same day he was well enough to return. But he never found the wagon. There was never any doubt that the men inside were dead. Their ankles had been shackled and the doors barred. At least that was what he had believed until the shooting a couple of weeks ago.

He scratched his bald head. It had never felt the same since the Indians scalped him some years ago. He jammed his hat on and once again looked up and down the road. For three days he'd been hiding behind the oak tree, hoping that shiny black carriage would return. He couldn't wait any longer. Though it was impossible that Joshua McCreed could still be alive, he had to know for certain. If it turned out that McCreed was alive, he'd know what had happened to the gold.

Loge grabbed the pommel and swung his big body up in the saddle. He looked in the direction the carriage had come from, then nudged his dun down the dirt road. He'd just go a ways and see if there was anything or anyone who might give him a clue as to where he could locate that woman the man had been with. If that didn't accomplish anything, he'd go on to Auburn.

Clothed in Zeek's brown trousers and faded blue shirt, Polly attended to her chores. As usual, Duchess was in the corral with her. Joshua had claimed it would be a way for them to bond.

Feeling something nudge her back, Polly knew it had to be Zeek. The boy loved to pull pranks. He particularly liked to sneak up behind her, then make her jump when he tapped her shoulder.

"Now stop it. I have work to do."

Again the nudge. Polly turned, ready to give the boy a good scolding. Instead of Zeek standing there, it was Duchess. Polly reached out and rubbed up and down her soft nose. The horse's friendly gesture was what made all this worth it. On more than one occasion, she had been ready to refuse to do any more of the grubby work. But it was the look on Joshua's face that kept her going. He expected her to quit, and she'd be damned if she'd give him the satisfaction of being right.

The mare nudged her shoulder, and Polly's heart immediately caved in. Until a week ago, she hadn't realized how much the mare's acceptance meant to her. "You stop that and let me finish," she scolded gently.

"Looks like you two are getting along just fine."

Polly didn't have to turn to see who had spoken.

"You might bring her a carrot tomorrow. I'm sure she'd like that. You know, I don't believe I've ever seen a stable hand who always wears a diamond necklace. I've been meaning to ask if you also wear that to bed at night."

"This is a strange time to ask such a question." She let her hand fall to her side and once again the mare nudged her. Laughing, Polly shook her head.

"Is there a certain time to ask a question?" Joshua asked when Polly left the corral.

"What are you talking about?"

"Your necklace."

Polly was in a joyous mood. Even her walk had a jauntiness to it. She was amazed at how Duchess's simple gestures always brightened her day. She reached up and fingered the diamonds. "I found this necklace," she said cheerfully.

"Oh? I don't think I would share that information with many people. They might get mean and insist you take them to where you found it."

"The place no longer exists. My friends blew it up with dynamite. Someday I'll tell you the story."

"How about this afternoon?"

Polly gave him a quizzical look.

"I've finished your study, and I think it would be good for both of us to dine out this afternoon. I also see no reason why we can't start your lessons tomorrow."

Polly danced around in front of him, unable to contain her excitement. "You mean I'm finally going to ride Duchess?"

Joshua shook his head. "Not exactly."

"What does that mean?"

"You'll find out tomorrow."

She gave him an ornery grin. "Who will pay for the dinner?"

Joshua reached out and pulled off the bandanna wrapped around her head, then handed it to her. "I thought when a man asked a woman out, he was expected to pay the bill. Am I wrong?"

"You're absolutely right."

"By the way, have you seen Malcolm Sawyer lately?"

"You're terrible! You know I haven't had time to see anyone. You're still going to take me to the ball, aren't you?"

"Uh-huh. How long is it going to take you to get ready? I'm starving."

"An hour."

"An hour?"

"Yes. An hour." Polly took off toward the house. This was the first time a man had ever asked her out. Even if it was Joshua, she was quite excited about it. She wanted to look her very best. Why, she might even meet her future husband today! She hurried on.

"Mary," Polly yelled to the cook when she entered the kitchen, "I'll need water for a bath right away. I'm going to town!"

Polly promenaded down the stairs. With her hair curled to perfection, and adorned in her finest linen suit, she was feeling quite the lady. She had just taken the last step when one of the maids rushed forward.

"Miss Polly, you have a visitor waiting in the parlor."

Polly beamed. "You mean Joshua?"

"No, ma'am. I've never seen this gentleman before."

"Thank you, Vera."

Curious, Polly hurried on. She was flabbergasted to find Malcolm Sawyer waiting for her. She watched his round face light up when he saw her enter the room. His thin lips spread in a slit of a grin. Strange that Joshua had just mentioned the gentleman a little over an hour ago.

Polly gave the visitor her best smile. "How nice of you to call, Mr. Sawyer."

Malcolm took her extended hand and raised the knuckles to his lips. The soft kiss lasted a bit longer than acceptable. "You look magnificent as usual."

"Thank you." Polly had to suppress a giggle upon remembering how she would have looked and smelled had he arrived earlier. "Won't you be seated?"

"No, I'll stand." Malcolm wanted to make this visit as brief as possible. His girdle was killing him.

Polly withdrew her hand and went to the only chair she could sit on while wearing a crinoline. As always, Malcolm's gray-streaked hair was perfectly groomed, his mustache trimmed and his clothes impeccable.

"I've missed seeing you at the hotel." When Polly made no comment, he continued. "I've come to ask if I may escort you to the dance. I realize your concern for propriety, but you needn't worry about that now. My wife has actually filed for a divorce." He reached up and smoothed his mustache with his finger. "I'm sure you would have found out about it eventually. It's a big topic for the gossipers."

"I'm sorry to hear that."

"Oh, don't be. We hadn't gotten along in years."

"I will be escorting Miss O'Neil to the ball."

Polly and Malcolm looked toward the doorway and discovered Joshua standing there. Confused, Malcolm looked back at Polly.

"I believe you have already met Joshua McCreed. He has been doing some work for me." Polly hoped Malcolm wouldn't ask where Joshua was staying.

Though concerned about what Malcolm might think, Polly was finding it difficult not to stare at Joshua. She had never seen him dressed so handsomely. Finally she gave up the effort and took a good look. His gray peg-top trousers, red-and-blue-striped cravat and black waistcoat were made of the finest wools. He looked magnificent. His wink made her grin.

"We were about to go to town for lunch," Joshua informed the older man.

Polly had momentarily forgotten Malcolm was still in the room. "Would you care to join us?" she asked cordially.

Joshua gave her a chilling look that she could feel all the way to her knees.

"Thank you, but I've already dined," Malcolm replied politely. "Since you will be going to the dance with Mr. McCreed, perhaps you will be kind enough to save me a waltz."

"Oh, you misunderstood. Mr. McCreed only agreed so I would have an escort." She turned to Joshua. "Isn't that right?"

Joshua nodded.

"I would be pleased to have you escort me, Mr. Sawyer."

Upon discovering the tall, handsome gentleman would only serve as a temporary escort, Malcolm's confidence grew. Unfortunately, Mr. McCreed gave no indication of leaving, which prevented him from having a private talk with Polly. "Until next week then," he said as he again kissed Polly's knuckles.

Polly watched Malcolm leave the room. "You acted terrible," Polly scolded as soon as Malcolm was out of hearing distance. "You could have been friendlier."

"I acted terrible?"

After being around Joshua for weeks, Polly was starting to see past his words. Though he kept his voice calm and controlled, she knew he was displeased about something.

"All right, Joshua," Polly said as she pulled her white gloves on, "what have I done wrong?"

"You're beginning to know me," Joshua said, more as a realization. He watched her go to the mirror and stick a long hat pin through the flowery affair she had placed on top of her head. "Friendly Malcolm wants only one thing from you, princess, and it's not a dance."

Polly looked at his reflection in the mirror. "I'm aware of that." She turned and faced him, her cheeks a bit flushed. "I'm not a virgin, Joshua. Does that shock you?"

"No, but it certainly does intrigue me."

Polly was surprised that his comment made her blush and look away. Strange how he made her feel like an innocent girl.

"You say you want to become someone in this town. Have you stopped to think that the biddies will be calling you the other woman? They may even accuse you of being the reason for the divorce. They'll say a pretty young woman like yourself wouldn't be going out with an older man unless there was a purpose to it."

Polly stared at her Berlin work she'd had framed and hung on the wall. Joshua could be right. Still… She swirled around. "On the other hand, if I act the lady of quality, they may want to get to know me. Once they learn I am in no need of Malcolm's money, they will start thinking in a different direction. Don't you see, Joshua? I can't turn down Malcolm's invitation. He can introduce me to all the important people about town."

Joshua knew he was going to have to take matters into his own hands. "Thomas is waiting for us. I hope you're not disappointed that Malcolm won't be dining with us?"

Polly's eyes sparkled with humor. "Not at all," she said truthfully.

Joshua laughed openly. "You have a cold heart, Polly O'Neil."

"I'll bet it's not nearly as cold as yours, Joshua Mc-Creed."

"You may very well be right."

Without a doubt, Joshua had the most devilish grin Polly had ever seen. Now that she was more comfortable around him, she was even willing to admit that his grin wasn't the only thing she found appealing. She flashed him a bright smile before placing her hand in the crook of his elbow. "I warn you, I'm going to order a huge meal. Especially since you will be paying for it."

"I don't blame you. If I remember correctly, that was what I did the night you paid for my meal."

"I'd forgotten all about that!" Polly stated good-naturedly. "Now I'm not only going to have a big meal, I'll have dessert, as well."

Seated in a quiet corner of the American Hotel dining room, Joshua and Polly waited for the waitress to clear their dishes away.

"I would never have believed that someone so small could eat so much," Joshua teased.

Polly laughed. "I warned you."

"Will you be wantin' dessert?" the waitress asked.

"Just coffee, please." Polly shrugged her shoulders. "I've no room left for more food."

"I'll take coffee, too," Joshua added.

"Joshua, are you angry because I accepted Malcolm's invitation instead of going with you?"

"I just wanted you to be aware of what you could be getting yourself into. What you do is really none of my business."

Polly experienced a deep feeling of regret. Why did she continue to think of him as always being around?

"Let's don't discuss the dance. I assure you everything is going to go exactly as it should. You said you'd tell me about that necklace you wear."

Polly became somber. "You'll never believe me."

"Maybe not, but I'd like to hear the story anyway."

Two ladies walked by, turned and took a good look at Joshua. Their inviting giggles aggravated Polly.

The waitress brought their coffee.

"Now," Joshua said when they were alone. "Tell me about the necklace."

Polly sighed as she resigned herself to relating the tale. Besides, she had Joshua's full attention, and she liked that. "I found the necklace in a town called Springtown. I also discovered poison oak while I was there," she added, trying to make light of the subject.

"You're joking with me about Springtown. I've heard old miners talk about that place. It's nothing more than a legend they created. Something about hidden gold and a ghost guarding it."

"It wasn't a legend," Polly said irritably. "I lived there! There was indeed buried gold and a ghost." Polly glanced around, then lowered her voice. "Of course there's no town now because Chance Doyer blew it up with dynamite."

"Who is Chance Doyer?"

Visioning Chance in her mind's eye, Polly sighed. "The only man I will ever love."

"The only man you will ever love?" Joshua repeated with humor in his voice. "You're much too alive and beautiful for me to believe that." He pulled a cigar from his pocket and held it up. "Do you mind if I smoke?"

"No." Polly opened her mouth to continue, but Joshua interrupted again.

"How come you didn't marry the man?"

"He was in love with my friend Amanda. They're happily married now and live in Sacramento. Are you going to let me tell the story or not?"

Joshua bit off the end of the cigar, lit it and took a couple of long puffs. "Do you expect me to believe this tale you're about to weave?"

"What do you mean?"

Joshua rested his elbows on the table. "Are you going to expect me to believe there really was a ghost and hidden treasure?"

"I don't know."

"What do you mean by that?"

"Listen to what I have to say, then you can make up your own mind."

Joshua fell silent.

"Amanda Bradshaw, Lester Adam and I left Columbia with the intention of going to Sacramento." She decided it wasn't necessary to tell him they were all wanting to start a new life. "From the very beginning, nothing went right. The map Lester had didn't make any sense, Lester up and died from a coughing fit, and Amanda and I were lost. Then we came upon Springtown."

"What did you say? You're talking too low."

"I said we came upon Springtown," Polly repeated a bit louder. "Maybe we'd better go somewhere else. I don't want others to hear what I'm about to say."

"There is no one seated close enough to hear you."

Polly glanced around the room again. They were indeed sitting off to themselves. The other people who had been sitting nearby must have already eaten and left.

"So you found Springtown. What happened after that?"

"It wasn't just what happened, it was also Springtown itself. The town was spread out in front of us, everything looking as if it had been recently built. Even the houses at the other end of town were in good shape."

Polly leaned even closer. "The only thing moving in the town was a burro, and a barking, black-and-white dog came running at us."

"Where were the people?"

"That's the strange part. I've never seen anything like it before and I hope I never see anything like it again. I have gooseflesh just thinking about it. There were cobwebs, but the stores were still stocked, and furniture, curtains and dishes were in the houses, as if the people had just stepped out for a minute.'' Polly's voice had started to quiver. ''And there were all these jewels and clothes. But no people.''

''And that is where you found your necklace?''

''I found it the first day we were there.''

''How did Doyer come upon the scene?''

''He arrived a week or so later, and ended up staying. We may never have made it out of there had it not been for him.'' Polly took a drink of her coffee.

''Did the people ever return?''

''No. He found out in a diary that they had either sneaked away at night, or they were murdered.''

''Who murdered them?''

''The ghost, Jack Quigley.'' Polly looked into space without seeing anything—her mind centered on Spring-town. ''It was Amanda who always saw Jack. He's the one who told her about the gold. At first he was nice, and we were very excited about being rich. We even talked about what we would do once we had money. Not long after that, Chance came to town and stayed. He also found out about the gold and wanted his share.''

Joshua watched her hand shake as she unthinkingly stirred her cold coffee.

''Jack claimed he loved Amanda and grew possessive of her. He was evil and deadly. Amanda, Chance and I joined forces, in an effort to locate the treasure and get away. We searched everywhere, but our efforts were all in vain. We even considered the possibility he was lying just to have control over us.''

Polly had to pause a minute to master her fears.

''Did you find the gold?'' Joshua asked quietly.

''Jack was threatening to kill us, and said he would never

let Amanda leave Springtown.'' Polly became very still, and her eyes turned glossy. ''To protect my life, Chance sneaked me out of town in the dead of night, then told me to continue on to Murphys. I never knew such terrifying fear. He gave me a sack of money and jewels Amanda had found, and said if they didn't meet me in a week, to go on to Sacramento without them. He went back for Amanda. I was sick with worry. The following week lasted a life-time.''

''You said they were married now, so apparently he succeeded in getting her.''

Polly's eyes slowly focused on Joshua. ''He not only succeeded, he located the gold. When they finally arrived at the hotel, they told me how Chance had demolished the town, and Jack Quigley, as well.''

''And did you believe him?''

Polly sat back in her chair, exhausted from the telling. ''I saw the wood and ashes that was once Springtown when we returned to get the gold. Everything had been leveled to the ground. For months after that I had dreams of being forced to return to Springtown, and Jack was there waiting for me to wreak his punishment. Even though I no longer believe there actually was a Jack Quigley, I can't rid myself of the fear.''

Joshua trailed cigar smoke from his mouth. ''Why don't you think there was a Jack Quigley?''

Polly smiled faintly. ''Amanda was always making up tales about something. Months later, I decided she had made up that whole thing about Jack. If he really was there, how come neither Chance nor I ever saw him? Chance believed every bit of it.''

Polly placed her napkin on the table. ''I'm surprised you're not laughing at such foolishness.''

Joshua shook his head. ''Not me. I believe that most

anything is possible. I may not even be what I seem. Did you ask Amanda if she'd lied?''

''Once. She denied it. Of course what else could she do? But even though I don't believe any of it, when I look back, I always feel as if I was touched by the devil.''

Joshua dropped his cigar into the spittoon, then reached across the table and took her cold hands in his. ''I'm sure the devil could manage to be more subtle. You'd probably never even know he was around.'' He released her hand and stood. ''Come along. Once we're outside, the coloring will return to your cheeks and your hands will grow warm again.''

Joshua went around the table and pulled Polly's chair out for her. ''Enough of this talk. We were supposed to be enjoying ourselves.''

''Joshua, I was only sporting about you paying the bill,'' Polly said quietly. ''I'll understand if you can't afford it. I know what it's like to have little or none.''

Joshua shook his head. ''What better use could I have for it than to take a beautiful woman out?''

Polly stopped and took a long, deliberate look at her escort. ''How come you don't have a woman?''

Joshua placed money on the table for the bill and tip. ''I do. She just doesn't know it yet.''

Polly was taken aback. The actual possibility of him having a lady friend hadn't even occurred to her. Maybe it was that horsewoman, Anne Graham. Well, she'd have to put a halt to that. The woman wasn't good enough for him. And just what was it that made her so special?

Once they were settled in the carriage and Thomas had the carriage headed toward home, Polly relaxed. She looked at Joshua, sitting across from her, and smiled. ''I thought you might like to know what I'm going to do about a husband.''

''You know what I like most about you, Polly?''

"My money."

"That, too, but also it is your commendable straightfor-wardness. You decide what you want and go after it."

"It doesn't always work out the way I plan."

"I assume you are referring to that man you said you loved. Wasn't his name Chance?"

Polly ignored the question by looking at the houses they passed.

"All right, you don't want to talk about the one love in your life. Then tell me about your plans to marry."

The twinkle returned to Polly's eyes. "I'm going to ad-vertise in the *Sacramento Union*."

"You're what?" Joshua was astounded. "What will you come up with next?"

"I thought you might help me write the ad."

"You can't do something like that."

"Why not? Men do it. I've seen more than one mail-order bride."

"That's different."

Polly's dander was starting to rise. She scooted forward in the seat and narrowed her eyes. "If a man can do it, why can't a woman?"

"Women are more docile and mold easier into a family. They know what they are letting themselves in for and are willing to follow their new husband's dictates. You get a man by mail, and he's going to expect to be the one to rule the roost."

"I'll interview them."

"Have you stopped to think that your money will be-come your husband's? After you're married, what's to stop him from spending it on his old cronies or girlfriends?"

Polly leaned back in the seat and glared at Joshua. "You're going to talk me out of this, aren't you?"

His humor tugged at the corner of his mouth. "It would

be easier to hire a lover instead of a husband. Men do that too, so why can't a woman?''

Polly stared in openmouthed disbelief. ''Just what do you find so amusing about a woman who wants to marry and have a family?''

''Surely you didn't expect marriage without sex? Now don't go getting yourself all upset. I realize this isn't exactly a proper subject, but forget I'm a man and you're a woman. Just think of us as…friends.''

''Getting married is very important to me, Mr. Mc-Creed.''

''Joshua.''

''I want a husband and children. I'm not likely to do the last part by myself. I want to be respected and be considered the upper crust of Auburn. I can barely read and write, I am not getting any younger, and I am not a virgin. All these things put limits on my selection of a husband. But one way or another, I intend to get what I want, even if I have to pay for it.''

''Very well, I'll help write the ad.''

''We'll do it when we get back to the house.''

''When we get back to the house, I had planned on you starting your riding lessons.''

''But you said we would do that tomorrow.''

''Why waste time?''

''Oh.'' Polly thought for a moment. ''Very well, then we'll do it afterward.'' She wondered why Joshua smiled as he nodded his agreement. Did he have something up his sleeve? ''Thomas,'' she called, ''can't you move the horses a bit faster? I'm anxious to get home.''

''I'm curious about that gold you and your friends found. Was it just nuggets and dust, or were there also gold bars?''

Polly thought for a moment. ''I don't remember seeing any bars, but Chance or Amanda could have loaded them. Why do you ask?''

"When I was a boy, I used to tell myself that one day, I'd find a buried treasure of shiny gold bars. I just wondered if you'd gotten there before me."

Polly laughed. "Remember that old saying about the early bird gets the worm?"

"How true. I think it would be a good idea for you to continue wearing Zeek's clothes while you're learning to ride. It'll allow you more freedom of movement, and there won't be any material to get in your way."

By dusk, Polly had forgotten all about writing an ad. The rest of the afternoon had been spent saddling and unsaddling the mare. The soreness she had previously overcome from her labors had returned. Never once did Joshua lift the saddle for her. Not until he was convinced she knew what she was doing and had learned to pull the girth tight, did he move on to the next phase.

The following afternoon they worked on mounting. It had to have been at least a hundred times that he had her place her toe in the stirrup, swing up onto the horse's back, then dismount.

As she fell asleep that night, Polly told herself she had reached the end of her rope. She couldn't continue on with this sort of treatment. The lessons were over. It just wasn't worth it. Joshua had won.

But by the time morning arrived, Polly was of a different frame of mind. Hearing Joshua whistling beneath her window helped with her decision.

Seeing the freshly cleaned pants and shirt hanging over the back of a chair was the final deciding factor. After all she had been through, she couldn't quit now. Just the thought of having to see Joshua's lips spread into a knowing grin was more than she could tolerate. Though her sore muscles still caused her to wince, she didn't falter once in her dressing.

When Polly finally walked out the back door, she was surprised to see Duchess saddled and tethered to the hitching rail. She didn't have to look far to find Joshua. He was standing beside the garden talking to Sable and Bidwell. They all had their backs to her, and it was apparent they didn't know she was there, or Bidwell wouldn't have reached over and patted Sable's fanny. She was going to have to have a talk with Sable about that little matter.

Then Joshua turned and looked right at her. Polly could feel his eyes peering into her very soul, causing her to quiver. It was that same wild, dangerous quality about him that always seemed to excite her.

Polly blinked several times to clear her thinking. Joshua was already walking toward her.

"Is there something in your eye?" he asked.

"No. Not at all. The sun is so bright it made me blink. Why is Duchess saddled?"

"Because, Miss O'Neil," he said in overly exaggerated politeness, "today you are going to ride your horse."

Polly clapped her hands and giggled. "At last!" The excitement immediately faded from her face. "By going for a ride, do you mean around the corral?" she asked suspiciously.

"No, I was thinking about going up a ways into the high country. Is that agreeable with you?"

"Yes." Polly rubbed her suddenly moist palms on her pant legs. "That would be wonderful." She had thought to say something about not having had any breakfast, but she didn't want to give Joshua a reason to change his mind.

"Then I'll go get my horse. By the way, I don't think I've told you that I've never seen a man who looked better in pants and a shirt than you do."

Polly laughed from pure pleasure.

Five minutes later, the pair rode away from the house. Duchess was a frisky horse. Once Joshua talked Polly into relaxing in the saddle and explained how to place the leather straps in one hand, the mare was easy to rein. He kept the horses at a walk, and quietly and calmly told Polly what she should do. He talked about using the stirrups to hold her weight, how to ride with a horse instead of against it, to think of a horse's gait as a rocking chair, and so forth. He even took her through bush and around trees to show her how to keep her balance and the horse under control.

By the time they were well into the mountains, Polly's tenseness had subsided. She not only rode with ease, she was actually enjoying herself.

Joshua led the way down an easy mountain slope, then brought his horse to a halt at the bank of the North Fork of the American River. "I think you need some exercise."

"Why?"

"Get down, and you'll find out."

Polly dismounted without so much as a second thought. She concluded that her lack of concern was due to all the times he'd made her practice mounting and dismounting yesterday. But when her feet were firmly planted on the ground, her legs turned to jelly. Even the insides of her thighs ached. She looked questioningly at Joshua.

"Now that's the part about riding I can't help you with," he said with a crooked grin. "I doubt that you would have been nearly as uncomfortable had you used a sidesaddle."

"You mean this is going to happen every time I ride?"

"No, not if you do it regularly. The aches eventually go away." He took the reins from her hand. "Come on, we'll walk for a spell. It'll keep your legs from getting stiff."

"I don't think I *can* walk."

"Of course you can. Just keep moving one foot in front of the other."

She didn't like it, but Polly forced herself to move.

"I think you're going to make one fine horsewoman."

Her face beamed with pleasure. "Do you mean that?"

"Indeed I do. Each day we'll ride a bit farther until I think you can handle everything on your own."

"Joshua, I want to thank you," Polly said as they strolled along the riverbank. She shoved some leafy branches away from her face. "I know you weren't pleased about having to teach me to ride. You have no idea how much this means to me."

"I believe I can make a good guess."

They walked on in silence.

"Joshua, do you think I'm pretty?"

"Are you searching for compliments?"

"No, just curious."

"I've told you before that you're beautiful."

"What about my figure?"

Joshua grinned. "Most appealing."

"Appealing? I didn't know you'd noticed."

"I noticed."

"You've never even tried to kiss me, so there must be something you don't like about me. Is it the way I act or talk?"

"Why are you asking all these questions?"

"Because if you find something wrong with me, I need to correct it. Like I told you, getting a husband is going to take some doing, and I want to be as perfect as I can possibly be."

"You're making quite a task out of this. Just be yourself, and you'll do fine. I think we'd better be heading back to the house."

They mounted up.

"When do you plan to tell me who your woman is?" Polly asked. "Is it Anne?"

"Nope."

Strangely, that piece of news made Polly feel much better. "Is it someone in Auburn, or does she live in a different town?"

They moved the horses up and over the rocky embankment.

"Someday I'll tell you about her."

"How come we're always talking about me, and never about you?"

"Because you're more interesting. What do you want to know about me?"

"Are you wanted?"

"Wanted?" The question came as a complete surprise, and Joshua broke out laughing. "Not that I know of," he finally said.

"How old are you? Thirty?"

"Minus a couple of years."

"Where do you come from?"

"Originally, Missouri."

"Are your folks still alive?"

"Nope."

Because Joshua was doing nothing to further the conversation, Polly fell silent again. As they rode through a thick stand of pine trees, they fell into single file. He was leading, but Polly wasn't in any particular hurry. Soon he was quite a ways ahead of her.

Polly inhaled the sweet smell of pine resin that permeated the air, and looked up at the high, feathery branches that nearly blocked out the sun. Then suddenly something struck her across the chest. The next thing she knew, the ground came up to meet her. She shook her head, then raised up on one elbow.

"Are you all right?"

Hearing Joshua's voice, Polly looked up. He was on his horse, holding the mare's reins. "I'm fine," she snapped at him as she stood. "You can wipe that smile right off your face, Joshua McCreed." She began brushing the dirt and pine needles off her pants. "What hit me?"

"An oak branch. If you're going to ride a horse, you'd

best learn to watch where you're going.'' He tossed the mare's reins to her. ''Do you need me to help you mount?''

''I don't need you for one damn thing, and I don't like you laughing at me!'' Polly swung the reins over the mare's head and climbed into the saddle. Without waiting for Joshua, she moved Duchess forward and out of the trees. She knew Joshua was right behind her because she could hear him still laughing.

When they returned to the house, Polly didn't bother to rub Duchess down. Instead, she told Zeek to take care of it. For today, she'd had all she wanted of being around horses, and Joshua. She would think of other things that gave her pleasure. For instance, the dress she would wear at the ball. In just three more days she would outshine every woman in Auburn.

Chapter Eight

Sable pointed at the large Ming vase sitting on the floor. "Do you see that?" Her gaze traveled from the pretty young girl, Ruth, to the rail-thin Vera, and finally to the chubby cook, Mary. "This is proof that one of you is lyin' about not movin' things around in this house. You all saw me put this on the end table yesterday. Now how do you suppose it's changed places with a brass spittoon?"

"You know I stay in the kitchen," Mary replied, her double chin shaking as she talked. "And why would I want to go around movin' things? I got enough work to keep me busy. But now that you have me in here, how come the rug is turned cattiwompus?"

The women looked down, then at each other.

"Even if me and Ruth was to give it a try," Vera said, "we couldn't move the rug like that. Not with all the furniture sittin' on it and for sure not without everyone knowing it."

Ruth giggled. "I think there's an ornery ghost living in this room, and it's giving you a bad time, Miss Sable."

"Don't you dare go sayin' something like that around Miss Polly," Sable warned, "or you won't be workin' here no more."

A bloodcurdling scream came from upstairs and walked its way up each woman's spine.

"Miss Polly!" Sable gathered her wits and hurried out of the sitting room.

The maids and cook followed. Another scream put all of them into a run.

When the women reached Polly's bedroom door, they barged right in and came to an immediate stop. Polly was sitting in the middle of her bed, her face and arms blotchy with what appeared to be a red rash.

"Look at me!" Polly screeched. "I can't go to the dance! I have poison oak!"

The women cautiously moved forward as one, until they could see the watery blisters.

"Looks like poison sumac to me," Vera said.

"No, that's poison oak all right," the cook confirmed. "I've seen it many times. I'll go soak oatmeal to—"

"No, no," Sable interrupted. "She should soak in Glauber's salts and drink magnesia to get it out of her system!"

"How could this have happened?" Polly groaned as she scratched an itchy spot.

"You went ridin' with Mr. Joshua," Sable reminded her. "Did you see any poison oak?"

"I don't know what it looks like."

"Mr. Joshua shoulda known. Especially if you was in the middle of it. Didn't you say somethin' about goin' to the river?"

Polly thought about the leaves and branches she'd pushed aside. Her eyes narrowed. "If Joshua is to blame for this, I'll never forgive him!"

Polly fell back and pounded the feather bed with her fists to keep from crying. Going to the dance had meant everything to her. Now she would have to spend the night at home. She wanted to die. "Sable, go to the druggist and get spirits of niter. And get a lot. I'm going to be drenched in it until this goes away.''

Polly jerked up on one elbow. "And Sable," she called just before the women left the room, "have Joshua go with you. He can stop at the Orleans Hotel and tell Mr. Sawyer that I won't be accompanying him Saturday night.''

"Won't you be cleared up by then?" Ruth asked meekly.

Polly shook her head. She was too upset to do any more talking. Instead, she released another earsplitting scream.

Saturday night, Polly lay on her back with her arms spread out, feeling sorry for herself. New blisters had stopped popping up on her skin, but she didn't have to go to the mirror to know she looked like a pitted melon.

She picked up the newspaper Sable had brought her, then tossed it back down, causing the beeswax candle to flicker. Though her reading had improved considerably, she was in no mood to decipher the big words. As for the articles, they were little more than gossip. Besides, instead of reading about people, she should be out meeting them face-to-face.

Sable had delivered Joshua's regret over her condition, but Polly wished he had come to her room and told her in person. She wanted someone to talk to. More importantly, she wanted to give him hell for taking her around poison oak. Maybe it was for the best. It would give her time to take hold of her temper before she fired him again. It seemed as if she was relying on him more and more for one thing or another. Now it was even conversation.

Polly stared up at the ceiling. She'd be willing to bet a toad that Joshua wasn't staying home tonight. No sirree. He'd be dancing with Anne Graham! He should be forced to stay at home, also, especially after what he'd done to her!

Would he move smoothly to the music, or would he be the type that constantly stepped on his partner's toes? Foolish question. He would be light on his feet just as he was when he walked.

Polly yawned. She was tired from boredom. She didn't try to fight sleep. Why should she? It would make the time pass faster.

Polly knew she was dreaming, but it was such a wonderful dream that she didn't want it to stop. She was standing in front of the mirror, but there was nothing else in the room that she could see. She had on the beautiful flounced gown of white silk brocaded with blue that Isabel had made for the ball. The capped sleeves left her shoulders bare, as well as her arms, neck and upper chest. The bodice was low, allowing a brief view of the rise of full breasts, and her tiny waist was shown off to perfection. She even had on stockings with openwork insets.

Surprisingly, her unruly hair was actually behaving itself. It had been parted in the middle and taken to the back of her head, then worked into combinations of glossy twists and braids. For the first time in her life, she truly felt beautiful.

Then she was standing in front of Joshua, who had been waiting for her. Just seeing him made her heart pound with excitement. The strong planes of his face and his dark looks were accentuated by the black evening suit and top hat. It didn't seem fair that one man should have so much sexual appeal.

Joshua took her hand and turned her in a circle. "Not only are you breathtaking, but your perfume is very intoxicating."

Polly suppressed a giggle. She had never had a man say such things to her, and she was enjoying every minute. "I bought the perfume just for tonight."

Joshua smiled. "Poor Malcolm. He never had a chance."

"Speaking of Malcolm, what will he think at seeing you escorting me to the ball?"

"What difference does it make? You owe him nothing."

Polly brightened. "You're right. I don't have to explain a thing."

"He won't matter in the long run."

Polly was about to ask Joshua what he meant by that, but he was already leading her to the carriage. To her wonderment, Thomas wasn't in the driver's seat.

"Thomas is passed out from drinking, so I had to find someone to take his place," Joshua explained.

During the ride to the Empire Hotel, Polly could feel the strange electricity that seemed to be flowing between the two of them. And when he took her hand in his, she had no desire to pull it away. Some part of her acknowledged that this was all a dream, so why not enjoy the fantasy to the fullest? And who else could make the fantasy more perfect than the dashing and daring Joshua McCreed?

When they entered the ballroom, it seemed to Polly that everyone in Auburn had chosen to attend. She held her full skirt up just enough so as to allow her to follow comfortably alongside Joshua.

"Since I escorted you," Joshua said after they had made their way through the crowd gathered near the doorway, "I believe I should be the one to claim the first dance."

"If that is a request, I'd be delighted." Polly was thankful for all the socializing she had done with her friends in Sacramento. Had it not been for them—and, of course, Mrs. Parker—she wouldn't have known how to dance.

The fine cotillion band consisted of a cornet, basso, clarinet, flute and two violins. Their wonderful music made dancing a pleasure. Of course—as she had expected—Joshua proved to be an excellent partner. Was there nothing this man couldn't do well? He was so light of foot that following him was like dancing on air. Everyone faded from view as he circled her around the room. There were only the two of them and the music.

After a rather rigorous dance, Joshua led Polly to one of the few open windows. "I'll get you something to drink."

Polly snapped her fan open and waved it vigorously to cool her face. While watching Joshua walk away, she caught sight of Malcolm Sawyer standing off to the side. Her interest shifted to the older man. She started to go to him until she realized he was having some sort of a confrontation with a handsome blond gentleman she'd never met.

The blond man walked away, but Malcolm went after him. He grabbed the younger man by the shoulder and jerked him around. They were now close enough for Polly to hear what they were saying.

"Dammit, I said I want an apology."

"I'm not going to apologize for a thing, old man. The drink spilled on you because you hit my arm."

"You young whippersnapper! Do you know who I am? I could have you roped and quartered. Now I want that apology!"

Polly was having a hard time believing such words were coming from sweet, gentle Malcolm. His face had turned red with rage, and his personality had become quite ugly.

Then of all people, Anne Graham appeared on the scene.

"Malcolm, do you know Joshua McCreed?"

"I certainly do, my dear," Malcolm replied in a sticky-sweet tone of voice.

"Have you seen him?"

"No, I don't believe he's arrived yet."

"Miss Graham," the attractive blond gentleman acknowledged. "Could I have the pleasure of the next dance?"

"Get out of here," Malcolm barked. "Can't you see we're talking?"

Polly was shocked at Malcolm's rudeness.

Anne smiled sweetly. "I don't believe we've met."

"My name is Berk Fritz. My mother owns the bakery in town."

Polly realized that he was one of Inez's sons.

"Never mind what your mother does," Malcolm said angrily. "I'm warning you to quit butting in."

"Malcolm, stop being so discourteous," Anne chastised. "I would be pleased to dance with you, Mr. Fritz. Malcolm, if you see Joshua, please tell him I'm looking for him."

"Don't say I didn't warn you, boy." Malcolm planted a fist in Berk's gut, causing the younger man to double over. "I didn't get where I am by letting young bulls like you walk over me," Malcolm grumbled.

Polly was shocked.

"Malcolm!" Anne said angrily. "What right did you have to do that?" She tried to help Berk straighten up.

"You'd best think about whose side you're taking, missy. Your pa and I have known each other for a long time. I'm telling you that I didn't get out of this boy's way, and he deliberately spilled lemonade on me."

"That's a lie," Berk persisted.

Malcolm took Anne by the arm and started leading her away. "You don't want anything to do with the likes of him, Anne."

Polly realized she had seen the punch being spilled, and it was all Malcolm's fault. Any thoughts she still had about marrying him were gone. It was frightening to think how badly she had misjudged the man.

By the time Joshua returned, Polly had regained her composure. However, she was grateful for the cup of lemonade he handed her.

"As I recall, Joshua, didn't you once tell me I was a woman who needed looking after. Do you still believe that?"

"More than ever."

Polly looked up into those wonderful dark eyes that practically danced with unspoken challenges. It made her wonder if she should have retained some of the old Polly O'Neil.

But what was she thinking? She didn't have her eye on Joshua, and she wouldn't be about to marry such a rascal. She'd met a lot of his kind. They were shiftless and could never be trusted. A woman might catch their eye for a while, but they eventually moved on.

Nevertheless, as the evening passed, Polly found that the only time she seemed to enjoy herself was when she danced with Joshua.

They danced several more times together, but in all fairness, Polly knew she shouldn't monopolize Joshua. He did come here to enjoy himself, and he appeared to be doing just that. It seemed every woman in the place wanted him to be her partner.

An hour later, Polly was ready to go home. To say the ball was less than she had expected would have been putting it mildly. Everyone snubbed her, and standing off to the side by herself made her feel as if she were on exhibition. She would never have guessed that such affairs could be so monotonous and meaningless. And to top all that off, she was still upset at the way Malcolm had acted.

After Joshua returned a dance partner to her seat, Polly motioned him to join her. She found it quite flattering that he always seemed to know where she was at any given time.

"Joshua," Polly said when he walked up, "I'm tired and I'm going home. I'll send the carriage back for you."

"I'll join you."

"That won't be necessary."

"But I want to."

Polly looked into his eyes. Was it her imagination, or had the words hinted of better things still to come? More likely she'd imagined it because she wanted something to happen. "Very well."

It was already nearing midnight when the driver moved the carriage away from the hotel. It had been a hot day, and the night air still held the warmth. The bit of a breeze the moving carriage created felt good brushing across Polly's warm face.

Suddenly Polly felt Joshua removing the pins from her hair. Shocked, she turned to look at him, but it was too dark to see his face.

"Let your hair blow in the breeze, and you'll be cooler."

His words were soft, like silk. Polly gulped as his hand came to rest on the back of her neck, making her temperature rise. How could she feel so innocent and inexperienced? Yet when she was around this man, that was exactly the way she felt.

Polly realized that as much as she might enjoy Joshua's advances, she couldn't permit them to happen. "Joshua, I don't want you to think that just because we're friends, or because we went to the dance…"

"Do I frighten you, princess?"

"No. Of course not."

"You said you aren't a virgin. How long has it been since you've had a man?"

"Well, I…I…it's been a while. But I haven't minded at all. I'm really not a very passionate person." She nervously brushed back a curl that had made its way to her cheek.

"If that's so, then surely there would be no harm in allowing one kiss."

Polly started to refuse, but she was more intent on his hand pressing against her neck, slowly drawing her to him.

She'd never experienced such a fatalistic feeling, and it frightened her. She stiffened.

"It's only a fantasy, Polly. Enjoy it."

Her resistance took wing. He had drawn her so close that his words brushed her face. He lowered his head, then his lips were on the curve of her neck, one of her most vulnerable spots. He sucked gently, and she put her head back so he would have better access. She savored the feel of his lips against her skin, but she couldn't let it continue. "We shouldn't do this," she murmured weakly.

"Do you really want me to stop?" His tongue trailed a path to her lips. "You're a woman who very much wants to play with fire, but you're afraid. Taste the fire, Polly, and savor it. Feel it. I can take you to worlds you've never even dreamed of. We've known that eventually it would come to this. Open your mind. Let it happen."

His lips came down on hers. Hot, searing lips that made every nerve in her body come alive. Passion raked its nails along the inside of her thighs and her breasts grew taut. She had never known such a feeling of pure lust. She wanted him.

"I've given you your night at the ball, Polly," Joshua whispered.

Polly sat straight up in bed. It took a moment for her to realize where she was and that the evening had all been a dream. But the dream had been so real that her body was damp with perspiration and her passion still paramount.

Breathing heavily, she climbed off the bed and went to the window. There was a full moon, and she could clearly see the carriage house. She wanted to go to Joshua and get the satisfaction her body craved, but how could she when it was all a dream? No, she was forced to bear the hell that gave no release.

It was at least another hour before Polly finally returned to her bed. Something had happened tonight that she would never be able to undo. At times, she had wondered what it would be like to have Joshua make love to her. But she had never openly acknowledged it. Now it would remain forever sitting in the back of her mind. She had never experienced such eroticism. Was Joshua really that capable of getting her so aroused with a few words and a kiss?

"You could have ruined everything!" Inez raved at her son, the following morning at breakfast. "What if someone had seen you kill Malcolm Sawyer?"

"I didn't knife him until he was by himself." Berk poured himself a cup of tea. "I wasn't going to let the old bastard talk to me like that!"

"I told you he couldn't keep that damn temper under control," Daniel said angrily. "And the way he was acting around that Graham woman, you'd think she was the one he was supposed to be wooing!"

"What difference does it make?" Berk said defensively. "Polly O'Neil wasn't at the ball and Anne is a fetching woman. And I would have had Miss Graham right where I wanted her if she hadn't left so early."

"McCreed was the one who had her right under his thumb, Berk. Not you. And when he left, she had no desire to stay."

"That's a damn lie, Daniel!"

"Stop it! Both of you!"

The two men looked at their mother.

"That's better. How can a person think with the two of you continually yowling at each other like a couple of tom-cats?" Inez tugged at an earlobe. "If I didn't know better, I would suspect the girl is deliberately avoiding us. Well, that's coming to a halt. The time has come for me to take matters in my own hands."

Chapter Nine

"I tell you, there's mighty strange things goin' on in this house!"

Polly continued looking out the front window and drinking her coffee. The poison oak was about gone, but after her dream four nights ago, she had deliberately avoided seeing Joshua. And, too, she still hadn't recovered from the shock of Malcolm Sawyer being murdered the night of the ball. According to the newspaper article, there were no clues as to who had done it. "What's wrong now, Sable?"

"Look at the rug! It keeps moving. And when Vera went to take the laundry out yesterday, she swore she felt someone trip her. 'Course, there wasn't no one around. The clothes fell from the basket onto the ground. She ended up having to wash them over again."

"She just made that up so she wouldn't have to admit she was clumsy."

"Me and Bidwell have been talkin' this over—"

Polly turned and looked at the woman who had kept her company for nearly two years. "Since when did you start discussing things with Bidwell?"

"Since you been runnin' about and doin' everything Mr. Joshua tells you to do."

Polly looked back out the window. She knew Sable was dying to find out why she hadn't spoken to Joshua, but Polly was in no mood to answer a bunch of questions and listen to advice. "What were you going to say about your discussion with Bidwell?"

"Knowin' how you feel about ghosts, I had warned everyone that if they even mentioned that word, they'd be fired. But Bidwell said that being as you is the mistress of the house, you had a right to know what was goin' on."

"What are you talking about, Sable?"

"Ghosts." Sable placed her hands on her slender round hips. "I think there's one in this house. It plays with me by movin' things around, and it knows I don't like it one bit!"

"There's nothing here that would attract a ghost. There wasn't even a death in this house before we moved in."

"At first that's what I thought. But this morning, I was talkin' to Mary about supper, and Ruth came in complaining about not being able to find the spittoon in the sitting room. Then we heard a woman laughing. Not just me, but all three of us heard it."

Polly couldn't hold back a shiver. She didn't like the subject, but she was through allowing the word *ghost* to intimidate her. "The windows are open. Remember, Joshua said when a breeze goes through the house it makes strange noises."

"But there's no breeze. I think we should get a preacher!"

"What's this about a preacher?" Joshua asked. "Is someone getting married?"

The women turned at the sound of the deep voice.

"Married?" Sable shook her head. "Who said anything about getting married?"

Memories of her dream flooded forth. Polly tried to stop

the dizzying current shooting through her as his gaze dropped from her eyes to her shoulders to her breasts.

Joshua chuckled. "You were saying something about a preacher. Don't tell me Bidwell has finally convinced you to marry him."

Polly had to fight an overwhelming need to be near him. She had never thought about a man having seductive lips, but Joshua certainly did. They looked as if they had been chiseled by a master artist.

"I was just tellin' Miss Polly that I think we got us a ghost in this house, and I'm gettin' mighty tired of all the fooling around it's doin'. Just look at this rug! Every day it gets turned more and more. And look at the spittoon sittin' on the end table. That's just the start of it!"

Polly had to clear her throat to speak. "I'm sure it's only the maids." She placed her empty cup on the secretary. "Neither is capable of doing anything right."

"You're looking well, Polly," Joshua said.

Polly reminded herself that it had been Joshua's fault that she'd been unable to go to the ball.

"Mary told me I'd find you here. How are you feeling?"

"Fine, no thanks to you!"

Joshua frowned. "Why me?"

"I had to have caught the poison oak while we were riding. How could you have done this to me? And just why didn't *you* break out with blisters?"

"Poison oak doesn't bother me. You should have said something."

"When I was telling you about Springtown, I also said I'd had poison oak!"

Joshua raised his eyebrows. "This is the first time I've heard you mention it."

For the life of her, Polly couldn't remember for sure if she had said anything. At the time, she'd been too emotionally affected by repeating the past. Now she'd never be certain if he'd done it on purpose.

"You must have thought you said something. Had I known, I'd have paid more attention to our surroundings. Are you sure you caught that while we were riding?"

"I haven't been anywhere else that it grows." Polly refused to retract her accusations.

"I've about finished the rooms you asked me to build in the carriage house, so I'll soon be on my way."

"Oh…but…who will watch after me?"

"I imagine it will be your husband," Joshua replied nonchalantly.

"You can't leave now! I…I've decided to add another room. Yes. That's it. Maybe even three." She ignored Sable's surprised look. "And what about the riding lessons? I still want to ride, I just don't want to spend any more days itching and miserable."

"I don't know. Once again you're accusing me of something, and it seems that we'd be better off keeping our distance. I think you'd best find someone else to handle the matter."

"But there *is* no one else! All right. If an apology is what you—"

"I'm not asking you to apologize. Very well, we'll give it another try. Duchess could use the exercise."

Polly had the strangest feeling that Joshua was the one who had control of the situation, not her. She tilted her chin and looked him in the eye. "I'll bet you came in here for the sole purpose of getting me back on that horse." Polly scratched an itch on her wrist. "I have to admit, it would feel good to get out of the house."

"I guess we can go in the morning."

"Why not now?"

Joshua shrugged his shoulders. "That's fine with me."

"Come along, Sable. I need you to help me out of this dress and into my britches."

Joshua's grin broadened. In a way, Polly was right. But he hadn't come to the house to get her to go riding. He'd come to stop the way she was avoiding him. "I'll meet you out back."

"You sure we won't be near poison oak?"

"Positive."

"But what about the ghost and the other things going on in this house?" Sable demanded as the two women hurried out of the room.

As soon as they had left, Joshua's eyes turned midnight black. "All right, Frenchy. You know you can't hide from me."

Frenchy slowly materialized. She was sitting Indian-style on the side table next to the spittoon. "Oh, Joshua, you should be ashamed of yourself the way you manipulate people. That Polly doesn't have the vaguest notion as to what you're doing to her."

"Don't try to avoid the issue, Frenchy. It sounds as if you've been keeping yourself busy."

Eyes downcast, she unfolded her legs and stood. "I was only having a little fun. I promise I won't do it again. You know I've only stayed so I'd be here if you needed me. Didn't I take care of you when you were shot?"

"There was nothing to take care of."

"You were unconscious."

"I came to."

The room faded from view, and the two were suddenly standing in a thick fog that lapped at their feet.

Frenchy hurried over to Joshua and was about to put her arms around his neck when a strong wind blew her back. "Don't be angry with me, Joshua," she pleaded.

"I warned you to stay away."

"I like the house. I want to live there. I promise I won't pull any more pranks."

"Find another house to haunt. You're in my way."

"You only want her for the gold!"

"The gold is mine."

Another strong gust of wind pushed her further back. Frenchy held her arms out. "It will never work," she cried. "Once the woman discovers the truth, she'll turn her back on you. Let me stay!"

Lightning danced around them and the thunder was deafening. Joshua's face looked as if it had been hued from marble. The strong winds continued, and Frenchy disappeared.

Knowing she would never be allowed to see Joshua again, Frenchy couldn't resist doing one last thing to try to get back in Joshua's good graces. She switched everything in the sitting room back to where it originally was.

"Mr. Joshua—" Sable stopped in the doorway and looked around the sitting room. How could he have left without her seeing him? She had only gone halfway up the stairs when Polly had sent her back with a message. Sable shook her head. Too many strange things were going on for her liking. Whoever heard of the sound of thunder on a clear summer's day?

As Sable started to leave the room, she glanced at the floor. Her eyes became larger with each passing second. "Well, I'll be!" she whispered.

The rug was positioned exactly as it had been the first day it was laid. Even the spittoon was back on the floor and the Ming vase on the side table. Polly would *never* convince her that there wasn't a ghost in this house! Sable's feet moved faster than they had in years. She didn't want to see any more!

This time, Joshua headed the horses south, where the land was open and sloped gradually. To Polly's delight, every now and then he would point out a deer or some other wild creature before it scampered away through the high parched grass. Polly not only appreciated the fresh air and the scenery, she also felt a considerable amount of pride at the way she was handling Duchess. Two months ago no one could have convinced her that she'd actually enjoy being on a horse.

"All right, Polly," Joshua said. "Let's start moving these animals."

"Oh, no. I'm just fine."

"You can't expect to always keep that mare in a walk."

Joshua leaned over and gave the gray a slap on the rear with his hand. With Polly keeping a tight hold on the reins, the mare only moved into a trot, causing Polly to bounce up and down in the saddle. But Duchess was eager to go, and kept tossing her head and dancing about.

Angry at what he had done, Polly managed a quick glance at Joshua. He was holding his own horse back in order to stay alongside her.

"Joshua, my insides are being pounded to death!" Polly said in staccato.

"Brace yourself with your stirrups. Come on, Polly, ease up on the reins—unless you like being jarred. A canter is a lot easier than a trot."

"I can't. I'm too scared! You should never have slapped Duchess!"

Joshua shook his head. Because Polly refused to do what he told her, she was unable to stop the mare. Seeing how white her face had become, he leaned over and grabbed hold of the mare's bridle and brought both animals to a halt.

Polly immediately dismounted and started walking.

"Where are you going?" Joshua called.

"Home! How dare you swat Duchess! I could have been killed!"

He turned the horses around and followed. "I thought you wanted to learn to ride."

Polly's breathing was quickly becoming labored. The slope hadn't seemed nearly as steep when she was on Duchess.

"You weren't even close to dying. Where's all that spunk?" He circled his leg around the pommel and relaxed as the horses continued to follow her. "Where's the woman who cleaned stalls because she didn't want to give me the satisfaction of saying she couldn't handle it?"

Polly continued to trudge forward. "It won't work this time, Joshua McCreed. You're not going to get me back on that horse. At least not while you're around." She was finding it increasingly difficult to talk and walk at the same time.

"You'd be in more danger if I wasn't around. Well, you started this, but it looks as if I'm going to have to finish it."

Polly stopped and spun around. "Just what do you mean by that?" she demanded. She watched Joshua let his horse's reins drop, then he unhooked his leg from the pommel and slid to the ground.

"As I recall, when we started this, you were the one who wanted me to do the teaching, and I was the one who wasn't interested. I know you were serious about it, because you wouldn't have worked so hard if you weren't. Now you're ready to call it quits. What do you think we should do about this?"

"Go home."

Joshua glanced up at the sun. "I don't think so."

Polly rolled her eyes, just as she had seen Sable do many times. "What do you mean you don't think so? It's up to me, not you."

"You see, that's where we disagree. I wouldn't be much of a teacher if I let you quit after one little hardship. So, we're both going to ride my black. I'll show you what to do."

"No!"

"Yes," he said in that soft voice.

Polly's breathing had returned to normal. Could she outrun him? She wasn't about to get on that horse!

"Are we going to do this the easy way, or the hard way?"

"What do you mean by the hard way?" It suddenly occurred to Polly that by riding behind him, she'd have to place her arms around his waist. No! As tempting as it was, she was not going to let him change her mind this time.

"It's quite simple. Either you mount up, or *I* put you up."

"You mean you want me to sit on the saddle?" she asked in shock.

"That's right."

"And you'll sit behind me?"

Joshua nodded.

"In the saddle or on the horse's rump?"

"On the rump. What are you getting at?"

"No, no, no. Not in a hundred years. If you slide off, you'll pull me with you! Besides, your stirrups are too long. However, I would be willing to get back on Duchess as long as I'm permitted to keep her at a walk."

Joshua started leading Duchess toward an oak tree about twenty-five yards away. His horse followed.

"Where are you going?" Polly asked. She didn't intend to budge an inch. "Has a cat got your tongue?" she called. When he didn't answer, Polly was feeling quite smug. At least she'd gotten in the last word.

She continued to stand and watch. Joshua tethered Duchess to a low limb, then walked to the side of his black gelding. When he lifted the stirrup flap and loosened the buckle, she knew what he was up to. He was shortening the length to fit her legs.

Polly started walking backward. "You can't do this, Joshua McCreed! You're fired! I never want to see you again! You're not going to make me get on that damn horse!" She started running.

It seemed to Polly that she hadn't even gone a hundred steps when she turned and saw Joshua swing up in the saddle. Polly sucked in her breath and stood frozen to the ground. Kicking the horse into a full gallop, Joshua took hold of the pommel with his right hand, then leaned down so low to the side that she was sure he would either fall right in front of her or knock her out cold.

Polly jerked around and once again started running. But her speed was nothing compared to the horse. Suddenly a strong arm wrapped around her waist and she was being lifted up and onto the saddle as if she were nothing more than a toy. The horse hadn't even broken stride.

"Stop this damn thing!" Stark and vivid fear swept through her upon seeing how fast they passed the low shrubs, and she clutched the pommel with a death grip. To her relief, Joshua slowed the big horse to an easy lope.

"Pick up the reins, Polly."

Polly wasn't about to release her grip.

Joshua placed one long arm around her waist. "Come on, darlin'," he whispered in her ear. "Didn't I tell you I wouldn't let anything harm you?"

To Polly, it was more like a caress than a question. It was that deep, lulling voice that always made her think she was being put into some sort of a trance. But now that she knew Joshua had control of the horse, her inhibitions began to fade.

"Put your feet in the stirrups. Don't worry, I won't let you fall."

When she had done that, he said, "Now place both of your hands in front of mine."

She released one hand at a time and took hold of the reins.

"Remember? Think of it as a rocking chair." His left arm forced her to feel the cadence of the horse.

Finally seeing what it was that he had been trying to tell her, Polly discovered that staying with the horse wasn't unpleasant at all. But other more pressing problems had cropped up. Joshua was much too close. She liked the feel of his arms around her and the—

The horse leapt over a rock, and Polly was thrown back against Joshua's hard chest.

"Polly, if you ever plan on riding by yourself, you've got to learn to watch where the horse is going."

Polly broke out laughing. "I think you're right, Joshua."

After five minutes, Polly was beginning to actually enjoy herself. She loved the feel of the wind blowing in her face. She laughed, and didn't hesitate a minute when Joshua had her hold the reins by herself. There was a strong feeling of power at being able to manipulate such a large animal.

For nearly an hour, Joshua showed Polly how to handle a horse, by using his hands to guide hers. As he explained how a rider and horse become as one, she listened to everything he said—and learned.

Polly had never experienced such exhilaration.

Her head was still in the clouds when they finally dismounted back at the tree where Joshua had tied Duchess. There was no doubt about it. Sable was going to have to rub her with liniment again, but she now felt every ache was worth it. She couldn't even wipe off the grin that seemed to be plastered to her face.

"Oh, Joshua, that was wonderful. I'll never ride in a carriage again!"

Joshua noted the way her hair hung in wild disarray, and

that, in her excitement, her cheeks had turned bright pink. Polly was definitely at her best when she was outdoors, or when she could turn loose and let the wild side of her nature go free. Today she'd been able to combine it all, and she was happy.

"I take it you're not still mad at me," Joshua commented.

"I should be."

"But you're not."

"I don't know. I'll think on it," she teased.

Joshua untied Duchess and handed Polly the reins. She started walking, and Joshua fell in beside her. It didn't take long for Polly to remember how it had felt having Joshua's arms around her. And of course there was always the dream that gathered forth other memories.

"Joshua, did you know Malcolm Sawyer is dead?"

"I read it in the paper."

"What kind of a man do you think he was?"

"He wasn't the gentleman he appeared to be. He was an unlikable codger who would stop at nothing to get what he wanted."

"So you didn't like him?"

"Nope."

"Why didn't you tell me?"

"Would you have listened?"

Polly grinned. "No."

"Be glad you're rid of him."

"Did you go to the ball?"

"Uh-huh."

"Did Malcolm ask how I was faring?"

"Nope."

Polly swatted at a pesky blowfly that kept buzzing around her face. The movement caused Duchess to toss her head, but Polly had a firm hold on the reins. "And...did you enjoy yourself at the dance?"

"Why are you asking me all these questions?"

"Since I didn't get to go, I would at least like to hear about it."

"It was no different than any other dance of its kind. After a few dances, the room became uncomfortable. The windows were open, but there was little air circulating."

Polly remembered how warm it had been in her dream.

"Anne Graham introduced me to many of the locals, and they were full of questions. Some of the ladies said they had heard of you and that they plan to pay you a call after you're settled in. I'm sure they are dying of curiosity and want to be the first with information they can spread to their nosy friends."

"What color was Anne's dress?"

"I believe it was a pale blue."

Polly fell silent. That was the same color she'd seen in her dream. But of course it was all coincidental. She certainly hadn't attended the ball. If only she could get that confounded dream out of her mind.

During the following week, Polly and Joshua rode farther every day. But when they weren't gloriously galloping across the land, Polly felt as if she were lying on a bed of hot coals. Part of it was anticipation, the other part worry. Anticipation of what it would be like when Joshua finally got around to kissing her. It was bound to happen eventually. After all, she was a woman and he was definitely a man. The old Polly would have gone to him and made it clear what she wanted. But there was something about Joshua that kept her at a distance.

Polly was at a difficult crossroad. As much as she wanted Joshua, she just as strongly didn't want anything to happen. What if he proved to be better in bed than any man she'd ever had? She'd heard the other girls talk about men who were so good a woman would gladly be his slave. Not that

Polly really believed a man could be *that* good. But in her dream, he'd certainly made a good start at it.

"I see no reason why you can't start riding to town and back by yourself," Joshua said as they were returning home one evening. "If you do it once or twice a day, you'll soon be a better rider than I am."

Polly laughed. "Don't get carried away with your flattery, Joshua McCreed. I'll never be that good."

"Someday you might even ride to Lake Tahoe. That's quite a sight to behold. I've never seen anything any prettier."

"Isn't that where they bring the ice down from in the winter?"

"Yep. But don't get it into your head to go alone. It's too far and dangerous."

Polly started to suggest they go together but quickly changed her mind.

As they rode up to the carriage house, neither Polly nor Joshua saw the man crouched in the shadows.

Loge Snipe's weathered face was several shades lighter than normal as he took another peek then ducked back around the corner. The sight of the tall, dark-headed man had Loge's mind twisted in confusion. He was the spittin' image of Joshua McCreed, but it couldn't possibly be him. He looked younger than the day they'd first met, some twelve years ago. Loge did some quick calculating. McCreed had been around thirty then, which would put him over forty now. Hell, it had been ten years since that desert storm. It had to be a son. No, that wasn't possible. The man was too old to be McCreed's son. Maybe a brother.

As soon as Loge had made his way unseen around the corral, he hurried toward the trees where he'd left his horse. For the time being, he didn't want anyone to know he'd been snooping around. Not until he could figure out what was going on. What he needed was a bottle of whiskey!

Even after all the drinking he had done, Loge was still dead sober when he made it to the room he had rented in a run-down hotel. He sat on the bed and pulled a tin of chewing tobacco from his pocket. Not until he had put a good-sized plug in his cheek, did he allow himself to think about McCreed.

One time Joshua had told him that he'd lived with Indians, and Loge had never had any reason to doubt it. The man had been the best tracker Loge had ever known, and lethal with a knife. But besides that, he was calculating and deadly.

Loge reached down and pulled the spittoon over by his foot. McCreed was the only man he should never have thought about crossing. Yet that's exactly what he'd done.

From the beginning, the plan had been McCreed's. He'd found out about the Mexican gold shipments that were moved across the desert in prison wagons and planned to rob it.

McCreed had asked Loge if he wanted to be in on the take. Loge had been quick to agree. McCreed made the plans and rounded up other men to help pull the holdup off.

Around that time, Loge had started making his own plans. He wasn't about to share the gold. He got hold of Clancy, an ex-army man who was as crooked as a snake, but knew the desert well enough to get them out of there.

The plan was simple. Let McCreed and his men attack and kill the Mexicans. Once the gold was secured, Clancy and four others would ride in and take over.

The plan had worked. McCreed and the men who were still alive after the battle were placed in the wagon. Loge wanted them all killed, but Clancy would have nothing to do with that. Seems Clancy had an old vendetta to settle. He and McCreed had gotten into a battle over some woman, and McCreed had shot him in the gut. Clancy wanted to watch him die a slow and painful death.

But again Loge had made his own plans. He already had the other two guards talked into killing Clancy and the kid once they were out of the desert. He'd told them he'd rather split the bounty three ways instead of five. After that, Loge would shoot the pair in the back, and the gold would be his. The sandstorm had changed everything.

Now, years later, a man shows up that looks like McCreed and uses the same name. Just the thought of it being Joshua made Loge want to run. But for the rest of his life he'd be haunted with the possibility of coming face to face with the one man who could be even meaner than he was. Joshua McCreed. The only man Loge had ever feared.

Loge lay down on the sagging bed and watched a cockroach crawl up the wall. As he saw the situation, he had two choices. Shoot the man and be done with it, or wait to see if *this* Joshua McCreed knew anything about the gold. The gold that he'd spent all those years searching for. There was no choice. He had to have the gold. And since the stranger couldn't possibly be the real McCreed, he had nothing to worry about. He could walk right up to him and never be recognized.

Chapter Ten

"Miss Polly?"

Polly was pulling weeds in the garden with Bidwell when the young maid, Ruth, came hurrying from the house.

"You have a gentleman caller," the young maid said excitedly.

"Oh?" Polly rose up from her knees. "Probably a salesman of some sort." She dropped the trowel and pulled off her gloves. "What does he look like?" She brushed at the dirt embedded in the knees of her trousers.

"Around Mr. Joshua's age, and nearly as handsome."

"Joshua isn't handsome, Ruth. He's just very masculine."

"You can call it what you want, but I wouldn't mind at all if he turned an eye toward me."

Polly felt a prick of jealousy. "Bidwell, I'm going to go see what the man wants. When I come back, I don't want to find you in the house chasing Sable around."

Bidwell chortled. "That Miss Sable, she's a fine woman."

"That she is, and I want her to stay that way. I don't want you to go testing the water before you decide to swim."

"Now you know, Miss Polly, that I've asked Miss Sable to marry me more than once."

"You just remember what I said." Polly headed for the house. Bidwell was a giant of a man, and no one would suspect a person that big would enjoy working with small plants.

"Aren't you going to change into a dress?" Mary asked as Polly hurried through the kitchen.

"It's probably Sable who should be talking to the man, not I. Where is Sable?"

"She's out of elixir. Said the kind she was using purifies the blood. I told her to get me some."

Polly shook her head and continued on. As she made her way down the long hall, the heels of her shoes made a clicking sound on the hardwood floor. She licked the palms of her hands, then smoothed back the sides of her hair. That was followed with a quick pinch to her cheeks.

Polly reached the sitting room and strolled in. If she could, she would have died a thousand deaths. At the moment she could think of nothing more pleasurable than to wring Ruth's neck!

She did indeed have a caller. But not one, two. Sitting on the big chair, with her back rigidly straight and one hand resting on the silver end of a cane, was a woman approximately sixty years in age. Her hat, her clothes and her bearing left no doubt that she was a woman of prominence. Seeing that Polly was dressed in men's clothing, her chin went up in the air and she looked away in disgust.

Standing beside the chair was a handsome gentleman of undeterminable age, but much younger than the woman. His clothes and stance also reeked of money and position. His relaxed smile was all the more disconcerting.

Polly knew she had no choice but to bluff. One of Mrs. Parker's golden rules had been that if you get caught in a dastardly situation, don't let the other person know it. "Act like you are someone and people will think you *are* some-one," she would say. "Never apologize for anything."

Polly smiled. "I'm Polly O'Neil. I must look a mess, but I refuse to ruin a good dress doing gardening."

"I have someone do that sort of thing for me," the older woman stated.

"So do I. But I also like to tend to my garden, and, personally, I find it far more satisfying than sitting around the house and doing handicraft."

"It is indecent for a woman to dress in such a fashion."

"Now, Grandmother," the gentleman said, "you were complaining just the other day about men's clothing being a lot more comfortable than all the garbage women had to wear these days."

"The least she could do is wear a sunbonnet to keep from getting her face burned!"

"Please excuse our rudeness, Miss O'Neil. This is my grandmother, Abigail Webber, and I am Ethan Webber."

"How do you do. To what do I owe the pleasure of this call?"

"Grandmother wa—"

"I wanted to meet you. All I hear from friends and ac-quaintances is constant guessing or speculations about you. I came to find out what you have to say for yourself."

Polly sat in the armchair across from the elderly woman. She also kept her back straight and folded her hands prop-erly in her lap. "I wasn't aware that I'd been noticed by anyone."

"How could you help but be noticed when you parade around in that big carriage?"

"Quite honestly, when I bought it, I had not realized its uselessness, nor did I know about the difficulty of maneu-vering a carriage over narrow and hilly streets. Because of the streets, I've taken up riding. The transportation is much easier to deal with. You might be interested to know that I ride astride instead of sidesaddle.''

Abigail looked at her grandson. ''What are the women coming to these days. Next thing we know they'll be wanting to have some sort of say in politics. Where do you come from, child?''

Polly was quickly tiring of the woman's rudeness. ''Since we are being so blunt, I don't mind saying that I find that question offensive. What difference does it make where I'm from? Nevertheless, I was born and raised in West Virginia. I moved here after staying with friends in Sacramento.'' Polly stood. ''Is there anything else I can do for you?''

Abigail Webber also rose to her feet. ''I think it is time you became acquainted with the better ladies of Auburn. I shall give a tea for you. Would a week from Wednesday be convenient?''

''Ye-yes, that would be fine. I will look forward to it.''

The older woman handed Polly a calling card. ''I will send instructions on how to get to my house, Miss O'Neil. Come along, Ethan. I still have other matters to take care of today.''

As Ethan assisted Abigail to the doorway, he smiled at Polly. Polly wondered if he was married. He'd make a perfect husband, and he was even handsome.

After the Webbers had left, Polly collapsed onto the sofa, and broke out laughing and clapping her hands. She had performed marvelously. Now maybe she'd start being somebody in this town!

It was nearing dark by the time Joshua left the saloon. After an early supper with the Grahams, followed by a ride back to town, a drink had sounded most appealing. He would have liked to spend some time playing poker, but he was in no mood to search for a private game. He still found it hard to believe that no gaming was allowed in Auburn.

He had started across the street, toward where he'd tied his horse, when he felt hard steel pressed against his back. He didn't have to be told it was the barrel of a pistol.

"I've got no money," he said to whoever was behind him.

"I want to know just who you are."

"Who's asking?" The barrel was jammed harder into his back.

"Answer the question!"

"Joshua McCreed."

"Can't be. You may look like him, and you may be usin' his name, but you ain't him."

Joshua slowly turned and looked at his accuser.

"You got the gold, ain't ya?"

Joshua's lips slowly curved into a cold smile. "I've been searching for you a long time, Loge. I knew we'd eventually cross paths."

Loge staggered backward. "Who told you my name?"

"No one."

Loge spit tobacco juice on the ground, trying to pull himself together. "A young greenhorn like you ain't foolin' me. The real McCreed would be in his forties, and you ain't got a gray hair in your head. Now, I want to know where you've hidden the gold."

"That's my secret. But you're right, I did get the gold." Joshua looked down the street. "You shouldn't have crossed me, Loge. There was plenty for everyone."

Everything about the man was like stepping back in time. Loge could still remember the quiet, deadly voice that had meant the death of more than one man. The dark, penetrating eyes and the lack of fear were all things McCreed had been known for. "Who told you about that? Did one of McCreed's men survive and say those things about me? It was a lie!''

Joshua turned his gaze back on Loge. ''It was no lie—I was there.''

Reminding himself he was the one with the gun, Loge grinned, pulling the skin tight on the top of his head. If the story had leaked out about what had happened, he needed to find out who had lived to tell it. ''Then why don't you tell me what happened?''

''Where would you like me to start? Or maybe you'd be more apt to believe me if I told you how it ended.'' Joshua looped his thumbs over his belt. ''I was the only one left after the sandstorm.''

Loge could feel sweat beading on his forehead. He shook his head. ''No. It can't be. You're too young!''

''What if I told you I made a pact with the devil?''

''I'd be more inclined to believe you are the devil.''

''I've waited a long time for this, but I'm in no hurry. You're mine now, Loge. I want to savor the pleasure I'm going to receive when I make you regret the day you turned on me.''

Hearing the cadence of hooves striking the ground, Loge jerked his head to the left. A horse was galloping straight for him. Apparently the rider wasn't even aware he was standing there. Left with no choice, he dived to the ground and rolled out of the way. The horse missed him by inches. He jerked around and aimed his pistol at where McCreed had been standing only seconds ago. Slowly he pulled himself off the ground, his eyes darting in one direction then the other. He wiped his mouth with the back of his hand. McCreed was nowhere in sight.

By the time Loge climbed on his horse, he was shaking so badly he could hardly hold on to the reins. How could someone just disappear like that?

Loge was ready to ride out of town and never come back.

But then he thought about the gold. The gold that would give him everything he'd ever wanted. The gold that should have been his in the first place.

He turned his nag in the direction of the Traveler's Rest Hotel. It beat that other place he'd been staying, and for a dollar he could get space for his bedroll and a decent evening meal.

The man had been bluffing! Loge thought. Still, he glanced behind him before turning his horse at the next corner. "He made it all up to scare me," Loge murmured. "And dammit, it worked. But it ain't gonna work the next time we meet."

As he continued down the road, Loge decided exactly how he was going to handle the situation. He'd tie a rope around the impersonator and drag him across the land until he begged for mercy. But he wouldn't kill him. Not until he made sure the man hadn't lied about the gold's location.

Polly sat in the library, reading the last pages of the book. She finally snapped it shut and held it to her breast. The story was wonderful. All about castles, knights and fair ladies. She sighed. How splendid it must have been to live in those days.

There was a light tap on the door, then it swung open. "You have another gentleman caller," Ruth announced, "and this one is mighty fine looking, too."

"Is there anyone with him?"

"No, ma'am."

Polly stood and put the book back on the shelf. For two weeks she'd spent every spare moment enthralled with the words on the pages. "Strange that for the last several months I've been here, no one bothered to even welcome me to town. Now I get visitors two days in a row. Did Mr. Joshua return last night?"

"He was at work on that new room first thing this morning. Miss Polly, what are you planning to use that room for?''

''I don't know. I'll decide when it's finished.''

Polly couldn't believe her eyes when she saw the man waiting in the sitting room. She knew him immediately, and was so shaken that she practically fell onto the divan.

''Are you all right?'' the gentleman asked worriedly.

''Yes! Yes. Just give me a minute.'' She had to offer some sort of explanation. ''I came in from outside, and I suspect I've been too long under the sun. Aren't you Inez Fritz's son?''

Berk's eyes narrowed. ''Have we met somewhere before?''

''No. It's just that…'' Polly was having difficulty talking. ''Please be seated.'' She had seen him in her dream talking to Malcolm Sawyer! ''Excuse my apparent ill manners, but like I said, I'm sure the heat got the better of me.'' Polly was having to fight to keep from swooning. ''I believe I was in town one day and someone pointed you out to me. Anne Graham. Yes. That's who it was. So what has brought you here?'' Polly noticed that upon discovering he had been the topic of conversation, his chest had to have swelled by at least two inches.

''Have you been ill? My mother has been worried that something had happened. She said you used to come by faithfully for a cookie, but you haven't been there for a long time. I told her I would stop by to see if you were all right.''

''As you can see, I'm fine.'' *He was probably looking at a woman who had turned milk white!* ''You can tell your mother that I will come by soon. I've just been very busy.''

Berk looked around the room. ''You have a lovely home.''

''Thank you.''

''Now that you're settled in, how do you like Auburn?''

Polly groaned inwardly. It was apparent the gentleman had no intention of making this a brief visit. "I believe I'm going to be quite happy here." He was a fine looking gentleman, but there was something about him that reminded her of Sam Logan.

"Have you been to the theater yet?"

Polly's interest perked up. "No, I haven't."

"Perhaps you would permit me to take you sometime soon."

Polly was genuinely tempted, but after seeing how she had misjudged Malcolm, she wasn't sure she should accept. "Possibly sometime in the future," she hedged.

As the time passed, Polly found Berk to be too full of himself. He constantly bombarded her with compliments, all of which sounded well rehearsed. Maybe she wasn't a good judge of men, but she knew she cared nothing for this one. She did, however, ask him to tell his mother she'd be in soon for another one of those delicious sugar cookies.

At one point during their conversation, her gaze shifted to the entryway. She had been certain that Joshua would be standing there. He felt so near. But there was no one. And still Berk lingered.

Joshua silently walked back down the hall. He was going to have to be more careful now. Polly was becoming sensitive to his nearness and it was becoming more difficult to read her thoughts. His lips spread into a whimsical smile. When Sable had told him Polly had a caller, he'd been ready to get rid of the buck. But this time Polly hadn't jumped into a situation without due consideration. Now he could wait and see what happened. His smile disappeared. Sable had also told him about yesterday's visitors. He wondered if the man would become another suitor he was going to have to watch. Obstacles were starting to be thrown at him, but he'd known all along that nothing was ever as easy as it may seem.

As Joshua passed through the kitchen, he nodded to Mary, then Sable and Bidwell. He continued on out the back door.

"What's wrong with Miss Polly?" Mary asked as she walked over to the table where the other two were sitting.

The chair scraped on the floor as Sable stood. "What are you talking about?"

"I can't understand why she hasn't set her sights for Mr. Joshua. That there is more man than any woman could ask for."

"I think that's the problem," Sable said. "As I see it, Miss Polly don't quite know how to handle Mr. Joshua. And she's not wantin' to lose her heart to no man. But that Mr. Joshua's a mighty smart man in more ways than one. He's makin' himself hard to get, and don't think Miss Polly hasn't noticed that he doesn't fall all over her with attention."

Bidwell handed his empty cup to Mary, and watched her refill it with coffee. "You're takin' a lot for granted, Sable. What makes you think that Mr. Joshua is even interested in Miss Polly."

Mary handed his cup back to him.

Sable gave him a knowing grin. "Because he hasn't left."

"Bidwell is right." Mary poured her own coffee. "Mr. Joshua's only staying here because of the work and the money."

"I don't believe that." Sable sat back down. She rested her elbows on the table and leaned forward. Bidwell and Mary also leaned forward.

"Do either of you honestly believe that Mr. Joshua would stay if he didn't want to?" Sable asked in a lowered voice.

Bidwell and Mary thought a moment, then shook their heads.

"And do you think Mr. Joshua would teach Miss Polly how to ride if he didn't want to?"

Bidwell and Mary again shook their heads.

Sable leaned closer. "I haven't seen him wantin' for a thing. He doesn't look like he's hurtin' for money. Miss Polly's not paid him much, 'cause she doesn't think about it. Now if he needs money, how come he don't remind her? And how come he was able to buy a new saddle and clothes? No, Mr. Joshua is stayin' around 'cause he wants to. And the only reason he would want to is Miss Polly. And though she won't admit it to herself, she wants him around or she wouldn't keep thinking of all these jobs for him to do."

Pleased at being able to share her observations, Sable sat back in the chair, crossed her arms over her bosom and waited for either of them to prove her wrong.

"If that's so," Bidwell commented, "how come he ain't tried to woo her?"

Sable shoved Bidwell's cup aside and leaned forward again. "I wondered the same thing. That was the only thing that contradicted everything else."

"Have you figured it out?" Mary asked.

"Yep."

"Well?" Bidwell whispered anxiously.

"He has been wooing her, but not like we think. He's smarter than that. First you gotta realize the things that's most important to Miss Polly. Nothin' comes before bein' a lady, bein' accepted by the wealthy people in town, gettin' married and havin' a family. In that order."

Bidwell and Mary nodded.

"Now, if a man makes advances, Miss Polly's gonna turn her back on him real fast 'cause gentlemen aren't supposed to act that way around ladies. Besides, she doesn't think of Mr. Joshua as bein' in that aristocratic bunch. So Mr. Joshua is coming at her from a different direction."

"How's that?" Her back hurting from leaning over for so long, Mary pulled a chair out from under the table and sat down.

"He's become her friend. Right now he's got her confidence and she can't wait to tell him things. She likes him. She trusts him."

"What does that accomplish?" Bidwell asked.

"He's got her to where she has feelings for him, though she probably hasn't even thought about it. It's quite a big start."

"You sure you got this figured out rightly?" Bidwell asked suspiciously.

"Did you see the way he hurried toward the sitting room when he found out she had a gentleman caller? He don't want anyone catchin' her eye. He wants that eye all to himself."

"You sound like you approve." Mary clicked her tongue. "What if he's after her money?"

Sable rose from the table. "All Mr. Joshua wants from Miss Polly is her love. I've been right so far, haven't I? I'll just bet ya Mr. Joshua is ready to start making his move."

Hearing approaching footsteps from the hallway, Bidwell stood and headed for the back door, Mary went to the bin table, and Sable moved in the direction the steps were coming from. A moment later, Polly came into view.

"Has your guest left?" Sable asked.

"Yes, but…" Polly ran her finger around the waistband of her midnight blue skirt with bold gold strips. "I was just coming to look for you."

"Do you want to go back in the kitchen?"

"No, let's just stand here where no one can hear us." Polly looked up at the ceiling, trying to decide how she should tell Sable what was on her mind. "Sable, did I go to the ball?"

Sable looked at her suspiciously. "What are you talking about? Of course you didn't go to no ball. You had poison oak."

"I've changed my mind. Let's go up to my room. I have something to tell you. Maybe you can help me make some kind of sense out of it."

When the women reached the room, Polly closed the door and had Sable sit. Polly began pacing. "I believe I must be losing my mind!"

"What is it, Polly? I've never seen you as upset as this."

"Sable, I had a dream that I went to that ball. It all seemed so real, and for days I've...well, never mind about that. In my dream, I saw a man who was the son of the bakery woman where I used to go get my cookie."

"Say that again."

Polly waved her hand. "It doesn't matter. Until today, I had never met the man. Yet when I went into the sitting room only a half hour ago, that very man was in there waiting for me. Everything about him was exactly the same, even to the point of being Inez Fritz's son! If it was all a dream, how do you explain that?"

"I can't. But it seems to me that you must've seen him before and just don't remember."

Polly lowered her head and rubbed her temples. "I know I never saw him before the dream." She looked up. "And other things in the dream have come true. I saw Anne Graham in a pale blue dress, the same color Joshua had told me she wore."

Polly finally sat on the bed, and Sable went over and sat beside her. She took Polly's hand and started rubbing it. "More than one of my family has had them kinds of dreams. They'd see things, and sure enough it'd happen." She felt Polly's hand tighten. "My mammy used to say it was a gift from the Lord Almighty. Black people from all around used to come and have her tell them what she saw for the future. That's how she kept all us children fed and clothed. Now I don't know if you're gettin' the gift, but if you is, it's not nothin' to be afraid of.''

Polly was becoming more confused by the minute. "I don't have any gift for such things. I don't *want* anything to do with such things.''

Sable smiled. "Then like I said, you musta seen this man somewhere and forgot all about it.''

Polly found Joshua standing out by the well. He had just poured a bucket of water over his head. He wiped his face with his hands, then shook the excess water from his hair. Rivulets of water flew in the air. He was naked to the waist, his strong body glistening in the sun where water had dripped down. As she approached, a shard of passion ran down the length of her body.

Fighting her womanly desire, Polly was about to return to the house when Joshua slowly turned and stared at her. It was as if he had felt her presence. He stood there, not saying a word, waiting. He looked dark, menacing and dangerous. Memories of her dream almost seemed like reality again. The words, the kiss, and the desire she still felt.

"I...I just had a caller,'' Polly said stiffly. "He just left.''

"Oh?''

"I've seen him before.'' Polly moved slowly forward. "I had a dream that you took me to the ball. I saw this man there. Everything about him was exactly the same.''

Joshua turned and grabbed his shirt from the wooden bracing around the well.

"Don't you think that is curious?'' Polly continued.

"There's a lot of curious things in this world.''

A foolish suspicion was building as Polly watched the

green-and-yellow-striped shirt soak up the water that was still on his body. "You know about the dream, don't you, Joshua?"

"Now how would I know about some dream unless you told me?"

Her suspicion was growing rapidly into positive belief. "It really happened, didn't it? You took me to the ball, but you drugged me in some way so I would forget." She stopped only a few feet away from him. "I want to know the truth."

Joshua buttoned his shirt. "You don't want to know the truth."

"What is that supposed to mean?"

Joshua dropped his hands to his sides. Polly's coloring was heightened by her determination, and her small chin was set. "I was just referring to what you said about having a visitor you'd seen in your dream and accusing me of knowing what that dream was."

Polly had to admit that by putting it in that context, it did sound ridiculous. Again, she had been reaching for straws.

"Then you turn right around and say you want to know the truth! You've obviously made your mind up about this, so whatever I say, you won't believe. So in reality, you really don't want to know the truth." He raked his fingers through his wet hair. "This has got to be the damnedest conversation I've ever had."

"Whatever it was you just said, you're probably right." Polly twisted her fingers in her skirt for lack of anything else to do. "But the dream seemed so real. And with everything that has happened—"

"I've had dreams that were like that. Took a long time for me to forget them. What did your caller want?" He rested a hip on the framing.

"His name was Berk Fritz. He's the son of the lady who

owns the bakery. I used to go there once a week for a cookie. His mother was concerned about me, so he came by to see if I was all right.''

''What's the matter?''

''What do you mean?''

''You had a caller and you're not even the least excited about it.''

Polly thought about telling him that there were several things about Berk she hadn't liked, but she smiled instead. ''He asked me to the theater,'' she gloated. ''Of course, I didn't accept. After all, I don't even know the gentleman.''

Joshua grinned. He stood and took Polly's arm. But as he proceeded to lead her back to the house, she jerked her arm from his grasp.

''Well, have you nothing to say?'' Polly persisted.

''What's there to say? You turned down an invitation to a play.''

Polly was becoming more and more peeved at his lack of interest. ''I also had visitors yesterday,'' she bragged.

''So I heard.''

''It was Abigail Webber and her son. A most striking gentleman. He could hardly keep his eyes off me.''

''I don't find that hard to believe, especially if you had on your trousers.''

''That wasn't the reason,'' Polly said through clenched teeth. ''And Mrs. Webber is giving a tea for me to meet the ladies about town.''

''So, someone has finally opened the door for you,'' he commented.

Polly had heard enough. He didn't even act excited over her good fortune! She stuck her foot out and tripped him. To her delight, he tried to regain his footing, then fell face-down in the dirt. Suddenly a hand clamped around her ankle, then she was falling through the air. She landed directly on top of Joshua. She tried to scramble to the side, but his arms circled her waist, pinning her body to his.

"Turn me loose, Joshua," Polly ordered.

Joshua laughed and rolled her over onto her back so he was on top. He straddled her and sat up, holding her wrists so she wouldn't start flaying him. "I have to admit, Polly O'Neil, you are a most tempting woman. Especially when you're angry and your eyes sparkle like fire." He brushed her hair away from her face.

Polly glanced up and fell silent. Those dark, fathomless eyes were watching her. She could feel the first prickle of excitement as her gaze drifted to his lips. It suddenly occurred to her that a kiss would be the answer to everything. She'd finally know, one way or the other, if the kiss she'd relived a hundred times had truly been nothing more than a dream.

Her lips parted as she eagerly waited for his lips to join hers. Instead, he slid off her and sat on the ground. She sat beside him, and he reached over and dusted the dirt from her back.

"Why didn't you kiss me?" Polly blatantly asked. "You were thinking about it."

"I plead guilty."

"Aren't I appealing?"

Joshua gave her a lopsided grin. "You are a most appealing woman, Polly. I'm not sure I'd be satisfied with just a kiss."

Polly was immediately infused with undeniable excitement. If she had to sacrifice herself, so be it.

"It would spoil our friendship." He climbed to his feet. "No, it just wouldn't work." He reached down and helped Polly up.

"Next thing I know, you'll be telling me you're shy," Polly snapped at him.

"Would you believe me?"

"No."

Joshua turned her around. "You're covered with dirt. I'm afraid I've ruined your dress. You'll have to go change."

"The conversation is over, isn't it. You're manipulating me again!"

"I don't know what you're talking about."

"You never do. And while I'm thinking about it, where is it you go so often? On a good many occasions, I've searched for you and you're nowhere to be found. I've heard Sable say the same thing."

"When are you talking about?"

"Well, I…I don't remember exactly. Sometime last week."

"If you don't know, how can I answer your question?"

Polly's eyes narrowed. "You never really answer anything, do you? You always avoid the question by changing the subject. You were right about one thing. Kissing would have been a mistake."

Polly walked away. She was angry, sad and at the same time glad that nothing had happened. She would probably have ended up regretting it. But damn! He'd looked so handsome standing there with his hair wet and water dripping onto his shoulders and down his back. And one kiss hadn't been much to ask for. Drat the man!

Polly stopped and turned. "Joshua!" she called when she saw him going to the carriage house. She waited until he had turned to face her. "Remember me telling you about Ethan Webber who came with his grandmother?"

Joshua nodded.

"That's who my husband is going to be!" Let him think about that! Satisfied, Polly continued on to the house.

Chapter Eleven

Ethan Webber escorted his grandmother from the dining room to the sitting room. Once she was comfortably seated in her favorite chair, he went to the liquor cabinet and poured each of them a glass of whiskey. For as long as Ethan could remember, Abigail Webber had always imbibed before going to bed at night. She had often said it was one of the few pleasures she refused to give up.

"How is your law practice going, Ethan?"

"Fine. I just settled a case where the husband wanted a divorce as well as his wife's mine. She had owned it before they were married. His contention was that she constantly mistreated him, and because he was a man, whatever she owned was his anyway."

"Oh, my. And which one were you defending?"

"The wife."

"And did she get to keep the mine?"

Ethan nodded. "I haven't had an opportunity to ask what you thought about our visit yesterday. I assume you must have liked Miss O'Neil or you would never have suggested giving her a tea."

Abigail took a long, appreciative drink of the expensive whiskey. "She reminds me a lot of myself when I was young. That one has a backbone. She'll not let anyone walk over her, though how she could stand to wear trousers is beyond my understanding. Makes her look like a man."

"Now there you're wrong. No one could possibly make that mistake."

"I noticed you didn't say much, and you were obviously smitten with the young lady."

"You're mistaken."

"Balderdash! Don't try fooling me. And it's long past time for you to start thinking about a lady in your life."

"I know, you want to see your great-grandchildren before you die."

"Precisely."

Polly went to the kitchen to find Joshua. "I need to talk to you as soon as you're through with your breakfast."

Joshua looked at the petite lady standing in the doorway. Her yellow dress made her look as fresh as a rain-swept prairie. "I just finished." He pushed his chair from the table and stood. "Thank you, Mary. I swear you have to be the best cook in these parts."

Mary giggled.

"So you've set your sights on this new man you met?"

Polly was pleased to know he hadn't shrugged off her statement yesterday. "That's right."

"Does he know it yet?"

"Not likely. I've only met him once."

Joshua followed Polly to the sitting room and discovered Sable waiting.

"Sit down," Polly said.

Joshua remained standing. "What did you want to talk about?"

"Can't you ever do anything I tell you?" Polly asked irritably. She plopped down into an armchair in a very unladylike manner.

"I do things you tell me every day."

"Then why do I always have the feeling…oh, never mind. Sable and I were having a bit of a tiff, and we decided to let you settle it. It's about Abigail Webber's tea. You always seem to be good at this sort of thing, so do you think I should wear dark colors or light colors?"

"I said light and she said dark," Sable spoke up.

Joshua decided to sit down after all. How did he manage to get himself in these fixes? "I would agree with Sable."

"Oh." Polly knew Sable was going to gloat about this for days. "What color?"

"I think she should wear that mint-colored town suit," Sable said, convinced that Joshua would again agree with her.

Joshua had to stop and think. He certainly hadn't stood about watching Polly parade her vast wardrobe. He tried to remember the various clothes she'd worn, and one particular dress came to mind. "The white dress. The one with yards of material and blue ribbons weaving in and out of the skirt. And carry that white lacy parasol."

"But that's off-shouldered," Sable objected.

Joshua grinned. "I would think that Polly would want to make as grand an entrance as possible. She should arrive in her coach and look as if she owned the world. Make them think she doesn't care what the others wear. She's a lovely young woman, it's summer, the weather is warm and she's dressed appropriately."

Polly laughed with delight. "It's daring. It's perfect!"

Sable shook her head. "I don't know."

"Thank you for your advice," Polly said when Joshua stood, apparently ready to leave. "I knew I could rely on your good judgment. Now I will be a nervous wreck until the day of the tea. Days ago, you mentioned Lake Tahoe. How far away is it?"

"I also said you shouldn't go alone. The distance is around ninety miles."

Polly was disappointed. She'd thought to have a nice ride by herself to pass the time. "I see you've started on the second room."

Joshua nodded.

"You know, I get very lonely at supper, especially now that Sable insists on eating in the kitchen with Bidwell and the others—" which she knew included Joshua "—and I was wondering—"

"You don't have to be lonely," Sable interrupted. "There's plenty of room at the table for another."

They all heard the knock on the front door. Sable scurried out of the room.

"I have to get back to work."

As Joshua entered the hall, he glanced at the front door. Sable had just let in a gentleman who wore a top hat. He had brown curly hair and appeared to be around six foot in height. He was trim of build and his suit was made of the finest material.

Joshua continued on down the hall. He suspicioned he'd just laid eyes on Ethan Webber, Polly's latest candidate for marriage. But this time was far more serious than either Malcolm Sawyer or her thoughts to get a mail-order husband. The gentleman appeared to have all the qualities a woman could want in a husband.

Joshua passed through the kitchen and gave Mary a quick smile. As he went out the back door, he knew instinctively his time was starting to run short. He was going to have to make a move of some sort. A small gap was forming between him and Polly, and it had every indication of growing larger. Especially if she became involved in Auburn society and Mr. Webber.

Ethan smiled at the slender black woman dressed in a blue, high-necked gown. "I've come to leave directions for

Miss O'Neil. Please see that she gets them.''

There wasn't anything about this man that Sable didn't like. But she liked Joshua better. That was who she'd planned on Polly marrying, but the woman was too blind to see what was right before her eyes. Refusing to tell the gentleman that Polly was in the other room, Sable reached out for the piece of paper.

''Mr. Webber,'' Polly greeted, ''how nice of you to return.'' She was pleased that today she was dressed in one of her better gowns.

Sable wanted to stomp the floor. Just a couple more minutes and she would have gotten rid of the man. Now, instead of handing the paper to her, he gave to it Polly.

''Good afternoon, Miss O'Neil. I had hoped you might be home. I remembered you saying you have taken up riding. I realize I'm being presumptuous, but I wondered if you might allow me to accompany you one morning.''

''I would enjoy that very much. I always like to rise early.'' Polly ignored Sable's click of the tongue. ''Perhaps you would have breakfast with me tomorrow, then we can leave around eight. So, shall we say seven in the morning?''

Ethan smiled with pleasure. ''Seven it shall be.''

''How can you act so brazen?'' Sable asked as soon as she'd shut the door behind the guest.

Polly laughed merrily. ''Because I'm not going to let this one get away.''

Polly and Sable spent the rest of the day showing and telling Vera and Ruth how to set the table and how to act. Mary was given instructions on what to serve. Several hours were spent just polishing the silver. Polly was making sure that everything went as smoothly as possible.

Polly went to bed early so she wouldn't have any difficulty getting up in the morning. Her black riding skirt, the white painter's shirt and colorful vest were all ready to put on. A wide-brimmed hat and leather gloves rested on the chair seat, and her boots were on the floor beside it. Even Zeek had been told to have Duchess ready at eight.

Sleep didn't come as quickly as Polly had wanted. Her excitement was too consuming. But when she did fall asleep, it was fretful. Feeling part awake and part asleep, she knew she was discontent. It was as if she were waiting for something to calm her down. Then she felt a hand sliding up the side of her leg as a hard body pressed against her back. She knew who it was, and she welcomed the feel of teeth tenderly nibbling her earlobe and his breath tickling the inside of her ear.

His hand continued its trail of fire across the flat of her stomach and came to rest just below her breast.

"Oh, Joshua," she murmured, "I had hoped you would come to me."

"I'll always be here for you. You just have to wish for me."

She reached down to help him remove her nightgown. As she pulled it over her head, she felt his mouth claim a taut nipple. She couldn't hold back the whimper of pleasure.

A single kiss had started it all, now Joshua had returned to make everything complete. His kisses, his hands, the feel of his body continued to escalate an already growing appetite for him. She wanted to feel him inside her, but he teased, kissed, nibbled and carried her to where she was sure she'd die for want of him.

Spasms of pleasure began the minute he entered her, and she had thought the lovemaking was over. She soon realized it had only begun. He drove her to delirious heights she'd never known existed. She couldn't get enough of him. She raked her nails down his back and bit his shoulder while his fingers entwined in her hair and drew her mouth to his. With each thrust he drove her closer to the brink of madness. She was a wild woman, always wanting more. And he never disappointed her. Then he gave her what she'd wanted. Her eyes squeezed shut, her heavy breathing became shallow, and everything exploded, sending her spiraling among the clouds.

Joshua pulled her into his arms and kissed the tip of her nose. Satiated and exhausted, she curled up against his marvelous body. She always felt so safe when he was beside her. She fell into a sound asleep.

"Miss Polly! Miss Polly! You have to get up! That man's going to be here in fifteen minutes, and you aren't even going to be dressed!"

Polly slapped away the determined hand that kept shaking her. She opened one eye and saw Ruth standing beside the bed. "What time is it?" she asked.

"Fifteen minutes to seven."

"How could you have let me sleep so late?" Joshua! Polly's eyes flew open and she looked to the other side of the bed. Just remembering Joshua's lovemaking turned her angry look into a radiant smile. Thank the Lord Joshua had had the good sense to leave before they were caught.

"I woke you at six," Ruth said worriedly. "You told me you were awake and to leave. You said you'd dress yourself."

Seeing the concern on the young maid's face, Polly had to assume she was telling the truth, though she had no memory of the incident. She'd just been too tired after her all-night romp with Joshua. She glanced back at the bed. There appeared to be no evidence of what had taken place, however, the sheet was rumpled. "Is Joshua up?" She climbed from the bed and quickly pulled off her nightgown.

"I wouldn't know, ma'am."

Polly stepped into the pantalets Ruth handed her. "What do you mean?"

"He left right after supper last night to go to the Grahams' place when one of their stable boys arrived. Zeek said the boy told Mr. Joshua something about a mare fixing to have a colt and his help was needed. He hasn't come back since."

Polly's hand paused in midair. "But that's impossible."

Ruth was crushed. "You can ask Miss Sable, Mary or Vera. I wouldn't lie."

Still trying to contend with Joshua being gone all night, it took a moment for her to realize what Ruth was talking about. "Oh, no, no." She patted the maid's shoulder. "I'm sure you told the truth. I was just thinking about something else."

Sable rushed into the room. "That Mr. Webber is here, and you aren't even started to dress!"

Polly rubbed her temples. Too many things were happening at once. She couldn't even concentrate. Had the lovemaking once again been only a dream? she wondered as the two women quickly dressed her. She could still feel Joshua's hands on her body.

Sable gave the thick, auburn hair a good brushing, then left it hanging down, with a ribbon to tie it back.

Still in a stupor, Polly let Sable guide her out of the room and down the stairs.

"What time did you go to bed last night? I swear, you're still half-asleep! I knew you shouldn't have told that man to come here so early. You'd best be careful you don't doze off while you're on top of your horse. If Mr. Joshua was here, I wouldn't worry. He takes care of you."

Polly gritted her teeth. "Sable, I've heard enough! Is breakfast ready?"

"Of course it's ready," Sable replied in a huff.

Polly plastered a smile on her face. "I'm sorry I'm late," she said as she entered the sitting room.

Ethan stood. "A woman as lovely as you has every right to keep a gentleman waiting."

"There was a little problem with the maids I had to take care of. Breakfast is ready. Shall we go on into the dining room?"

Polly was proud of what Mary and the others had accomplished. The table was set to perfection, with crystal water goblets, china and polished silver. Sterling silver containers lined the sideboard and offered a feast of food. In fact, there was so much that Polly wondered if the others were waiting to eat after she and Ethan had finished.

When they'd completed their meal, Zeek was already standing out front with Duchess. Polly couldn't believe how smoothly everything was going. Not thinking to wait for Zeek's assistance, she swung up into the saddle.

"Has Joshua returned from the Grahams'?" she asked the towheaded boy.

"No, ma'am."

"Are you sure he didn't come back during the night?"

"Oh, no, Miss Polly. I would've woke up. I was waiting to take care of his horse 'cause I knew he'd be tired."

Polly gave Ethan a quick smile. She probably should have waited to ask the questions, but how could she after what had taken place? She needed to talk to Joshua! "Do you know why he had to go over there?"

"Mr. Joshua's got a way with horses. Them people has a mare that's had a mighty hard time carryin' the foal. He's been showing them how to ease her misery. He wanted to be there when she delivered."

At least he hadn't gone to keep Anne company. Polly looked toward Ethan, who was already mounted and waiting. "Are you ready?"

Ethan nodded. "That is a spectacular mare you have,"

he commented as they rode off. "If it would be all right with you, I'd like to discuss breeding arrangements with this Joshua."

"Joshua?"

"Why, yes. I assumed that is who takes care of your horses. I would never presume to discuss such matters with a lady."

"Of course not."

By the time they returned to the house two hours later, Polly had a splitting headache. She had thought the cool morning air would have put her in better spirits, but she hadn't been that fortunate. She wanted to kick herself for being less than pleasurable company, but she couldn't stop thinking about what had happened last night, or maybe it was in the wee hours of the morning. She didn't know. It seemed that at this point, there was very little she knew. At least Ethan had been nice enough to keep a running conversation going, although he would probably never want to see her again.

"I enjoyed our outing, Miss O'Neil," Ethan said graciously. He dismounted and helped her down from Duchess. "I hadn't realized what an excellent horsewoman you are."

Polly blushed at the compliment. "Thank you." He may not have been so gracious with his compliment had he known what Joshua had gone through to teach her.

"As I stated earlier, it's been a long time since I've taken a ride just for the pleasure. I very much enjoyed it. Would it be possible for us to make this a weekly occurrence?"

Polly couldn't believe her good fortune. "Yes…I'd like that."

He tipped his hat. "Then I'll be looking forward to next Friday." He swung back up on his horse and rode off.

After turning Duchess over to Zeek, Polly went straight upstairs. She fell facedown on the bed, wanting to once again experience the feel, the smell of Joshua. She ran her hand along the bed beside her—where he had lain only hours ago. She couldn't have dreamed something so real. If only she could prove it, if just to herself. To know she wasn't going mad. A thought suddenly occurred to her. There might be a way.

Polly jumped to her feet and yanked back the covers. The sheets were clean. She hurried downstairs.

"Where are the sheets that were removed from my bed?" Polly demanded when she barged into the kitchen. She didn't care what anyone thought. She had to find out if there was any kind of stain that would prove she and Joshua had coupled.

"Vera is out back doing the laundry," Mary replied over her shoulder.

Polly rushed out the door. The big copper vats used for laundry were off to the side. As she neared them, she could see the steam rising in the air. Too late to stop her, Polly watched Vera drop what appeared to be bed linen into the boiling water.

"Were those my sheets you just put in the tub?" Polly asked when she was close enough.

"Yes, ma'am," Vera said proudly. "Before long they'll be clean and smelling of sunshine."

Polly's shoulders slumped. She returned to the house, went to her room and again fell facedown on the bed. All morning she'd thought of hardly anything but the sensations and wild ecstasy Joshua had created. At one point, her desire for him had become so strong that she had stopped at a stream to splash cold water in her face. Fortunately, Ethan had accepted her excuse about it being a hot morning. Even now, her flesh came alive just thinking about what Joshua had—was she going mad? Had it only been another dream? All morning she'd asked herself the same questions and she was no closer to an answer.

She buried her face in the pillow and gripped it tightly with her hands. She wanted to feel Joshua inside her, making her body come alive. The girls had been right. There were indeed men so good that you couldn't get enough of them, even in dreams.

Joshua rolled his shirtsleeve down and chuckled as the colt tried to get up on long, spindly legs.

"We'd have lost that colt, and possibly even Lady if it hadn't been for you, Joshua," Ned Graham said. "After what I paid for that mare, I'd have hated to have to put her away."

Joshua stroked the mare's neck. "Well, Lady, you should be real proud of yourself. You've got one fine-looking boy there."

The mare nickered as if she understood what Joshua was saying.

Anne stepped aside so Joshua and her father could leave the stall. "Breakfast is ready. I know you're both hungry."

"I could eat an ox." Ned gave Joshua a good-natured slap on the back. "How about you, son?"

Joshua nodded. He looked up at the sun and smiled. It had been a long night.

They all walked back to the house, each feeling good about the way everything had turned out.

After steak, eggs, biscuits, gravy and apple pie, Joshua and Ned went back outside to enjoy a cigar.

"You know, Joshua," Ned said as they strolled back toward the barn, "I'd always hoped to have a son. Of course when my wife, Martha, died, I knew it was never going to happen. I'd like you to come in as a partner with me. I think you and me could turn this place into the best horse farm in the country."

"That's good of you, Ned, but you don't even know me."

"I know you've got a way with horses, the likes of which I've never seen before. You were like an angel the way you made that mare fight instead of giving up. Horses don't take to just anybody. Besides, I'm getting old, and though Anne doesn't know it, the doc told me I got a bad heart."

"You and Anne are good people, and I'm glad I could be of help. I thank you for the offer, but I can't accept. One of these days Anne is going to marry someone, and he's the one who should work with you."

Ned didn't like it, but he accepted Joshua's decision. And there was always the possibility that Joshua could change his mind a couple of months down the way. "You know, Anne was sort of hoping you'd be the man she wed. She hasn't said anything to me, but I can tell in her eyes that she's interested in you."

"She'll find someone else, and you'll be pleased with the man she picks."

"I only hope he likes horses."

Joshua laughed. "I can guarantee you he will." He looked down the road that led to Auburn. "I need to be heading back."

They walked to the barn. Ned waited while Joshua saddled his horse.

"Will you be having Sunday supper with us next week?"

"I think not." Joshua mounted the black.

"Then come back when you can."

Joshua pulled his hat down firmly on his head, smiled and rode out of the barn. When Ned stepped outside, he watched Joshua until the tall man and horse disappeared from view.

Polly was standing by her bedroom window when she saw Joshua ride up to the carriage house. "I'm surprised

you could finally pull yourself away from sweet Anne,''
she muttered.

She watched him swing from the saddle with that lithe-
ness that she'd come to recognize, then lead his horse inside. He didn't look tired, but Joshua never looked tired.
She thought about what he looked like naked, and every
inch of his body her hands and mouth had trailed over. She
turned and flattened her back to the wall. What was she
thinking? She was doing it to herself again. She was allowing her dreams to become reality. And why was she letting
all this have such an effect on her? She had Ethan, and if
everything went the way she wanted, he'd eventually become her husband.

Since she hadn't changed her clothes, Polly decided a
ride to town was exactly what she needed. It was time she
became interested in other things besides Joshua McCreed.

When Polly entered the carriage house, there was no one
around. Even Zeek seemed to have taken off somewhere.
She'd hoped to see Joshua, but he was probably upstairs in
his room. After picking up the bridle, she stuck the bit in
Duchess's mouth, then buckled the strap. She turned to lead
the mare out of the stall and discovered Joshua standing
right in front of her. Her knees turned to pudding, and having him so close, her desire was immediate. She wanted to
kick herself for letting him have this effect on her. Somehow, she managed to detour around him.

"I thought you'd be asleep after being up all night."
Polly couldn't believe her voice sounded so normal.

"I managed to rest some at the Grahams'."

"Did you rest alone?" Polly wanted to cut her tongue
out for letting that pass by her lips.

"Do you care?"

"You can take that smug smile off your face, Joshua. It
doesn't matter to me."

"Then why the question?"

She tied Duchess to the post, then placed the wool blanket on the mare's back. "I had a dream that you were here at the house." The saddle followed.

"That was it? That's all the dream was about?"

"It was like the other one. So real that I would have sworn we—" Polly cleared her throat. "It doesn't matter."

"We what?"

"I don't know what you're talking about."

"You started to say we did something. You seemed to be upset, so what did we do this time? Did we go to another ball, or did we make love?"

Polly had just leaned down to grab the end of the cinch. At hearing Joshua's question, she jerked back up, hitting her head on the mare's underbelly, causing her to kick and the blanket and saddle to slide to the ground. But Polly was more interested in how Joshua knew what they'd done.

Joshua stared at her, then burst out laughing. "From the look on your face, I'd say I hit the nail right on the head."

Polly reached down and snatched up the blanket. She shook it then put it back on the mare's back.

His mouth was still curved into a mischievous grin. "If this was another of your vivid dreams, I hope you weren't disillusioned. Perhaps we should go upstairs. The real thing is always better."

Polly's eyes darkened and turned stony. After that statement, she wasn't about to admit to anything! "Weren't you the one who said we shouldn't even kiss because it might ruin our relationship?" She slung the saddle up. "But now, because of a dream you *think* I had, you're not only willing to take me upstairs, you actually think I'll go!"

"Are you giving me a no for an answer?"

"That's right." She reached under the horse's belly and grabbed the cinch. "Besides, I wouldn't want anything to ruin our friendship," she said sarcastically.

Joshua laughed again. "Tell me, Polly, don't you ever feel the need for a man?"

"No."

"I think you're lying."

"I don't care what you think." Polly grabbed hold of the saddle horn and wiggled the saddle to be sure it was tight enough.

"Where are you going?"

"To town."

"Did you enjoy your ride this morning with your... future husband?"

"Yes. It was so enjoyable that we've decided to make it a weekly occasion." She untied the mare, gathered the reins in her hand and mounted.

"Maybe I could say something to Anne, and we could all ride together."

Polly gritted her teeth. "I'm sure you must be tired after your all-night session, and you have enough to do here at the house to keep you busy for some time!"

"I suppose you're right. Have a good afternoon, princess." He headed for the stairs leading to the loft.

"Joshua," Polly called. "You did say you spent *all* night at the Grahams', didn't you?"

"Where else would I have been?"

Polly's already sour disposition worsened when Joshua didn't even bother to look at her. "Next time you talk to me, have the courtesy to look me in the eye!" She rode Duchess out of the carriage house.

After traveling a short distance, Polly released a heavy sigh. One thing was certain. Joshua hadn't come back last night and made love to her. It had been another dream. But, oh, what a magnificent dream it had been.

Chapter Twelve

Polly came out of the dry goods store and would have bumped into a man had she not been able to stop in time. She groaned at seeing who the man was. Berk Fritz.

"Miss O'Neil. I've waited for you to leave the store."

"How nice," she acknowledged. She smiled at the big man standing beside Berk. He was a bull of a man and far from being handsome, but there was something about him she liked. Maybe it was his quick, almost shy smile. "Aren't you going to introduce me to your friend, Mr. Fritz?"

"Oh. Yes. This is my brother, Daniel."

"I'm glad to meet you, Mr. Fritz," Polly said with a broad grin.

Daniel was perplexed by the gesture. Most people expressed shock at the difference between him and Berk. Polly O'Neil not only didn't do that, she actually seemed to prefer his attention over his brother's.

"You are truly an amazingly beautiful woman," Berk said. "Most ladies would refuse to show their faces in the heat of the day. Because it is so warm, I thought perhaps I could talk you into letting me buy you an ice cream."

Polly looked at Daniel. "Will you be coming with us?"

"No, he has other things to do." Berk gave Daniel a cutting look.

"Too bad. Well then, I guess I won't—"

"But it isn't anything that can't wait." Daniel nudged Berk aside.

"Well…then maybe…"

Berk was furious, but he'd learned a long time ago how not to let his feelings show.

Both men extended their elbows. Polly took the easy way out and chose neither.

Berk tossed his hands in the air to show his frustration. "The son of a bitch wouldn't leave, so our Miss O'Neil had the grace to ask him if he wanted to get an ice cream with us. Then he had the nerve to push me aside! He actually thinks she liked his ugly face!" He banged his fist on the table. "He doesn't have the social manners of a pig."

Inez poured herself a glass of brandy. "Where is Daniel now?"

"Probably with some whore and pretending it is the O'Neil woman." Since his mother didn't offer, Berk filled his own glass.

"Do you think she's attracted to you, Berk?"

"Of course. She's just shy." He took a quick sip. "Has there ever been a woman I can't win over?"

"I don't know. I'm not with you all the time."

"You tell Daniel to stay out of my way. I don't need him dogging my tail all the time, and if anything goes wrong, it's going to be his fault."

Inez glanced at her son. He looked like an angel and had the heart of the devil. He was far more deadly than either Daniel or herself, but he had always been a bit of a mama's boy and did what she told him. She swirled the brandy around in the cheap glass. "I'll talk to Daniel when he returns. You'd better be telling the truth about her attraction to you, Berk. I don't like throwing money away on a scheme that isn't going to work.''

Berk finished off his drink. ''In no time I'll have her exactly where I want her—providing you keep Daniel out of my hair.''

To Inez's aggravation, her older son had an entirely different story to tell. There was no question that Daniel had his eyes set on the O'Neil woman.

After Daniel left, Inez took an honest view of what was happening. Though the boys had never cared for each other, they'd always united when the family conspired to relieve someone of their money. But what with the attractive redhead wiggling her seductive fanny about, the boys were becoming increasingly further apart.

From the beginning, everything about this plan had gone wrong. It was almost as if some guardian angel was keeping Polly O'Neil safe from harm. Inez had a premonition that she should leave Auburn and forget trying to relieve Polly of her money. She'd had the same feeling in London. Had she not left when she did, she wouldn't be alive today. Still, Inez chose to wait for a few more days before making a final decision about Polly.

As Thomas drove the carriage away from the large brick house, Polly held her head high. At least no one could see that her hands were twitching.

Though her knees had been shaking when she had arrived for the tea, she'd managed to appear confident and in perfect control. As always, Joshua had been right. The ladies had oohed and aahed over her white dress, and had even gone so far as to ask for her seamstress's name. Yes, indeed, she couldn't have asked for a better introduction into Auburn society.

However, all feelings of elation were replaced with anxiety when she realized several of the women looked familiar. It had taken another fifteen minutes to jar her memory, but the moment she realized she had seen the ladies at the ball, it became difficult to breathe, let alone concentrate on what she was doing or saying. With a determination she didn't even know she possessed, she'd somehow managed to hide her emotional trauma. Nevertheless, as soon as she felt it would be socially acceptable, she had left the tea.

Polly rested her back against the soft, cushiony seat. Now that she was riding in the carriage, the refreshing breeze brought her back to her senses. She needed to do some rational thinking, and hopefully she'd be able to assemble her thoughts.

There was no longer any doubt in Polly's mind that Joshua had not made love to her, nor had he escorted her to the ball.

So, where did that leave her? Dreams. All dreams. But there was another possibility that had been floating around in her mind. A possibility that made no sense whatsoever. Still, her friend Amanda had claimed to have had unexplainable things happen to her, and even Sable had spoken about her own mother having some sort of sight. In West Virginia, folks had also spoken about strange things happening. It all served to strengthen an idea she'd been playing around with in her head.

What if she had wanted to go to the ball so badly that she had somehow felt the experience of going. But if that were so, that would also mean that she had actually felt her desire for Joshua. The possibility of that being true was startling, to say the least. She couldn't deny that she'd given considerable thought to what it would feel like to have him make love to her, especially after his kiss following the ball. Strange that she didn't feel the same desires with Ethan.

It really didn't matter that she couldn't understand how

it could happen. What was important was her ability to use it to her advantage. Just knowing it was possible and that the options could be endless already had her fidgeting in her seat. She stifled a giggle. What wonders she could accomplish! She sat up straighter. Why, she could even have Joshua make love to her every night, and no one would be the wiser. Not even Joshua! Just thinking about it had already created an ache in the pit of her stomach.

As they drove down Main Street, Polly slowly became aware of the people walking or traveling. Could they tell what delicious thoughts were running through her mind? Of course not! Seeing Daniel Fritz standing in front of the tailor shop, she nodded and smiled. There was something about the man she rather liked, though he could never be described as handsome. He seemed more down to earth than that impossible brother of his. She pitied the woman Berk Fritz married.

All afternoon, Polly watched the sun slowly descend, and fought with her thoughts and the desire to see if she could bewitch Joshua into joining her. By nightfall, she was a nervous wreck. This morning she'd thought to swallow her pride and start eating supper with the others, but she wasn't sure she could look Joshua in the eye without turning a dozen shades of red. He always said her face mirrored her thoughts, and surely he'd see her anxiety. So again she ate alone, listening to the voices and laughter coming from the kitchen.

The moment the sun went down, Polly had to force herself not to run upstairs and hop in bed. Sable, who Polly suspected had eyes in the back of her head, would notice it immediately and start nagging her with questions about being sick.

She spent an hour in the library, leafing through one book then another until she could no longer stand the delay.

Her body was already alive with the expectation of sweet delights to come.

As she went up the stairs, it occurred to Polly that she'd never paid attention to just how many there were. She counted every single one of them. Nor had she given any thought as to the distance from the landing to her bedroom. It seemed to take forever.

When she entered her quarters, Polly closed the door behind her and glanced at the big bed. The covers had already been turned back and it looked most inviting. She could practically picture Joshua waiting there for her.

She began undressing. When she'd changed·after her return from the tea, she'd made a point of selecting a gown that buttoned down the front so she wouldn't have to break her arms trying to get out of the confounded thing.

The dress slipped to the floor. As she stepped away, she was already untying her petticoats and letting them fall. Her fingers didn't want to cooperate.

After what seemed like a lifetime, she pulled on her most daring, blue nightgown. The lantern was quickly extinguished, and she jumped into the bed. Lying on her back, she arranged the pillows beneath her head, and closed her eyes. Thirty minutes later, frustration began to take over. She wasn't tired. She tried willing Joshua to come to her, but nothing happened. She rose from the bed and paced the floor, trying to wear herself out.

After being up and down most of the night, Polly finally fell into a fretful sleep around three in the morning. When Ruth delivered her morning hot chocolate, Polly was sure she'd been dragged behind a galloping horse. At least that's the way she felt.

Vera was polishing the dining room table when Sable entered the room. "Is Miss Polly upset about something?" Vera asked.

"You just never mind. Tend to your own business. I know she's been snappin' at everyone today, but she's got a lot to think about." Sable had no idea what was making Polly so irritable. She checked the dining room chairs to be sure Vera hadn't missed polishing anything, then went in search of Ruth, who was examining all the rooms for spiderwebs. It seemed there was never any end to the troublesome creatures.

"Miss Sable," the young girl said when she saw the housekeeper headed toward her, "is Miss Polly feeling all right? She was in here a few minutes ago and said she couldn't think with me busying around the room."

"She's not feelin' well." Sable made a mental note to say something to Polly if this continued tomorrow.

That evening Polly chose to have her supper in her room.

"Why didn't you have Vera carry that big tray?" Polly asked when Sable brought the food. "Vera is a lot stronger."

"You make me sound like I'm a hundred years old." Sable placed the tray on a small round table by Polly's chair. "I've carried heavier than this in my day." She handed Polly her plate, well filled with roast beef, gravy and vegetables. "I'm glad to see you're dressed for bed. Maybe if you get a good night's sleep you'll be of a better disposition tomorrow. You wouldn't want Mr. Webber seeing you at your worst."

Polly's fork paused in the air. "Friday! Tomorrow is Friday! I'd forgotten." She cut a piece of meat and stuck it in her mouth, savoring the taste. "Hmm. Tell Mary the roast is delicious."

Sable shook her head at seeing how quickly Polly's disposition had improved. Why couldn't Polly have that attitude toward Joshua instead of Mr. Webber?

With a suddenly ravenous appetite, Polly continued her meal, paying little attention to Sable's departure. Riding with Ethan in the morning was exactly what she needed to take her mind off Joshua. All day she'd been disillusioned with her inability to conjure up Joshua in a dream. She had to have done something wrong. Apparently it was going to take a few tries to get it right. But tonight, she had every intention of getting a good night's sleep. This time she would be well rested for her outing with Ethan.

As soon as she had satisfied her hunger, Polly turned out the lamp and went to bed. After last night, she was exhausted. She turned onto her side and tucked the pillow under her head. "Joshua," she murmured as she drifted off to sleep, "when will you come make love to me?"

Polly wasn't sure of the hour when the mattress sank down behind her. She was only aware of the hand on the flat of her stomach and the soaring excitement as his hand moved up to claim a ripe breast. She had called to Joshua, and he had answered. "I've been waiting for you," she murmured. "I wanted to feel you beside me."

"I told you I would always be here for you." He nibbled at the soft, creamy flesh at the bend of her neck.

"I wanted you last night, but you didn't come. What did I do wrong?" A pleasurable groan escaped her lips as his hand moved down between her legs.

"You wanted me, but your need wasn't strong enough. You must want me above all else."

His breath tickled her neck as he pulled her tightly against him. There was no question that he was ready for her, but he continued to take his time.

"Say you're mine for all eternity, Polly."

"Oh, yes."

"Say it."

"I'm yours for all eternity. Oh, Joshua, you make me wild with wanting."

"Remember the words, Polly, and I will come to you once a week."

"Why just once a week?" she asked with a pout.

"When one waits for the fruit to ripen there is more pleasure in the eating."

"What is that supposed to—"

Joshua rolled her over and claimed her ripe lips, lips that were made for kissing.

Polly was trying to reconcile her feeling of guilt as she rode with Ethan through the Sierra mountains. Worn out from lack of sleep, once again she wasn't good company. What kind of woman was she that she'd allow Joshua to make love to her all night then spend the following day with the man she planned to marry? A smile tickled the corner of her lips. She had to be a witch if she could conjure up such a night of wild abandonment and ecstasy. Unthinkingly, she ran her tongue across her lips. What would Joshua do if he knew how she was using him? Was she truly being bad? After all, it didn't really happen and no one knew about it but her.

She glanced at Ethan. He looked so handsome and tall in the saddle. He was exactly what she needed and wanted in a husband. The least she could do was try to carry on a conversation. "Ethan, your grandmother told me you're a lawyer and that you have a very successful practice."

Ethan laughed. "And did she tell you that she often encourages me to marry?"

"No, she didn't."

"She says she wants to see great-grandchildren before she dies. How do you feel about children, Polly?"

Polly was momentarily taken aback by the question. "I always thought I would like five children. Three handsome boys to watch after their two beautiful sisters."

They fell silent as they moved their horses up a rocky embankment. When they reached the top, Polly dismounted and looked out over the land and the tops of the tall pine trees stretched out below. Ahead and to the sides were mountain peaks that reached toward the sky. "What a breathless sight," she whispered in awe.

"Almost as breathless as the sight of you."

Polly had been so enthralled by the spectacular view that she hadn't realized Ethan had dismounted and was standing beside her. She turned and completely forgot what she'd been about to say when she saw him staring at her. She stood very still, waiting for him to claim a kiss. To her disappointment, he cleared his throat and stepped away.

Ethan glanced toward the mountains. "I suppose you've already guessed that I'm attracted to you."

Polly smiled. "No, but I had hoped you were."

Ethan reached out and pulled her toward him with gentle authority. "You don't mind me wooing you?"

Polly unexpectedly felt guilty for deceiving Ethan. He was everything a woman wanted in a man. Handsome, considerate, masculine yet very much a gentleman. She lowered her head. "This is happening too quickly. We've only met three times. You don't even know me."

"Is there a deep secret hidden in your past? If so, tell me and we'll get it out of the way. If it has to do with another man in your past, I'm already aware of that."

Polly's head shot up. "But…but how could you?"

Ethan dropped his hands to his sides. "I'm thirty-two years old, Polly, and I'm well aware of the difference in a virgin's eyes and the eyes of a woman who has experienced a man."

Words failed her. Apparently Ethan had known more women than she'd realized.

"I have a feeling that we could be very good for each other if we trust and take the time to become acquainted."

"I'll not go to bed with you," Polly stated defensively.

Ethan laughed. "I never thought you would."

Polly was embarrassed all the way down to her toenails.

Would she ever totally conquer the habit of saying what was on her mind?

"I haven't spent my life living with my grandmother. Quite the contrary. She dragged me back here. But no one will ever make my mind up for me, and that includes picking the woman I choose to marry." Ethan grinned. "I don't care for the possibility of leading a dull, private life, nor do I care about maidenly virtue. Is there anything else you'd like to know at the moment?"

Flabbergasted, Polly could only shake her head.

"Then do we have an understanding?"

Polly laughed. "I believe we do."

Ethan grinned and helped Polly back up on her horse. "You're a very beautiful woman. How come you've never married?"

"I guess I never found the right man."

Ethan mounted his chestnut. "Then let's continue our ride and exchange tales of our growing up. I think you should know about what a hateful child I was."

Polly was thankful for the way he had deliberately put her at ease. He hadn't asked any questions about her past, nor had he condemned her for it. Ethan Webber was a most extraordinary man, and the more she was around him, the more appealing he became. It was nothing like the animal magnetism she felt toward Joshua. Ethan gave her a contented peacefulness, while Joshua kept her blood stirred and her desire constant. Well, that wasn't exactly right, either. Joshua had done nothing. It was her imagination. Damn. It was all so confusing.

During the next three weeks, Polly spent a considerable amount of time with Ethan. He took her to the theater, they went for long walks, rode together, enjoyed picnics or played card games at her house. But though she enjoyed her time with Ethan, she couldn't give up her nights with

Joshua. Even though she tried to convince herself that the act really wasn't taking place and she was innocent of any wrongdoing, she still felt guilty. She wasn't being faithful to the man she expected to marry.

Polly avoided Joshua as much as possible during the daytime. She even felt guilty about that. After all, she and Joshua had become good friends. When he finished one project, she still found something else for him to do.

Sable was an entirely different matter. The woman no longer gave unwanted advice or complained. It had been replaced with dirty looks. Polly had no idea why.

On a Saturday, Polly finally decided to confront the problems that seemed to get worse daily.

"Vera said you wanted to see me," Sable announced as she entered the large study. She'd planned to tell Polly she was quitting, so it didn't please her to see the petite redhead sitting behind the large desk and looking very unapproachable.

"Sit down, Sable." She waited to continue until Sable had made herself comfortable in one of the deep leather chairs. "I wanted us to be alone so we could talk."

"Well, that would be a change!"

"What do you mean by that?"

Sable folded her arms across her chest. "You never talk to anyone anymore, less it's somethin' to complain about. You sure have changed since you been around that man."

"Ethan. His name is Ethan."

"I don't know of anyone else you been with."

"Is that why you've been acting so distant?" Polly rose and walked around the cherry wood desk. "But Ethan is a wonderful man. You've known all along that I intended to look for a husband."

"Has he asked?"

"No, but he will."

"That don't mean you have to spend all your time with him until he gets around to it."

Polly suddenly realized that Sable was jealous of Ethan. "But I want to spend time with him. Besides, you've got Bidwell," she stated defensively. "Why can't I have a man in my life, as well?"

"'Cause you got other responsibilities. You don't see me shirking my duties. How can I make the others do their work if they don't think you is standin' behind me. You haven't even taken the time to notice that the herb garden is growing more weeds than herbs. Or that the house isn't as clean as it used to be, because of Vera and Ruth spending so much time in the kitchen samplin' Mary's cookin' and talkin' about anything that comes to mind. And what about Mr. Joshua?"

Polly sat on the fat arm of one of the chairs. "What about him?"

"Seems he stays gone more and more. I wouldn't be surprised if one of these days he don't return."

"Where has he been going?"

"How do I know? I got enough troubles without trying to keep up with him."

"Has he said anything about the Grahams?"

"You talkin' about that pretty brown-headed woman that comes by every now and then?"

Polly jumped to her feet. "She's been here?"

"Isn't that what I just said?"

"She's got no business coming here!"

"Yes, she does. She comes to see Mr. Joshua, just like you see Mr. Webber. She's a real nice lady." Sable scratched the back of her head. It was plain to see that Polly was upset. Maybe there was still a chance that something might happen between Polly and Joshua. "Miss Anne ate supper with the rest of us on several occasions. She's got her eye on Mr. Joshua."

"I've decided that tonight I'll start eating in the kitchen."

"That's a mighty quick decision. Is it because of Miss Anne's visits?"

Polly folded her hands in her lap. "Of course not. I've intended to do it for some time. I just hadn't got around to telling you." She looked up at the ceiling, appearing to be looking for spiderwebs. "It seems rather foolish to continue eating in the dining room alone."

"That it does."

"You're right, of course. I haven't spent much time attending to duties. Where are Ruth, Vera and Mary?"

"In the kitchen, working butter and putting it in molds."

"Have them come in here, then go tell Thomas and Bidwell the same thing. Is there anything I should reprimand them about that you haven't mentioned?"

"No." Sable had changed her mind about leaving. Things were starting to get interesting again. "You want me to get Mr. Joshua, also?"

"No, I'll talk to him privately. Is he here?"

"He's here." Sable stood and started for the door.

"Sable, has Bidwell talked you into marrying him yet?"

"He's too lazy." She cackled as she left the room.

After warning her employees that if they didn't attend to their duties they'd be looking elsewhere for work, Polly went in search of Joshua. She finally found him in the paddock area, sitting on a bale of hay and talking to Zeek.

The minute Polly's gaze landed on the tall, dark man, her heart started pounding against her chest. Everything about him was exactly as she remembered in her dreams. She suddenly realized he was staring back at her, and she looked away. "I think I'll get up in the morning and help with the horses, Zeek."

"That would be great," Zeek said excitedly. "Duchess seems more content when you're around."

"Zeek, I want to talk to Joshua privately. I'm sure you wouldn't mind going to the kitchen and getting some of those lemon cookies Mary baked this morning."

Grinning from ear to ear, he hurried off.

Polly turned to Joshua, who so far hadn't said a word. "I've missed our talks," she said.

Joshua didn't comment.

"I'd like to hear your opinion of Ethan Webber."

"He seems all right."

"Seems all right? Haven't you anything else to say?" She reached down, pulled the back hem of her gingham skirt between her legs, then brought it up and tucked it in her waistband. Satisfied, she joined him on the bale.

"Like what? That he's the wrong man for you?"

"Is that what you think?"

"That's what I know."

"I've never known love until I met him. Oh, Joshua, he's so wonderful."

Joshua broke out laughing.

"What's so funny?"

"You. You haven't even a hint as to what love is about."

"That's a lie! I suppose you think you're speaking from experience? Do you expect me to listen to you when some time back you admitted you had a lady friend, yet you keep spending time with Anne Graham."

"At least I don't give Anne any false hopes for the future."

"And just what is that supposed to mean?"

"You know exactly what I'm talking about." He leaned forward and rested his left arm on his leg. "How do Ethan's kisses make you feel? Do you cling to him because you don't want him to stop? Do you want him to make love to you so badly that little else matters? Or can he—"

Polly jumped to her feet. "That is none of your business!"

"The hell it's not."

Joshua reached out and pulled her to him. She tried to get loose, but she couldn't deny the thrill of being placed on his lap.

"Look at me, Polly."

"No." She knew what trouble that could lead to. More than once those eyes had persuaded her to do what he wanted. Dreaming about him making love to her was a lot different than the actual thing. She felt his finger under her chin. Then slowly, he forced it upward. She turned to tell him she'd scream if he didn't release her, and immediately realized her mistake. He pressed his lips to hers. Warm, soft lips that she knew so well. She couldn't—didn't want to—fight her desire that he so easily aroused. It was as if she had been trained to do his bidding. Then she was kissing him back with fervor.

To her disappointment, she was suddenly lifted up and placed back on her feet.

"Like I said, darlin', you're a long ways from being in love with Ethan Webber."

Mortified, Polly ran out of the carriage house. Fortunately, Joshua didn't try to stop her. How could she have been so brazen, especially with Joshua? If she had wanted to act like that, it should have been with Ethan. Hearing Joshua's devilish laughter, she picked up her pace.

In the dead of night, Loge crept into the carriage house. Holding a rope in one hand, he silently made his way up the wooden stairs to the rooms in the loft. He already knew which one belonged to the man who had claimed to be Joshua McCreed.

Loge was through putting up with the impostor's antics and weeks of doing without a good night's sleep. Too many times he'd awakened in a cold sweat after dreaming that Joshua was coming after him to wreak some terrible revenge. During the day, it seemed that everywhere he went, McCreed stood waiting. In the saloon, sitting on a stool and staring at him. On some corner when he rode by. Even looking through a window as he sat in a restaurant eating.

No matter how often he had told himself that he couldn't be the real Joshua McCreed, Loge was finding it harder and harder to believe his own common sense. How could he forget what Joshua had said the night Loge had stuck a gun in his back? But this time he was going to do what he should have done from the start. Drag Joshua away and make him reveal where the gold was hidden.

The door to Joshua's room squeaked loudly as Loge slowly opened it. There was enough moonlight coming in through the window that he could see the still figure on the bed. The noise hadn't wakened McCreed. He walked up to the side of the bed. With his rope held in readiness, he gave the sleeping man a hard shake. The minute McCreed sat up, Loge quickly looped the rope around him.

"Now you're going to answer to me," Loge growled.

At that moment, the moon shone directly through the open window, and Loge's loop fell limp onto the empty bed. What had happened to the man he'd just tied up? A man's laughter rang through the room, raising the hair on Loge's neck.

"As I said before, Loge, you're mine now."

Loge dropped the end of the rope and ran. When he reached the steps, he was trembling so badly that he missed the first one and tumbled end over end all the way to the bottom. The nausea and excruciating pain in his arm told him it was broken. Still, he pulled himself to his feet and continued running, the terrible laughter following him as he went. He knew now with whom he was dealing. The devil. Joshua McCreed had returned from the dead.

Chapter Thirteen

Polly couldn't cut off her tears of happiness as the preacher said the words that would unite Sable and Bidwell in matrimony. It was all so romantic, and they made a perfect couple. Sable gave the orders and Bidwell was happy to oblige. Since joining everyone for supper in the kitchen, it had quickly become apparent to Polly that no matter how much Sable denied any feeling for Bidwell, a wedding was just a matter of time.

Polly glanced at Joshua, who was acting as Bidwell's best man. It was hard to tell what he was thinking—but it had always been impossible to second-guess him. Having to sit across from him every night hadn't been easy. But at least with the others being at the table, plus taking part in their conversations, it made it much easier to handle.

Joshua shifted his gaze and Polly was once again caught up in those dark, devouring eyes. Though they weren't even standing close, she felt as if she were being made love to. She could even feel his hands on her body, his lips teasing, tempting and demanding. In all actuality, he was probably wondering where he was going to build the hothouse she had said she needed.

''I pronounce you man and wife.''

The words broke the spell, but it didn't stop the overpowering desire to ask Joshua to make love to her. The smile that had come so easily only minutes ago now had to be forced. Even the tears had stopped. She hugged and kissed Sable, then congratulated Bidwell. Joshua would soon be adding another room onto Sable's so the pair could have some privacy.

A big party followed, and even the carriage driver, Thomas, joined in the spirit of the occasion. To everyone's delight, he brought a fiddle and was very good at playing it.

Polly tried avoiding Joshua, but finally she had no choice but to dance with him. Had she refused, the others would have wondered why.

Thomas played a waltz, and Bidwell and the women stood back and appreciatively watched Joshua guide Polly around the room. She looked lovely in her pink dress with lots of ruffles and lace, and he dashingly handsome in his black suit, towering over her like a protective eagle.

Polly was thinking about how attractive they looked. Being held in Joshua's arms made it difficult to think of anything other than his nearness. She was positive that when he moved her around in circles, he deliberately pulled her close so her sensitive breasts rubbed against his strong chest, sending bolts of lightning through her body. She was beginning to think Thomas would never tire of playing his violin, when the music stopped.

Joshua stepped away and made a sweeping bow. "Thank you, madam, for allowing me the privilege of being your partner," he said eloquently and loud enough for everyone to hear.

The devilish grin on his face was enough to convince Polly that he was aware of her wanton thoughts. Refusing to let Joshua think he had the upper hand, she gave him an outrageously flirtatious smile. "But, my prince," she mocked as she curtsied, "it is I who should be thanking you. Never have I had a more worthy partner—or one so light of foot."

Joshua laughed and the others clapped, thoroughly enjoying the antics.

With all the champagne that was devoured, everyone was soon ready to call it a night, including Polly. However, with everyone going straight to bed, she had been left with the task of extinguishing the candles and lamps.

Using an oil lamp to guide her way through the house, Polly had just stepped out of the kitchen when an arm circled her waist and a hand covered her mouth. At first she thought it was Joshua, so she didn't fight. But the moment she felt herself being dragged in the direction of the front door, she kicked, moaned, tossed her head, bit the large hand over her mouth, and tried hitting him with her elbow. Still the intruder managed to keep his hold on her.

In her desperation to free herself, she dropped the lamp. She tried to dodge the burning oil, but even though she was still being pulled backward, the flame caught the bottom of her skirt. Her glassy eyes were focused on the red glow that seemed to grab at the ruffles and sheer lace. Her ears were already ringing from sheer panic. Good Lord in heaven! She was going to be burned to death!

Whoever it was behind her released his hold as Polly screamed and frantically swatted at the flame with her hands. Having no success, she tried to yank her clothing off. She gasped for breath, but her lungs received more smoke than air.

Suddenly she was thrown to the floor and rolled. That was followed with something heavy tossed over her. Convinced she was being smothered, she tried fighting, but her strength had been sapped by the smoke. Bile spewed into her throat from the pain and the terrible realization that the rancid odor she smelled was her own burning flesh. The pain was unbearable.

Reality faded away, then she was aware of being carried up the stairs. She knew it was Joshua carrying her when he let out a thunderous yell that had to have wakened the entire household. He gently laid her on the bed.

"You're going to be all right, Polly," Joshua said, trying to make her think it was true. He lit two lamps, then pulled a bowie knife from his boot. He had to get her clothes off as quickly as possible.

"Polly! Can you hear me?"

Her mouth was so dry it hurt to speak. She placed her hand on her throat, forced her eyes open and nodded.

"Don't speak. I just wanted you to know that I have to get to where you were burned. I know it isn't easy, but try to relax as much as possible."

He began to carefully cut away her clothing, layer by layer. What was left of the once pink dress went first. The work seemed to take forever, even though it hadn't been more than five minutes since he'd placed her on the bed. Hopefully the horsehair petticoat had protected her enough that the cloth wouldn't stick to the raw skin.

Dammit, where was everyone? He remembered the champagne. They were probably passed out. He sliced through the corset. His blood ran cold. He could see where the fire had burned its way through her clothing, from her navel to her graceful neck. He clamped his teeth together, causing his jaw muscles to flex. The pain had to already be excruciating, and it would get worse. He had yet to pull the remaining material from Polly's charred flesh.

He hurried to the door and again yelled for one of the servants. Still getting no response, he took off down the stairs, taking three at a time.

When he came to Sable and Bidwell's door, he barged

in without even knocking. After some hard shaking, he managed to rouse Bidwell.

Bidwell jumped from the bed. "What's wrong?"

"Go tell Zeek to fetch a doctor immediately. Polly's skirt caught on fire from an oil lamp. Tell Zeek to use my horse."

Without further explanation, Joshua hurried back into the house, grabbed bottles of whiskey and milk from the kitchen, then ran back to Polly's room. She was still awake. This was one time he wished that she would pass out so she wouldn't feel the pain. He opened the bottle of whiskey and looked down at her.

"Honey, I have to remove your clothes, and it isn't going to be pleasant."

"I hate pain," she managed to squeak out in a weak, raspy voice. "Joshua, am I going to die? Will I be scarred for life?"

"Not if I have anything to do with it. Now take this bottle and drink until you think your eyes are swimming. I not only want you drunk, I want you passed out."

He poured milk over her to keep the fabric wet, then proceeded with the job at hand. It wasn't easy to pull the cloth away from the wounded area and see parts of her flesh go with it. But it had to be done. He couldn't allow the material to become hard and glued to her skin.

Joshua wasn't sure when Polly had passed out, but it was a blessing.

He heard the thud of heavy boots coming up the stairs.

"Where is the woman?" a deep voice boomed.

"In here," Joshua called back. He was surprised to see a big-bellied, slow-moving man with thick glasses enter the room. Joshua was convinced the man could not be very competent. But he'd have to settle for what he got.

"Name's Kenneth Hubert." The doctor shoved Joshua

aside so he could examine the patient. "How the hell did this happen?"

Joshua suddenly realized that he didn't want to give out the details. Perhaps he could use that piece of information in locating the man responsible for all this. "An oil lamp fell and the flame caught her skirt."

Kenneth nodded. "You did a good job of getting her clothes off. Are you her husband?"

"Nope. I just work here."

After seeing as much as he needed to, Kenneth sent Joshua to fetch the whites of two eggs, a cup of lard and lots of cotton cloth. He took alum from his black bag. As the doctor mixed the ingredients, Joshua ripped wide strips of material. Their work was swift and efficient. The concoction was then spread onto the strips and applied to Polly's body. Joshua had already changed his opinion of the good doctor.

It was dawn when Dr. Hubert left the house with the assurance that he would return by two that afternoon. The poultices had to be changed at least once a day. He also left laudanum and instructions to get hold of him should Polly take a turn for the worse.

Joshua pulled a chair up to the side of the bed and made himself comfortable. He sat staring at the small figure on the bed. At least her backside was fine. She'd be able to lie on it until the front part healed. It would have been an entirely different story had he not entered the house to extinguish any lamps that had been left lit. That was when he'd heard the struggling.

Wracked with guilt and anger, Joshua leaned his head against the high-backed wooden chair. This was all his fault. He should have taken care of Loge Snipes before he caused the fire. Maybe he had meant it to be a warning to Joshua. He already knew what would have happened if

Loge had successfully kidnapped Polly. It wouldn't be the first time the scalped rat had raped a woman.

The bastard had already sent too many men to early graves. It was time he received payment for those deaths and for the men who had screamed and begged for mercy as the blowing sand had suffocated them one by one. And he should have never put his filthy hands on Polly! "I'm going to get you, Loge."

Polly moaned softly, causing Joshua to flinch. She was still sleeping off the whiskey she'd downed. Few men could have withstood the pain the way she did. She didn't scream or beg. She drank her whiskey, gritted her teeth and bore the torture.

When there was no longer any possibility of Polly's burns getting infected, he would make sure Loge rotted in hell alongside of him.

He stared at Polly's face. Her eyebrows and eyelashes had been singed, but they would grow back. He'd learned a lot about the beautiful and feisty woman since that first day they'd met outside of Springtown. Beneath her bluster, she had a soft heart for anyone she thought was being unjustly treated. Brave and determined were two more qualities he admired. She was determined to weave her place in society, but she also knew she was vulnerable, which she did a good job of covering up. But what she didn't realize was that all the things she desired so badly would never make her happy. And that included Ethan Webber.

An hour later Sable silently entered the bedroom. Joshua was sitting in a chair with his head bent in sleep. As soon as she took a couple of steps toward the bed, his head snapped up and his eyes flew open. He was looking right at her.

"Is she going to be all right?" she whispered.

Seeing who it was, Joshua took a deep breath and slowly

let it out. "She'll make it. The doc said it could have been a lot worse. Even so, she's going to go through hell."

Sable moved to the side of the bed. Polly's frail body lay stretched out with only a sheet to cover her. Sable was consumed with anguish and ladened with guilt at not having been here to help with her mistress. "Oh, my poor baby. Why did this have to happen to you?" She fought the desire to cry. "I gave Bidwell hell for not wakin' me earlier."

"I told him to let you sleep. I knew you'd need the rest. Someone needs to be with her twenty-four hours a day." He stood and stretched. "You get the next shift. There's laudanum—" he pointed to it "—in case the pain becomes too unbearable."

Polly started whimpering and thrashing. Joshua was immediately by her side. Shortly after he managed to get the laudanum down her throat, she settled back down.

"Go to bed and get a good sleep, Mr. Joshua. I'll watch after her. If I get tired, I'll have someone else up here to watch after her."

"Wake me up when the doc returns or if Polly takes a turn for the worse."

"I will. Thank you, Mr. Joshua. Bidwell told me it was you who saved her life and probably ours, as well. You kept this house from goin' up in flames. I saw where you put it out in the hallway."

"I guess I did manage to do that. I hadn't thought about it." An ironic smiled played at the corner of Joshua's lips. "Believe me, I used to be more adept at taking lives than saving them."

Sable stared at Joshua's broad back as he left the room. Just what did he mean by that statement? She had never doubted that if roused, Joshua could be meaner than a snakebite. And she'd seen a display of his strength. The heavy kitchen door that led to the hall was splintered and completely broken off its hinges. The wall table had also been shoved aside and broken, along with a vase and other items sitting on top.

She had also seen a much gentler side. Like when he'd brushed strands of hair from Polly's face after the laudanum had taken effect. Polly was such a fool.

She looked down at Polly's peaceful face and smiled. "I'll tell you what I think." She gently smoothed out the sheet. "I think Mr. Joshua is fixin' to take matters into his own hands. Real soon he's gonna put an end to your notions about marryin' Mr. Webber."

Mr. Webber! She had forgotten what day this was. He had to be informed as to what had happened before he arrived in the morning to go riding.

Sable reached over and pulled the cord by the bed. Only minutes later, Vera was poking her head into the room. Ruth and Mary were right behind her. As she hurried toward the three worried women, Sable pressed her finger to her lips to warn them to be quiet. As soon as she had them back in the hall, she told them of Polly's condition.

"Did you see the way Joshua tore through the kitchen door and hallway?" Ruth asked in awe. "He wasn't about to let anything stop him from getting to the mistress."

"I saw. Now you all stop your worrying. Miss Polly is goin' to be just fine. Mr. Joshua said so, and I wouldn't be about to doubt anything that man says. Ruth, I want you to go directly to Mr. Webber's house and leave a message with a servant. Vera, I want you to take a nap so you can relieve me tonight."

Two hours later, Ethan arrived at the house. After a lengthy conversation with Sable, he went to the carriage house to see if Joshua might be awake. To Ethan's surprise, when he entered, he saw the tall man leaning against a post and looking as if he were expecting him.

"I wanted to thank you for saving Polly's life." The cold

look on Joshua's face set Ethan's nerves on edge. "How can I repay you? Name anything you want."

"I didn't save her in order to reap a reward, *Mr. Webber*," Joshua replied. His lips slowly twisted into a grin. "However, since you asked, there is one little favor you could do for me. Get out of Polly's life. She doesn't love you."

Ethan's shock quickly yielded to fury. "Why? So you can take my place?"

"Take your place? I already have."

"Are you insinuating—"

"I'm not insinuating, I'm telling. I know you plan to ask Polly for her hand, but you could save yourself a lot of embarrassment if you just stop seeing her. I guarantee there will be no wedding. At least not between the two of you."

"You can't guarantee a damn thing. Or are you threatening murder?"

Joshua chuckled. "A most interesting thought."

"What is it you're after? Polly's money? Because you saved Polly's life, I'm going to ignore this conversation. But if you ever make a threat again, I'll shoot you without a moment's hesitation. I'm not afraid of you, McCreed."

"You should be. Believe me, I'm being merciful."

Ethan turned and walked out of the carriage house, all the time listening for the sound of a pistol being cocked. He had never been a coward, but as soon as he was convinced there would be no shot in the back, he released his pent up breath.

The days passed slowly and painfully for Polly. She was sure she must have thanked Joshua at least a hundred times for saving her life, and had asked the doctor every conceivable question she could think of about her condition and if she would have scars. His standard reply was that there would probably be some, but they would eventually fade. And, yes, the day would come when she could once again wear a corset.

Joshua had made her promise not to reveal that she had been attacked, his explanation being that someone might make a slip of the tongue and get caught. It would also make the others feel more comfortable.

Each day, when Dr. Kenneth Hubert was due to change her bandages, Polly was tempted to run away, hide under the bed, or anything else that might prevent it from happening. But she doubted that she could make it off the bed. She couldn't even complain, because she'd chosen the pain over taking laudanum. She didn't like how groggy it made her feel.

Joshua seldom came to her room. It seemed rather foolish since Kenneth had told her it was Joshua who had had the foresight to cut away her clothes as quickly as possible. It was also Joshua who had helped apply the treated cotton to her body. However, according to Sable, Joshua always questioned the doctor thoroughly after he left Polly's bedroom. She also pointed out that it would be unseemly for a man to be in a woman's room, especially with her having nothing but a sheet over her body.

The chocolates and beautiful flowers that filled her room were from Ethan. She particularly enjoyed the little notes that accompanied the gifts. Especially the one that asked her to marry him. Of course he wasn't allowed to visit so she penned replies. One being her acceptance to his proposal.

Oddly, the two things Polly missed the most about being bedridden had nothing to do with Ethan, or no longer having her weekly dreams of making love with Joshua. What she missed were her talks with Joshua and being able to go on long rides.

Slowly and mercifully, she began to heal. It was a glorious day when Kenneth informed her there would be no more poultices. It was even better when he informed her that she could start having her head raised, but only for short periods at a time. She was starting to heal.

Sable made sure the pillows were properly supporting Polly's back. She was still weak, and her face turned white when her skin was stretched so she could raise up a bit further.

Sable picked up the bowl of soup she'd placed on the bedside table.

"All right, Sable. You might as well spit out what's on your mind."

"I don't know what you're talking about," Sable protested. She dipped the spoon in the soup. "Do you feel like feeding yourself today?"

"I'm not ready to eat. We've known each other too long to try and slip something by me. Something is bothering you, and you're not sure whether or not to tell me. I'm not going to eat until you spit it out."

"I guess I might as well. I don't know of any other way to do it. Mr. Joshua has left."

"Is that all? He's always coming and going. How many times have we commented on how quickly he could disappear? He'll be back, so I don't understand why you're concerned."

"This time it's gonna be some time before he returns."

Suddenly feeling chilled, Polly carefully pulled the sheet up to her chin. "What makes you think that?"

"Besides his horse, he had six pack mules. One of them was loaded with supplies. Wherever he's headed, it's gotta be a long ways off."

"What?" Polly jerked up, but the pain forced her to fall back down on the pillows.

"Polly! Are you all right?" Sable sloshed the soup on

the floor when she slammed the bowl onto the table. "He said he'd come back."

Polly opened her eyes as the constriction in her throat suddenly eased. She'd thought she'd lost Joshua forever. "Sable, how could he leave me alone like this?" she asked sadly.

"I don't know, baby, but somethin' mighty powerful caused him to go away. I've never seen anyone with as much hatred as he had in his eyes. I sure wouldn't want to mess with him."

Maybe he discovered who attacked me, Polly thought.

"Whatever his reason for leaving, he went and hired some men to watch over this place."

"Oh, Sable, I feel so bad. He saved my life, watched after me, and now he's making sure I'll be safe. I'm so grateful to him."

"He knows."

"Do you honestly think he'll come back?"

Seeing the color returning to Polly's face, Sable continued on. "Honey, there's not a doubt in my mind. I got a mighty strong notion that when he does, he plans to take you away from Mr. Webber."

"Oh, that's ridiculous. There has never been anything between Joshua and me." *Only in dreams.*

Sable picked up the bowl of soup again.

"Instead of eating, why don't you try brushing the tangles from my hair?"

"Then you'll promise to eat this soup?"

Polly no longer had any interest in food, but she nodded just to keep Sable happy. "What does it feel like to be married, Sable?"

Sable giggled. "That Bidwell is one fine man." She went to the dressing table to get the brush. "You said there has never been anything between you and Mr. Joshua. You mean he's never even kissed you?"

"No. Well, once, but he was only playing with me."

"Are you sure?"

"Of course I'm sure." Polly rolled partially onto her side so Sable had better access to her hair.

"Hmm. I wonder what the reason for that was?"

Polly laughed. "Once I even *asked* him to kiss me, and he refused."

"Is that right? It don't make no sense. If he don't have no feelings for you, how come he's stayed instead of movin' on? And it's as plain as the nose on your face that you're always making up jobs for him to do to keep him here."

"That's not so. I've needed everything I've had him do. Ouch! Must you pull so hard?"

"It's the only way I'm going to get the tangles out. What about that staircase you had him build from the end of the hall to the outside wall? It don't go nowhere!"

"I have plans for it."

"What plans?"

"I don't have to explain everything I do."

"Especially when it don't make no sense!"

"Oh, Sable! You don't know what you're talking about."

Sable smiled but said nothing. Polly cared more for Joshua than she wanted to admit.

"Besides, by the time Joshua returns, I'll already be married."

"I told Joshua about that."

"Oh? And what did he say?"

"He just laughed."

"Well, he's certainly going to be in for a big surprise."

Down the street from the mercantile store, Joshua sat atop his horse in plain sight, patiently waiting for Loge to leave with the goods he'd purchased. Now that Joshua

knew Polly was going to be all right, the long awaited time
for retribution had arrived. Since knowing Polly, he had to
admit he'd become a changed man. He no longer looked
forward to a good fight. Robbing didn't even have any appeal. But one thing had remained constant—his need to get
even with Loge. Not just for the men Loge had left to die,
but also for what he'd done to Polly.

Joshua shifted in the saddle. He had already made up his
mind to return Loge to where it had all began, some four
hundred miles away. Back to where they both should have
died years ago.

Joshua's lips spread into a cold smile. To insure Loge's
participation in his scheme, Joshua had silently entered the
Traveler's Rest Hotel before dawn to stuff money into
Loge's saddlebags. The craziness, combined with his greed,
would overpower any common sense Loge had left.

Joshua watched the bull of a man walk out of the store
onto the boarded walk, his arms loaded with supplies. Holding the lead line to the mules, Joshua nudged his black
forward. He moved the animals in a slight zigzag motion,
just enough to attract Loge's attention. A surreptitious
glance over his shoulder confirmed that Loge had spotted
him. Smiling, Joshua continued on his way.

Loge couldn't believe his luck had finally turned. He'd
caught sight of McCreed riding out of town. He hurried to
his packhorse and loaded the last of the provisions he'd
bought. He wasn't about to let McCreed out of his sight,
but he needed to stay far enough back so the devil wouldn't
realize he was being followed. He chuckled with satisfaction. After all these years, what he had been waiting for
was apparently about to happen. With that many unloaded
mules, the bastard had to be on his way to collect the gold.
The gold that belonged to him—not McCreed!

Loge curled his lip. Since he'd first laid eyes on McCreed
in the stand of trees, he'd turned to smoking monkey weed

again, and going to the Chinese section for opium to rid the fear that threatened to consume him. After what had happened when he'd tried tying his hated enemy up, he had imbibed even more. He laughed, remembering how he'd even plundered and raped in small, nearby towns, to prove he was meaner and stronger than McCreed would ever be. It hadn't worked, and the day before yesterday, he'd decided a quiet exit out of town would be his wisest choice. Besides, he was broke and those coolies didn't take credit.

He tightened the last strap then quickly mounted his mouse-colored gelding. After sleeping for nearly twenty-four hours straight, he felt good and ready to take on anyone—including McCreed. He kicked his horse into a trot. His whole life was about to change for the better. The money he'd found in his saddlebags was an omen of good things to come. He still didn't remember putting it there, but it had to be part of the money he'd robbed from the bank in Hangtown before coming to Auburn.

Loge pulled his hat lower on his head, and laughed aloud at the irony of his situation. Just two days ago he didn't even have the money to get his packhorse out of the livery stable. Flat broke, he'd even considered stealing his pack-horse and robbing another bank on his way out of town. As it turned out, he'd not only been able to pay the boarding fee, he'd bought supplies as well and still had money left over.

Ahead, the road sloped downward, and Loge watched the man and his animals slowly disappear from sight. When he reached the top of the hill and saw McCreed still moving south, he pulled back on the reins, slowing his mount to a walk.

Now that his mind was clear and he understood how McCreed had supposedly disappeared the last two times, he was no longer afraid. It had been the opium playing tricks with his head. Besides, the man up front couldn't possibly be the real Joshua McCreed.

Loge started humming a tune that he'd heard at some time and place. Taking the gold and killing the tall man up ahead was going to be such sweet vengeance. But until he tired of the fun, he planned to inflict his own brand of pain and watch the bastard suffer.

Polly was sure she would burst from joy when the doctor said he wanted her to start taking short, slow walks three times a day, to help regain her strength.

She hadn't realized how weak she still was until she tried getting to her feet. Even with the doctor and Sable's help, she wasn't able to take more than two steps. But as the days and weeks passed, she became stronger. Everyone, including herself, was justly proud of her accomplishment.

Her strength grew. The most magnificent day so far was when she was permitted to go downstairs. Once again the doctor and Sable held on to her to make sure she didn't fall, but she didn't mind in the least.

Because she wasn't to tire herself, Ethan was only allowed short visits. But those visits were made daily. Polly and Ethan discussed everything—from planning their wedding to the foreign capitals she'd read about. To her delight, Ethan suggested that for their honeymoon, they take an extensive tour of Europe. But something wasn't right. As of late, when she looked at Ethan she saw Joshua's dark eyes staring back at her.

The days turned into periods of rest, doctor visits, concerned servants watching and waiting on her, Sable hovering over her like a protective lioness and visits with Ethan. But with the passing of time, she came to miss Joshua more and more. And as her body healed, her passion returned. She told herself that things would change once she was married. After all, it was Ethan she loved, not

Joshua. But until they were married, it was Joshua she needed. She tried calling him to her again, but as the Thursday passed by, she deduced he was too far away for her to conjure him up. Still the words, ''I'm yours for all eternity,'' continued to float through her thoughts, even when Ethan was able to steal a kiss.

Nearly two weeks had passed before Loge realized McCreed was headed back to the Mojave Desert. It infuriated him to know that the gold had been there all along.

Loge could feel his bravado starting to fade when the desert came into view. He began to have second thoughts. Why hadn't McCreed ever turned in the saddle to see if he was being followed? There was something else he couldn't understand. Sometimes he considered the man he'd been following a stranger, but most of the time he was thinking of him as the real Joshua McCreed. The man even sat in the saddle like Joshua! He shook his head. The heat was making him confused. But no matter what was real or not, he couldn't give up now. The gold was nearly in his hands.

Loge licked his dry lips. His water was getting low.

Chapter Fourteen

Daniel Fritz stepped out of the Young America tobacco shop and glanced up and down the street. Spotting Polly walking about a half block ahead, he hurried to catch up with her. ''Miss O'Neil,'' he called as soon as he was close enough.

Polly stopped, turned, then smiled warmly. ''Why, Mr. Fritz. How good to see you.''

''I haven't seen you in town lately. Here, let me carry that hatbox.''

Polly gladly handed it to him. She should have had it delivered to the house. ''Thank you, Daniel. My horse is just ahead at the livery stable.''

Daniel was pleased to hear her call him by his first name.

Polly sighed tiredly. ''I shouldn't have come to town. Don't breathe a word that I sneaked away today. I'll never hear the end of it.'' A mischievous light entered her blue eyes. ''Only to you would I admit that everyone was right. I'm not as strong as I'd like to be. But it did feel wonderful to be on Duchess's back again with the wind blowing against my face.''

''I heard about your accident. It's good to see you finally

out and about.'' He suddenly realized that she was making no effort to move.

''Accident? I'm not supposed to say anything, but I don't see what harm it would do now. It was no accident. I was attacked by a man in my very own house. As he was trying to drag me to the front door, the lamp I was holding fell and caught my dress on fire. I wouldn't be alive today if Joshua McCreed hadn't managed to put the flame out.'' Just the memory caused Polly to shudder.

''Have you any idea who did it?''

''None whatsoever. He got cleanly away. Nor do I know why anyone would want to do such a thing. I've wondered if he's waiting for me to get well before trying again.''

Polly swayed, and Daniel reached out to steady her. ''I shouldn't have kept you here talking. Come along, and I'll take you home.''

''I'll be all right, but I would appreciate your walking with me to the livery.''

''I'll do better than that. I'll personally take you.'' Daniel set the box down, then swung Polly up in his arms. She was as light as a feather. He leaned down and hooked his fingers beneath the pink ribbon wrapped around the box, then took off toward the livery stable.

Polly giggled. ''I know that this is terribly improper, but it does beat having to walk.''

Her laughter reminded Daniel of bells, and it was quite infectious. He also broke out laughing, something he hadn't done for a long time.

''I hear you and Ethan Webber are planning to marry. Is that correct, or just a rumor?''

''Word carries fast. Mr. Webber only asked for my hand a few weeks ago. And, yes, I accepted.''

''Congratulations.''

''How nice of you.''

''When is the happy occasion to take place?''

Polly spied Mrs. Carver and her daughter walking on the other side of the street. "I'm going to have to do some explaining. The Carvers are the worst gossips in town." Her tone of voice made it clear that she wasn't particularly worried. "Ethan wants a big wedding, but I have to get my strength back first, and there's a lot of arranging to be done, food to plan and invitations to send. So I doubt that the nuptials will take place before three months. Much too long, as far as I'm concerned. If you would give me your card, I'd like to send you an invitation."

Daniel had never experienced such a deep sense of sorrow. He was hopelessly in love with Polly, even though he'd known it was futile. The beautiful redhead would never think of him in a romantic sense, nor did he have anything to offer her. Like Polly, Ethan Webber had always taken the time to stop and talk to him. Yes, they were well suited for each other.

They reached the livery stable, and Daniel soon had her settled on her horse. "I'll ride with you in case you get dizzy again."

After escorting Polly home, Daniel returned to town. He would never be able to tell anyone that his wedding present would be a gift of silence. He couldn't remember which gold town or which saloon, but he'd never forget her standing behind some gambler's chair. Her youth and beauty had made it difficult to concentrate on his cards, causing him to lose a bundle of money that night.

Once he'd returned his horse to the livery, Daniel broke out with hearty laughter that shook his big frame and made his bulbous nose even redder. His walk took on a definite jauntiness. His mother and Berk were going to be mad as hell when he told them of the forthcoming wedding. For once it felt good to know their investment was a total loss and that all their planning had gone awry.

* * *

Daniel sat quietly, nursing his glass of whiskey as he listened to his brother and mother quarreling. He grinned. He hadn't informed either of them that he planned to take off on his own. He'd even been giving some serious thought to becoming a Texas Ranger.

"I can't believe that slut would do such a thing!" Berk drew his eyebrows into an angry frown. "All along she's led me to believe I was the only man she cared for!"

Daniel sprang to his feet. "You're a damn liar," he accused.

With the quickness of a cat, Berk spun around and sneered at his brother. "Shut up, Daniel, or I'll slit your throat from ear to ear."

Daniel laughed. "You'd be smart not to try it."

Berk looked back at his mother. "If you want to know what went wrong, look to that ox you're too embarrassed to call a son. He's so smitten, he probably told the O'Neil woman our plan. Everything was going fine until he stuck his face where it wasn't wanted. Polly O'Neil was so horrified that she's stopped talking to me."

Inez rubbed her chin. "Did you know she was going out with Ethan Webber?"

"I'm sure she went to him on the rebound."

Inez continued on with her game of solitaire. "It was your business to keep an eye on her. Why didn't you get rid of Webber?"

"I don't think that's a good idea," Daniel spoke up. He leaned his shoulder against the wall. "The lawyer is not only well liked in Auburn, his grandmother would never quit looking for his killer. Even if it meant hiring every man in California."

"After making such a mess of everything, you should be the one to handle that end of it," Berk bit out.

"I've heard enough of your accusations, you lying son

of a bitch!'' Daniel pushed away from the wall, but he hadn't taken two steps before Berk pulled his knife.

Inez stood and slammed both hands down on the table. ''Stop it! If you want to kill each other, do it somewhere else. I'm finished with this whole scheme. I've decided to sell the bakery and get away from here. I don't want to have to clean up blood or have to explain where the stains came from.''

Berk turned his fury at his mother. ''I'll not let you leave until you hand over my share of money,'' he stated in a dangerously low voice. He dropped his hand holding the knife, but backed up so he could still keep an eye on Daniel. ''I haven't given up on Miss O'Neil. I've already made plans for that one. We'll marry, no matter whether she likes it or not. But I need *my* money to pull it off!''

Inez's face mirrored her shock. ''I had no intention of leaving without giving you and Daniel what you have coming! Haven't I always been fair?''

''Let me remind you that my share includes a third of what you get for the bakery,'' Berk reminded her.

Inez turned her back on them, and headed straight for the front of the shop. With it being closed for the night, she would at least be to herself. She needed to plan her departure.

What kind of a fool did Berk take her for? She plopped down onto a wooden chair by the oven. She had no intention of leaving either boy any money. They were young and could still learn how to work for a living. However, her years were limited. She was tired of figuring out schemes, and she was tired of them hanging on her skirt tail. Maybe she should leave them a note with a little truthful information. Like how they'd been kidnapped from different families when they were young so she could put them on the street to beg. She could also say that considering what it had cost her to raise them, she owed them nothing.

Berk still stood by the sofa, glaring at the doorway Inez had passed through. "As sure as hell, that witch is planning to sneak away without leaving us a cent."

"You know, Berk, we have never had anything in common. You always spend money as fast as you can lay your hands on it. By the time I was ten, I had already learned to tuck my money away. When we were begging, I made sure that I pocketed at least half of the take before I turned it over to Mums. It was the same with anything else. And unlike you, I saved. I would venture to say I have even more money than Mums."

Daniel set his glass on the fireplace mantel. "So you see, Berk, the money makes no difference to me. But I'll tell you what does matter. Polly O'Neil. Now we both know that she never looked twice at you. And we know that because of it, you could never talk her into marrying you. The only way it would happen would be for you to force her into it. So, I'm giving you a warning. If you lay a hand on Polly O'Neil, I'll kill you."

Berk smiled. "Well, well. How touching. But you're too slow and clumsy, *brother dear.* I could throw this knife quicker than you could get your sights on me. You two probably deserve each other. Her all scarred from the fire, and you looking as if you belong in a circus. She'd have been better off if she'd let the man pull her out of the house."

Daniel's eyes narrowed. "Don't forget the warning." He left by the back door. Had Berk been the culprit, or had he just heard what had happened?

Berk's smirk quickly faded. Daniel never gave haphazard warnings. Maybe he should kill Daniel and get the hulk off his back. It would make things a lot easier. All of this

would have already been taken care of if Polly hadn't
dropped that damn lamp.

Well ahead of where Loge sat motionless on his horse,
Loge watched McCreed dismount and remove a shovel
from his supply pack. Loge's excitement superseded any
thoughts of wariness, exhaustion, or heat. He finally knew
where the gold had been hidden for the past ten years.

Loge moved his mount forward, then pulled him to a
stop at the bottom of the next mound of sand. He quickly
secured the animals, then crawled on his hands and knees
to the top of the ridge. For some time, Loge had suspected
that McCreed knew he was being followed. Loge was also
sure he himself was being led into some sort of trap, but
still he followed, already envisioning the yellow bars resting in his hands. Still, wasn't so stupid as to not be careful
and stay far enough back so that no tricks could be pulled
on him. No, this time it would be McCreed who would
come up the loser.

With his body hugging the ground, Loge felt like a lizard
as he cautiously edged forward. He paid scant attention to
the salt that clung to the sweat on his face and damp
clothes.

McCreed had already started digging. With McCreed's
back turned and giving no heed to danger, there was no
doubt in Loge's mind that he had the upper hand. He'd
thought about shooting the bastard, but he'd never been a
good shot from this distance. And what if it wasn't gold
being dug up? He'd need Joshua to tell him the real location.

Joshua stood straight and turned. Loge fell flat against
the hot earth. Then he saw what had attracted Joshua's
attention. The mules and his horse had started to drift away.
McCreed hurried forward, but his movements frightened
the animals. Loge laughed to himself. The man had the

brains of a rabbit. Or was this a trick to get him close enough for McCreed to overpower him? He had to be careful.

Loge was close enough now to hear Joshua speaking softly to calm the critters. But each time Joshua moved forward, they moved farther away. Soon the beasts had gone to the other side of another ridge of sand.

Loge hesitated only a moment. With the slyness of a weasel, he stood and ran forward, ready to drop to the ground should McCreed make an unexpected appearance. He made a wide circle and came around on the far side of where Joshua was securing the mules. Keeping his body crouched over, he crept toward Joshua's backside, being careful not to make a sound or frighten the animals. His mouth tasted as if it were full of cotton as he edged closer and closer. Joshua suddenly jerked around, but it was too late. Loge was already bringing the butt of his pistol down on Joshua's head.

When Joshua fell to the ground unconscious, Loge couldn't hold back his giggle of delight. With his finger on the trigger, he pointed the pistol at the prone man. His hand shook with anxiety, and he had to grit his teeth to keep from firing. He forced himself to shove the gun back in his waistband, then reached down and grabbed hold of the back of Joshua's shirt.

After dragging the unconscious man back to where the digging had started, Loge let go of his captive and let him fall to the ground. He glared down at the hole. He could see a part of a wagon wheel as well as parts of a skeleton.

Loge eagerly snatched up the shovel. Saliva drooled out the sides of his mouth and sweat was already dripping down his temples onto his soaked shirt by the time he started to dig. The sooner he got what he'd come for, the sooner he could get away from this hellhole.

A few minutes later, Loge began to notice that every time

he pulled out a shovelful of sand, the ground gave way beneath his feet. Then the sides of the hole caved in, covering his feet and ankles. He tried lifting them free, but he continued to sink into the hole. He was quickly being buried alive!

Frantically he resumed his shoveling, faster and faster. He was losing ground. Terrified, he dropped the shovel and clawed at the sides of the hole. But they gave way, burying him even deeper. He hollered and yelled, trying to awaken Joshua. The sand was up to his shoulders. He turned pure white when he felt hands grab his ankle and pull. He let out one last desperate scream before his mouth, then head, disappeared.

Joshua groaned and sat up. He reached up and felt the goose egg on the back of his head. When he brought his hand back around, it was covered with blood. Then he remembered Loge. He jumped to his feet, ignoring the pain. He glanced around, but Loge was nowhere in sight. Then, as if someone had whispered in his ear, he looked down and saw a hand disappearing beneath the sand. He didn't have to be told who it was, nor did he have to confirm the man was dead. Loge's old comrades had been waiting for him.

Joshua returned to his black gelding and the mules. A few minutes later, he was mounted and riding away. He'd brought Loge back here to kill him. He still couldn't figure out how Loge had managed to get behind him. But maybe he wasn't supposed to know. Maybe his job had been just to make the delivery. He wasn't even sure how Loge died, nor did he want to know. The matter had been taken out of his hands, and he was actually glad. Since meeting Polly and becoming part of her family, he'd lost that killer instinct somewhere along the way.

For the first time, he realized how much he'd changed. He glanced up at the bright sun and smiled. Just maybe something good was going to come out of this after all. He gave his horse a kick in the sides. He was anxious to return to Auburn. He was through playing around. From here on, Polly was his territory. He'd had enough of her looking toward other men for happiness.

He brought his horse to a halt, turned in the saddle, and once more looked back at where Loge Snipes had been buried. Joshua sneered. It was too bad that the turncoat hadn't found out before his death that the gold had been removed years ago.

Polly stood by her bedroom window, watching the yellow sun slowly dip beneath the horizon. She knew supper was nearly ready, but still she lingered. She looked toward the carriage house below. She'd never noticed how gray it looked in the waning sunlight. The darkness was closing in, and the small house seemed to change colors by the minute.

She squared her shoulders. Her sadness of late couldn't possibly have anything to do with the realization that Joshua wasn't going to make it back before the wedding. However, she was willing to admit that it seemed like an eternity since they'd last made love. Could Ethan satisfy her passion after the wild ecstasy she'd experienced with Joshua in her dreams?

Polly's blue eyes suddenly came alive. A man had just ridden up to the front of the carriage house. Though she couldn't see his face, she would have recognized the easy way he swung from the saddle and that lank body, even if it had been pitch-dark. Joshua had returned home.

She licked her hands, then pulled them across the sides of her hair to pull back any straggly wisps that may have worked their way loose from the soft knot at the top of her head. Quickly she smoothed the purple bodice of her dress, and shook the purple striped skirt to be sure it hung properly over her petticoats. Satisfied, she hurried out of the room. She didn't want Joshua to know she had been looking toward the carriage house when he rode up. She certainly didn't want him to think she'd been pining for him.

She raised the hem of her skirt and ran down the stairs, all thoughts of decorum forgotten. She wanted to be seated at the kitchen table when Joshua made his appearance. As soon as she neared the kitchen, she slowed down and inhaled deeply several times. She didn't want the others to suspect that she had been running.

Even after they had all filled their plates with food, Joshua still hadn't made an appearance. Polly was having a difficult time trying to appear normal and force food down her throat. She had already dropped one of the serving spoons on the table. Where was Joshua? Surely he had to be hungry.

Another five minutes passed before the back door finally opened and Joshua strolled in. His dark eyes immediately locked on to Polly. She knew her heart had stopped beating and she was going to faint dead away. How could she have forgotten how commanding he was?

Everyone welcomed Joshua back at the same time. Mary practically shoved him down on a chair, then went to fetch a plate and silver. Polly couldn't even speak, let alone act impersonal to his return. All she could think about was the way he had filled the doorway and that it was indecent for a man to be so devilishly appealing. More importantly, would she now be able to summon him into her dreams? Joshua smiled, and she felt like melting wax.

"You look much better than the last time I saw you."

Polly poked at the snap beans with her fork. "It's good to have you back, Joshua," she said sincerely.

After they finished their meals, the others quietly left the table.

"I thought for sure you'd miss the wedding," Polly began as soon as she was alone with Joshua.

"Wedding?"

The way his eyes narrowed and his jaw muscles twitched made Polly nervous. Even his eyes darkened. She jammed a forkful of beans into her mouth. She needed a moment to regain her composure. She swallowed her food and looked directly at him. "Yes. I told you I was going to marry him, and he finally asked. Of course I accepted."

"But of course." He started spooning food onto his plate. "You know you don't love him."

"You don't know that. Why would you even say such a thing? And even if it were true, I'll make him a good wife."

"You said the same thing about Malcolm Sawyer." He took a roll, then opened and buttered it. "How are you feeling, Polly? Is everything back to normal?"

Polly couldn't squelch the laugh that bubbled forth. "I swear, Joshua McCreed, I've never known anyone better than you when it comes to changing the subject, or avoiding questions. Yes, I'm just fine. I wouldn't be about to marry Ethan if I weren't."

"I've missed you. Have you missed me?" He took a bite of the delicious roast chicken.

Polly shrugged her shoulders. "I've been so busy I hadn't given it much thought. But yes, I suppose I have. I missed our talks and arguments, but now Ethan fills my time."

Joshua nodded.

"You act as if you don't believe me."

"I didn't say that." Joshua chuckled but continued to eat his supper.

"What's so funny?"

"I was thinking about when we first met."

"What is that supposed to mean?"

"Nothing, I was just thinking aloud. You know, Polly, you're a very beautiful woman. It seems such a waste to throw yourself away on a man you don't even love."

"I'm very fond of him. Love will come."

"You have no guarantee of that. What happens ten years from now when you're still cursing yourself for not holding out for the few joys life has to offer? If you knew how wonderful life is, you would never have considered Ethan's proposal."

"You just returned, and you're already trying to change my mind. I'd much rather marry a man who has both feet on the ground instead of a man like you."

Joshua wiped his mouth, tossed the linen napkin onto the table and stood. "That, my dear, is an out-and-out lie. You're just too afraid of the consequences. I don't think the old Polly would have been."

"You don't know what you're talking about. By the way, where have you been for so long?"

"I had to go visit with an old friend and tell him some other friends were looking forward to seeing him."

"Was it that woman you once mentioned as being a special friend?" Though she didn't like to admit it, she could feel molten jealousy filling her insides.

Joshua grinned. "Nope."

He's gloating, Polly thought.

He finished up, then left by way of the back door.

Polly stayed up late reading that night, afraid of the disappointment she'd experience if Joshua didn't appear to her tonight. What about all the nights she'd called to him but he hadn't come to her. Or the nights she couldn't sleep and her body became wet with perspiration from the unrelenting need to have him make love to her.

When she was ready for bed, and the lamps had been extinguished, she pulled back a corner of the heavy drapes and peeked down below. She could see a glow behind the curtains, which meant Joshua was still awake. She closed her eyes and allowed her hands to trail to her breasts.

"I'm yours for all eternity," she whispered.

"Then come to me."

Polly's eyes flew open and her hands dropped to her sides. She glanced around the dark room and listened for any noise. She was terrified. This had never happened before, and she was definitely not asleep. Had the man who had tried to drag her away returned?

"I'm yours for all eternity." She waited for a reply so she'd know where the man was standing in the shadows.

"Come to me, Polly. Don't be afraid. It will be the night you've waited for."

The voice wasn't coming from any particular place. It seemed to be coming from everywhere. She pulled the curtain back again. The light in Joshua's room had been extinguished.

"Come to me. Didn't you say you were mine for all eternity?"

This time the words seemed farther away. As if in a daze, she went over and opened the door. She didn't even bother to put on her robe. She continued down the stairs. Would Joshua really want her?

She could feel the cold ground as she walked barefoot along the path to the carriage house, but it wasn't uncomfortable. Neither were the steps that led to Joshua's room. When she came to his door, she silently opened it. There was enough moonlight to see him lying on the bed. He pulled the cover back and silently waited for her.

"How did you know I'd come?" she asked in wonderment.

"Though you refused to admit it, we've wanted each other for quite some time. I could tell by the light in your eyes that tonight was the night."

"Were you in my room or did you talk through the door at me?"

"Of course not. I've been right here. Come, Polly, let me show you the pleasure we can give each other."

Polly walked over and climbed into bed with him. When he pulled the cover over both of them, she felt as if Joshua had finally made his claim. He pulled her to him, and all thoughts and questions left her mind. At this moment, she could think of nothing but her desire to finally have him make love to her. It seemed as if she had waited an eternity for it to happen. This time it was no dream.

Chapter Fifteen

Polly sneaked into her room, hopped in bed, and waited for the first rays of the sun to climb up the opposite wall. Though she'd just left Joshua's side, she could already feel the need to have him again smother her with kisses and take her to physical heights she'd never known existed.

But the last two weeks had taken its toll. Indecision was eating at her. She could no longer tell herself that being with Joshua didn't matter, or try to deny that she was being unfaithful to the man she planned to marry.

Polly pulled the covers up to her chin. The night and mornings were much cooler now. Winter was knocking at the back door. She released a heavy sigh. She couldn't continue on like this. She had to make a decision. Either ask Joshua to leave, or tell Ethan there would be no wedding.

There was no question that Joshua should be the one to go. Though he'd saved her life and was wonderful in bed, he didn't love her. She would much rather have the man in love with her than to be in love with a man who didn't return the feeling. And there would never be any permanency or commitment between them. He might even decide to ride out of her life tomorrow.

There were also other concerns. She knew instinctively

that if she called the wedding off, she would never get a second chance with Ethan. But what if his lovemaking didn't do anything for her? Joshua was right. Ten years or more of discontent could be an awfully long time. Would she end up running back to Joshua's arms?

She needed to get away from both of them and think. Someplace where she could be alone without either of them influencing her decision. Maybe she should take a trip to Sacramento and visit with Amanda and Chance. She could see the baby and discuss her dilemma with Amanda. Suddenly she thought about Lake Tahoe. It was close by. And if it was as big as Joshua had said, it couldn't be hard to find. It was still very early. If she hurried, she could put a good many miles behind her before anyone even discovered she'd left.

She leapt off the bed and ran to the armoire. The floor was cold on her bare feet. As soon as she came back, she'd have wool carpeting installed. While rubbing her arms to warm them, she studied the clothes before her. During some past conversation, Ethan had said that to go to Tahoe would take two days up and two days back. All she'd need was a bedroll, clothes and supplies to last five days. She began tossing clothes onto her bed.

Oh, what an exciting adventure this was going to be! But she didn't want to frighten anyone or give them reason to believe that her attacker had returned. She'd have to leave a note.

Light hues of orange were just starting to light the sky as Berk left Madam Suzie's place of business. He sniffed at the smell of the crisp morning air and mounted his horse. As he rode toward the bakery, he noticed how the tree leaves were already starting to change their colors.

Any thoughts of nature were completely forgotten when he caught a glimpse of Polly O'Neil crossing the street in front of him. Though the broad-brimmed hat and dim light prevented him from seeing her face, no one would fail to recognize that mare she was riding.

When he reached the corner, Berk brought his horse to a halt, then rested his hand on the saddle horn and watched the beauty continue down the road. Now just where would she be headed this time of a morning? he wondered. Most folks were still settled warmly in their beds. She wouldn't be taking a bedroll and saddlebags if she planned to return soon.

Berk turned his horse back toward the bakery, then sank his heels into its sides. Polly was giving him just the opportunity he needed. Very soon she would be going by the name of Mrs. Fritz. And if Mums or Daniel got any ideas in their heads about sharing the money, they were going to be in for a big surprise.

As soon as he reached the house, Berk entered on cat paws. It only took a minute to grab his pistol and shove it into the waistband of his trousers. He might need it to convince Miss O'Neil that he was serious about them getting married. He grabbed a warm coat from the peg as he quietly sneaked back out of the house. He leapt onto his horse and had it in a full gallop before he'd even shoved his right foot in the stirrup.

Daniel also hurried out of the house. He'd heard Berk come in and he'd watched him leave. Berk was up to something and he was going to find out what that something was.

Berk's anger had long since reached its peak. For two hours he'd gone around pine trees, along streams and over rocks, trying to catch up with Polly. He'd never been much good at tracking, and she wasn't helping matters.

The woman had to be loco. She would be headed in one direction, then turn off in an entirely different direction.

Each time that happened, he'd had to search around until he located her mare's tracks or caught sight of a broken limb. It seemed as if she were lost, but that wasn't likely. No one would be stupid enough to take off into the wilds without knowing where they were going. No, she was trying to confuse anyone who might follow her, and she was doing a damn good job of it!

Again, Berk had to dismount. This time Polly had gone over a rocky area, and again he was going to have to pick her trail back up. Holding his horse's reins in one hand, he began looking around the outer portion of the rocks for anything that might give him a clue as to where she'd gone this time.

Five minutes later, he was still searching. He was so intent on planning ways to make Polly pay for all the trouble she'd caused him that he ignored how his horse was snorting and tugging on the reins.

Suddenly the sorrel reared up on his hind legs, taking Berk completely off guard. The horse's reins were pulled from his hand and all he could do was stand and watch the damn animal gallop away.

"Son of a bitch!" he yelled. He pulled off his hat and slapped it across his leg. Now he not only didn't have a mount, he wasn't even sure which way Auburn was! A loud scream sent shivers up his spine. He looked up at the rocky ledge above him. He grabbed for his pistol, but he was too late. The mountain lion had already made his leap.

Daniel also heard the big cat's scream and got a quick glimpse of Berk's horse running away. Daniel nudged his animal forward, but the beast was frightened and it took several minutes before Daniel could finally get him under control and moving forward.

When Daniel came upon the scene, the mountain lion was dragging Berk away. Daniel shot but missed. The cat turned loose of his kill and darted off.

Daniel slowly dismounted. There was no question that his brother was dead. His neck had been broken and his eyes had already glassed over. He was too mangled to return home.

Daniel glanced around for something he could use to dig a grave. After that, he'd go home, collect his things and make his way to Texas.

"Mr. Joshua!" Sable yelled to the tall man talking to Bidwell.

Joshua looked up at the woman running toward him. He didn't think he'd ever seen Sable run before.

"Mr. Joshua! Polly's gone! Somethin' terrible must have happened 'cause she left a note."

"But that's impossible." Joshua snatched the piece of paper Sable was waving in front of him.

"Well, what does it say?"

"I needed time alone to think," Joshua read aloud. "I'll be gone five days. Don't worry, I'm fine."

"I hope she's not in any kind of trouble," Bidwell said.

"What could she have to think about?" Sable asked.

Joshua grinned. "Marrying Ethan. She should have asked me. I could have told her it will never happen."

Sable reached over and squeezed Bidwell's hand. She had been right. Joshua wasn't about to let Ethan have Polly, that is, if nothing had happened to her.

Joshua glanced up to see if there were any clouds building. There were a few puffy ones, but nothing to worry about. "Sable, get me enough stores for a week. Polly has a habit of thinking she can go anywhere and ending up lost."

"I'll go with you," Bidwell offered.

"No, I can travel faster alone."

Sable's expression turned from worry to surprise. "You know where she's going?"

"No, but I intend to find out."

Joshua went in search of Zeek. He found the boy in back of the carriage house, sitting on the ground. His face was pale and he looked sickly. "What's wrong with you?" Joshua asked.

Zeek held up a tin. "I bought me some chawin' tobacco. Made me sick as hell."

"I did the same thing when I was young. Never touched the stuff after that."

"Oh, yeah?" Zeek felt better knowing that he wasn't the only one this had happened to.

"Where did Polly go, Zeek?"

"I don't know what you're talking about."

"I haven't time to fool around. You had to have noticed her horse was missing. I want an answer, and I want it now."

Zeek rose to his feet and dusted the dirt from the back of the new trousers Polly had bought for him. "Honestly, Mr. Joshua, if I tell you, I ain't gonna have a job."

"All right, let me put it differently. If you wanted to take a trip, where would you go?"

Zeek gave him a puzzled look then suddenly broke out in a smile. "Well, I reckon I'd like to go to Lake Tahoe."

"And what would be the best time in the morning to leave?"

"I reckon about five-thirty."

She had taken off right after she'd left him this morning. Joshua tossed the boy a gold piece.

Before Joshua rode away, he left instructions with Sable that should Ethan show up, tell him Polly had to go to Sacramento to visit with friends.

Polly sat on a rock, her elbow resting on her knee and her chin on her hand. Not once had she come upon a well-traveled trail. According to Ethan, people traveled up to the lake and back all the time. So there had to be some kind of road. She was probably lost. How could that have happened? This morning she'd headed in the direction the sun came up. Of course she'd had to make a few direction changes as it rose higher in the sky. But all she'd seen were trees and more trees. Even the mountains continued to get higher and higher and more difficult to climb. She hadn't even spotted any animals other than deer.

She sat up and stretched her back. She'd have to quit for today. It was turning uncomfortably cold and getting dark. She needed to make camp before it was too dark to see. She went to Duchess and untied the saddle strings that held her coat. After slipping it on, she unsaddled the mare and hobbled her. She giggled softly at remembering the last time she'd left Columbia. She felt sorry for that poor nag she'd left the buggy attached to. And she still wouldn't have known anything if it hadn't been for Joshua.

She began collecting wood to make a fire. There were a lot of things Joshua had taught her. It wasn't that she was dumb. If that were so, she could never have taught herself to read and write. No, the problem had been her lack of experience in so many things. And she still had so much to learn. One being to never again take off alone on a trip. It was doubtful she would ever learn direction. She so admired those men who went out on ships and ended up exactly where they had planned.

Once she had a fire going, Polly rolled out her bed, well away from the flame. She was terrified of the possibility of being burned again. But she had heard someone say that a traveler should always build a big fire at night. Not just for cooking, but also to keep hungry animals away.

Though she wasn't really hungry, she ate a couple of the cold biscuits she'd taken from the kitchen. The darkness now enveloped her, and she felt frightened and very alone.

Leaving everything on, including her coat and boots, she

lay on her bedroll and pulled the covers over her. Joshua should be here to keep her warm. That was ridiculous! Wasn't that what this trip was all about? Hadn't she wanted to get away from him? However, if she planned to do some thinking, she'd best get to it instead of constantly admiring the scenery. Tomorrow she was going to start back down the mountain. Heaven knows where she'd end up.

Polly looked up at the black sky, amazed at the multitude of stars. It was beautiful! Then she imagined seeing Joshua's eyes looking down at her, as if he were watching over her. She felt safe and protected. In a matter of minutes, she was sleeping peacefully.

Polly awoke feeling wonderful. She sat up and glanced around the forest as she inhaled the sweet smell of the trees. Her perusal came to rest on the man sitting on the ground with his back against a tree and looking right at her. She realized that somehow she'd known all along that Joshua would find her.

Polly smiled. "I shouldn't have made the trip alone, huh?"

Joshua grinned back at her. "With realization comes hope."

"How did you find me?"

"I'm very good at tracking. Your big fire did the rest of the work."

She raised her knees and wrapped her arms around them. "Zeek told you where I was going."

He stood, walked over to Polly, then held out his hand to her. She took it and allowed him to pull her up. Her arms circled his waist as he drew her to him.

"You know, you're even beautiful when you sleep. A claim few women could make." He leaned down and nibbled at her earlobe. "We fit perfectly together." His lips brushed the bend of her neck as he spoke.

Polly closed her eyes and tilted her head to the side so he'd have easy access. His hand cupped her buttocks as he accepted the invitation. He sucked on the sweet hollow of her neck and delighted in the taste of her soft, creamy white skin.

"Am I so wanton that all you have to do is hold me and I'm overcome with lust?"

"But being wanton is what I like the most about you." His tongue trailed a path to her lips, then she was kissing him back with the fervor of a woman besieged with desire. But when Joshua began unbuttoning her shirt, she pulled away, her breathing still heavy from the passion he had ignited.

"What's wrong?"

Polly leaned down and picked up the small wool horse blanket sitting by her bedroll. "I have a decision to make, but now that you're here my need for solitude is gone."

"What kind of a decision?"

"It's none of your business."

"Do you want me to leave?"

"Yes…I mean no." She settled the blanket on Duchess's back. "We both know I'm lost. I'm not even sure I could find my way back to Auburn."

"Then you want to go back?" he stated flatly.

"What does that mean? Where else would I go?" She picked up her saddle and was about to swing it on top of the blanket when Joshua took it from her hands. She stared in disbelief as he saddled the mare for her. This was an absolute first.

"I had thought that since we were already in the high country, I'd take you to see the lake." He tightened the girth. "But I'll warn you here and now, we've already shared too much for me to keep my hands off you." He crooked his arm around the saddle horn and stared at her. "So, what's it going to be?"

"But you're not being fair. Whether I go home or to the lake, you'll be with me."

Joshua's eyes traveled down her neck to the last button he'd released. "All kinds of thoughts race through my mind just knowing you aren't wearing a corset." His knowing eyes suddenly shot back up to hers. "I'm not really an unfair man, so I'll make you a proposition."

"You've never saddled my horse before. What are you up to? If need be, I'll go back down by myself, even if it takes a week."

"Next thing I know, you're going to say you don't want me to make love to you anymore. Aren't you even curious what the proposition is?"

Polly snatched up her bedroll and tied it behind the cantle. "All right, tell me and get it over with."

"Let me make love to you now, in the sunlight, and I'll never touch you again—unless you ask."

"No."

"You'd make it a lot easier on yourself if you agreed."

"Are you threatening me?"

"I simply mean that refusing something you really want can be awfully hard on a person."

"You think too highly of yourself."

Joshua pulled her back into his arms, and planted a kiss on her lips. When she backed away, her knees were still shaking. Would he always have this effect on her?

Furious at her weakness, Polly turned away. "You will never touch me again. I'm going to marry Ethan. I should have listened to my mind all along, instead of my body. I've always known that Ethan was the right man for me."

"You're a passionate woman, and I give you what you want."

Polly wasn't about to admit it was true. This was all her fault. For the past couple of weeks they'd made love every night, and now he expected her to perform when he was in the mood.

"Have I told you that you have the most perfect body of any woman I've ever known. Better yet, have I told you how much I love you?"

Polly didn't believe him. She didn't even believe the warm smile that accompanied his words.

"What? No reaction to my confession of love?" he asked, obviously amused. "One of these days, Polly O'Neil, you're going to learn to trust me. Tell me, had I asked after I kissed you, would you have willingly shed your clothes? You wanted me to make love to you, so why did you turn away?"

"That's all you think about! Bedding me! I wasn't fooling when I said I'm going to marry Ethan."

Hearing an eagle screech, Joshua looked up at the big bird flying above him. "So you've finally admitted that you can't have us both at the same time."

Polly flinched at hearing the truth spoken aloud. She wasn't proud of sleeping with Joshua while continuing on with her plans to wed Ethan.

"Did you come here to decide which one to give up?"

Polly tilted her chin up. His guesses were always so uncannily correct. "Yes, and as before, Ethan won."

Joshua became serious as he settled his black, penetrating eyes on her. "If you marry Ethan, you'll be back in my bed within a week. We both know that's your dilemma."

"That's not so," she stated angrily.

"To hell it isn't! What's wrong, Polly? Can't you even admit to yourself that I'm the man you really want?"

Polly spun around, fire dancing in her blue eyes. "You? Why would I want you when I can have Ethan? Maybe I'm using him to give me the kind of respectability I long for, but I'll make sure he never knows, and that he'll never regret marrying me!'' She straightened her shoulders and looked him straight in the eye.

"Why don't you just come right out and say you're using him?"

"He's not like you and the rest of the men I've known who are only interested in my body."

"Are you saying he's not? If that's so, how could you even think of him as a man?"

Polly narrowed her eyes and stepped toward him, wanting to slap that smug face. "I know you will find this hard to understand, but he respects me as a lady and is willing to wait until we're properly married. And even if nothing physical were to even happen, I'd still be content."

Joshua's bitter laughter was like a shot ringing through the pine trees. "Now you're really getting carried away with yourself."

"What's so damn funny?" Polly snatched the bridle from the ground. "I'm tired of listening to your comments. I'm going back home, either with or without you!"

"If you have no sexual attraction to Ethan, that means you haven't even thought of him in terms of making love."

Polly started to come back with a rebuttal, but couldn't. She suddenly realized Joshua was right. She had never thought *seriously* about making love with Ethan.

"I wonder why?" Joshua continued, his deep voice suddenly soft. "Could it be because I keep you content? Or are there even deeper reasons?"

His self-assuredness aggravated Polly. Again she opened her mouth to speak, but it took a minute before she managed to form words. "What are you saying?"

"I'm saying don't ruin our lives by making the wrong decision. Though you choose to ignore it, we both know that I meant it when I said I love you, and I believe you love me. Why are you afraid to admit it?"

Polly tried to fight the rays of hope that he was building

inside her. She wanted to stay angry at him. It was safer. But she couldn't. God help her, she did love him. But Ethan... She didn't bother to try and keep up her argument in Ethan's favor. Once again, Joshua had won out, and once again her heart soared from the pleasure of it.

When he held out his arms, Polly dropped the reins and ran to him. It felt so right when he wrapped his arms around her. She hugged him fiercely. An unspoken commitment had been made, and she prayed she had made the right decision.

After a few minutes of holding each other, Polly gently pushed him away. ''Joshua, what about the other woman you told me about? If I'm giving up Ethan, you have to give her up as well.'' Polly wasn't sure she wanted to hear his answer, but it was time she knew the truth.

Joshua chuckled. ''I thought you would have realized by now that the woman was you, my love.''

''You're just trying to avoid the question.''

''Not at all.''

Excitement ran up Polly's spine. ''You knew way back then that you wanted me?''

''I knew the first day I set eyes on you, but don't let it go to your head. Now button up your shirt while I fix us breakfast.''

''And coffee?''

''Absolutely.''

''Can I do anything to help?''

''Add some wood to the fire. We'll be enjoying our meal in no time.''

Bursting with happiness, Polly sat on the ground and fed wood she'd collected into the campfire. Her dilemma was over. Joshua loved her as much as she loved him. At least that's what she wanted to believe. She was afraid to question him further about his love. She wasn't going into this blindfolded. If they only had several months together, she'd be heartsick at the separation. She'd cry and carry on for days and weeks. But later, she'd relive all the wonderful memories she'd have to look back on. It wasn't going to be easy telling Ethan that she couldn't marry him. He was a good man. In many ways, a better man than Joshua. But Joshua had a fire in him that Ethan would never be able to conjure up. "When will we get to the lake?" she asked.

"This afternoon." He set the skillet on the hot coals, then leaned down and kissed her cheek.

Polly drew a heart in the dirt with a twig. If this new-found love was going to get off on the right foot, she knew she would have to tell Joshua about her past. They could never build a life together on lies. She took a deep breath and slowly let the air back out. Her next words could end how Joshua felt about her.

"Joshua, there's something I need to tell you. Before I knew you, I was a dance—"

"I don't want to know," Joshua cut her off. He turned the bacon he already had cooking. "If you tell me your secrets, I'll have to tell you mine. There is no past, only a beginning."

Polly felt cheated, but said no more. She didn't need to be told that Joshua didn't want to reveal his past. Maybe that information would come in time. She had a sneaky hunch that what he chose not to talk about was far worse than her being a dance hall girl.

Lake Tahoe was without a doubt the most beautiful place Polly had ever seen. The water was varying shades of green and as far as the eye could see. Polly had thought to bring a bar of scented soap, and was perfectly willing to bathe in the water as long as Joshua stayed by her side. She had planned to go in with her underclothing still on, but he talked her into shedding everything.

The plan quickly changed when Polly waded out and

discovered how cold the water was. She turned, ready to run back to the bank, but Joshua wouldn't permit it. Laughing, he carried her out a short distance, then settled her back on her feet. To her delight, he had her dunk her head in the water, then proceeded to wash her hair for her. After it was thoroughly rinsed, he scrubbed her back. The water heated up considerably when he reached around and glided his soapy hands over her sensitive breasts and gently nipped her shoulder. His hands slid down and disappeared below the water. She sucked in her breath when he washed between her legs. Once again Joshua had her body singing with desire.

Crouched, Joshua turned her around and lowered her body down onto his throbbing manhood. His need was every bit as strong as hers. As she worked her hips against him, her arms wrapped around his neck and they kissed deeply, unable to get enough of each other. She leaned back and he suckled the pink buds of her ripe breasts. ''You taste and feel so good. I've never known any woman who could make my blood race the way you can.''

His lips pressed against hers as he thrust deeply within her, sending them both into the world of exalted pleasure.

When the sun had dried them off, Polly sat up on the blanket and reached for her green flannel shirt. ''I must truly be a hussy.''

''Why do you say that?''

She looked down at Joshua. He was lying on his back. The fact that he had nary a stitch on didn't seem to bother him in the least. Polly looked across the lake and smiled. ''I so wanted to be a lady, but here I am, as naked as I was the day I was born, lying in the open for all to see.''

Joshua rolled over onto his side and laughed. ''I wouldn't allow you to be seen by others. You are only for my eyes to behold. Besides, we're in a hidden cove. There are trees all around us, and the land juts out on either side. Not to mention that the distance across the lake is too far to even worry about. You have to admit that the sun feels mighty good after the cold water.''

Polly didn't even bother to button her shirt. ''I wonder how long I've loved you.''

''You asked me about my woman, what about that man by the name of Chance Doyer? You said he was the only man you'd ever truly loved.''

''How did you remember his name?''

''When something is important to me, there's very little I forget.'' He sat up beside her. ''You also said you could never love another man.''

Polly turned and gave him a kittenish grin. ''And you once said I had never known what love really is. Which one of us do you think was right?''

''The one who stayed around until you came to the right conclusion.''

''You mean you've known for some time that I love you?''

''Some people never really know how deep their love is until it's put to the test. I think you're one of those people.''

''That's a strange thing to say. You said you loved me. Would such a statement apply to you?''

''Oh no. I know exactly how I feel.''

''And?''

''You're trying to get me to say I love you again.''

Polly tilted her head. ''What's wrong with that? I would feel a lot more comfortable about saying it to you.''

''There is nothing wrong with it. But there are some things we have no control over.''

Polly shuddered. ''You're beginning to scare me.''

Joshua pulled her back down onto the blanket and rolled on top of her. ''Yes, my redhead beauty. I am madly in love with you.'' He pushed her shirt back and ran his tongue across an inviting nipple.

Polly sat looking across the room at Ethan Webber. She felt as guilty as a child caught holding the candy he'd just stolen.

''Am I to be allowed the reason for your decision?''

''I'm so sorry, Ethan. I never wanted this to happen. I truly thought I was in love with you. When I realized I was only fooling myself, I had to tell you the truth. A marriage is difficult enough. And when there isn't a strong bond between the man and woman, it's made twice as hard.'' *Where had she heard that before?* ''You are too deserving a man to have to settle for that.''

Ethan stood and went over to where Polly sat on the armchair. He raised her hand and kissed her knuckles. ''Thank you for your honesty.''

''Did you love me, Ethan?''

''I believe so. But now I'll probably never know if it was truly love, or your beauty and charm that had me so fascinated.'' He smiled fondly. ''Goodbye, Polly.''

Polly pursed her lips as she watched Ethan leave the room. The least he could have done was lie and say he was madly in love with her. Had she chosen him over Joshua, the marriage would have been a complete disaster!

The following two months were the happiest Polly had ever known. She and Joshua went everywhere together. Polly had finally come to realize that there was a lot more to life than just respectability. The servants, and especially Sable, were excited that Polly had finally found the sense to take a good look at Joshua. There was no doubt in anyone's mind that the couple was madly in love.

Chapter Sixteen

Polly carefully walked over the rocky-bottomed shallows of the American River and onto the bank. Her wet underclothes clung to her body like a second skin. During their short stay at Lake Tahoe, she'd discovered a definite fondness for bathing in the fresh water.

"The water is cold," she called to Joshua, who lay under a big shade tree. She noticed he had pulled his trousers back on, something he normally didn't do after they'd made love, unless they were ready to return home. Something was definitely wrong. Joshua had been acting strange for the past couple of days. Maybe it was because she'd put on her underclothing before getting in the water. But she'd been afraid someone might see her. She was reaching for straws. Maybe he was tired of her and ready to move on. In all the time they'd been together, he'd never once mentioned marriage.

"Oh, that felt good," she said as she joined Joshua. "You should have gone in with me." She wiped back the wet hair clinging to her cheeks. "Surely this wonderful Indian summer can't last much longer."

Joshua remained silent. He couldn't put it off any longer. Today he had to tell Polly the truth. Every last dirty side of it. And he could do nothing to sway her opinion. It was against the rules. His hands were tied. He couldn't tell her that by falling in love with her he'd become a changed man. She wouldn't even recognize the man he was before she entered his life. But even though his life literally hung in the balance, he could not coax, woo, or threaten. If he did, whatever her decision, it would not be considered valid.

Polly lay beside Joshua and propped herself up on one elbow so she could look at him. His hands were crossed beneath his head and he was looking up at the cloudless sky. With a tapered nail, she twisted the short black chest hairs into tiny ringlets.

"Polly, how much do you love me?"

Her finger paused. "More than you love me."

"Enough to die for me?"

Polly laughed nervously. "That's a strange question. You've taken me to many wonderful deaths on more than one occasion." She sat up and proceeded to braid her hair. "For the first time in my life, I have everything I've ever—"

Joshua sat up and grabbed a handful of pebbles. One by one, he threw them into the center of the river.

"You're serious, aren't you?" Polly stopped fussing with her hair. "Are you in trouble? Do you need money or something? Joshua, I have—"

"I know what you have."

"But that's impossible."

"Is it?" He turned his head and looked directly at her. The ramifications of what he was about to say could cost him his life. But from the very start, it had all been a gamble. "I'm afraid that for us to stay together, you're going to have to prove the depth of your love."

"That sounds like a threat! Nothing could be that serious. I hate it when you try to manipulate me like this." She pulled her wool shirt on over the wet chemise. "Why

can't you just say what you want? I'll tell you what I want.
I want to stop this discussion right now and go back to the
house.''

"I'm going to tell you a story about what you, I and
Springtown have in common.''

Polly's eyes darkened at the mention of Springtown. That
old tentacle of fear was already starting to twist around her
neck, threatening to cut off her breath. ''I don't want to
hear any more. I'm leaving.''

"No, you're going to stay and listen to what I have to
say. The time for nurturing your love has run out. Don't
you want to know the answers to all the things you've
wondered about since we met?''

Polly was tempted, but something warned her that she
wouldn't like what she heard. She shook her head. ''You're
deliberately trying to scare me!''

"When we were up at the lake, you said you wanted to
tell me about your past. You were going to admit that you
were a dance hall girl before gaining your wealth.''

Polly chewed at her bottom lip. ''How could you know
that? You were in Columbia, weren't you?''

"It doesn't matter. What matters is that I'm ready to tell
you some things about me.''

"I said I don't want to hear any more!'' Polly started to
stand, but a powerful hand on her shoulder prevented it.
His set jaw was enough to warn her that he had no intention
of allowing her to go anywhere. But at the same time, she
could also see a strange sadness in his eyes. She folded her
legs beneath her and waited. ''Very well, say what you
want to say, and I hope you'll make it short.''

Joshua leaned back against the tree. ''I won't go into my
past other than to say I was raised a gentleman. From there
on, the story isn't pretty. What you need to know is that
from the moment we first met outside of Springtown, I've
used you.''

She sucked in her breath. Suddenly the memories of their first meeting flooded into her mind. "You came out of Springtown," she accused, her apprehension growing.

"Yes."

His voice was absolutely emotionless and it chilled her. "You're making this up to tease me. You know I can't stand much of this sort of thing. You're being cruel."

"Springtown never dies, Polly."

"And I suppose you're going to tell me Jack Quigley is still haunting the town?"

"No. He's gone. There are different people and different situations now. I made you forget about the circumstances of our first meeting."

"How?"

"Just knowing I did it will have to suffice."

Polly hugged her arms about her chest, trying to ward off the panic she was already feeling. "I always thought it was strange the way you knew when I was around or what I was thinking. What are you? The devil? An angel?"

Joshua raked his fingers through his hair. "Maybe both. See how the water rushes around those boulders stranded in the middle of the river? I'm like that. A man trapped between the living and the dead. I don't know what I am. I can't explain it."

"I don't understand."

"I don't, either. The one thing I do know is that I never grow old. At times I am like you, then I disappear. I can see my surroundings, but no one else can see me."

Polly thought of all the times she turned to tell him something or when she searched but could never find him. "Blessed Lord! You're a ghost!" She scrambled to her feet, but she wasn't quick enough. Joshua grabbed her ankle. Desperately she kicked at his hand, trying to free herself, but slowly she was being dragged back to him. She could swear his eyes had turned red. She screamed, twisted, dug her fingers in the thick grass, but none of it had any effect. She held her breath, determined to pass out and avoid having to face the demon she had thought she loved.

"All right, Polly," Joshua said in a thunderous voice, "we'll have to handle this a different way." Polly faintly heard the words as she passed out.

But to Polly's shock, everything didn't turn black. It was as if she were in a dream, surrounded by a thick fog. She looked over her shoulder, instinctively knowing Joshua would be there. There had to be a way of escaping. She started running but couldn't even see where her feet were landing, and she didn't seem to be going anywhere. There was no escape.

"This time you can't escape me. Not with your mind or your body."

She turned and faced him. "The dreams were real!" she gasped.

"Yes. We shared our souls with nothing to prevent us from doing whatever we pleased. Your passion was ripe for the taking, and I took it. And you can never deny you savored every minute of it. You couldn't get enough of me, even when you were planning to marry Ethan."

Polly tried to run forward, determined to scratch his eyes out for what he was putting her through. But once again she was going nowhere. She couldn't even reach him. Drowning in defeat, she stopped fighting and looked him in the eye. It wasn't fair that he could make her want him so desperately. Even her fear couldn't erase the overwhelming desire she still felt to once again let his hands glide over her body.

Joshua laughed bitterly. "Can't you see, my dear, that it is the dark side that draws you to me? The danger, the unknown? How much of it is truly love, and how much is only what I give you in bed?"

Polly lowered her head. "I...I don't know," she answered truthfully.

"We will soon find out." He walked up to her and took her hands in his. "Look into my eyes, Polly, and listen."

Polly gazed into the black, fathomless pits, then suddenly she was standing in what appeared to be a desert. There was a ferocious storm, and sand was blowing and covering everything. But she couldn't feel it. Then she realized she was witnessing a scene. The mules and a wagon of some sort were slowly being covered. She shuddered at the sound of screams that slowly died as sand filled in the holes and gaps that were still left open. She wanted to go dig the men out but knew she was helpless. Tears began streaming down her cheeks as she watched everything being covered like a blanket. Yet she could hear Joshua's deep voice talking to her.

"I was in that wagon, but I made a pact with the devil to live. My soul for the gold and a traitor's life. But for some reason I can't explain, I was given a way to escape the devil. If I could find a woman who would be willing to make a supreme sacrifice for me, I could keep my soul and become human again.

"So I waited, because I knew the woman would be selected for me. In the meantime, I came back here to the desert and collected the gold. When I came upon Springtown, I hid the gold in an old mine shaft for safekeeping. As the years passed, I never aged, I came and went as I pleased, and I never again wanted for money."

"Is it the gold we took?"

"No. You only found a part of it."

"I don't want to hear any more!" Polly closed her eyes and put her hands over her ears, but still the voice continued.

"You were the chosen one. I was riding down the main street of Springtown when I saw you and your friend approaching. To this day, I'm not sure how any of this works, but I knew you were the woman who had been selected for me. I also knew I had been given a seemingly impossible task.''

Polly opened her eyes. The storm had stopped, and she could see a man walking away from the buried wagon, the heat waves from the desert floor distorting his image. Then he disappeared. She didn't have to ask who the man was.

Joshua came back into focus. ''So you waited until I moved to Auburn to see me again,'' she stated bitterly. Somehow, it all seemed so clear now.

''I knew there was only one way I could get you to make the sacrifice.''

Polly already knew the answer. ''Have me fall in love with you.''

Joshua nodded. ''But the devil still had a trick up his sleeve.''

''What was that?''

''He turned the tables. It was I who fell in love with you.''

Polly's heart was pounding against her chest. Was he telling the truth or was this just another ruse to get her to do his bidding? ''How can I ever again believe anything you say? What I thought was real wasn't. You were only playing tricks on me. You've gone too far this time.''

''I haven't finished.''

''Very well, Joshua. What is it you want of me?'' She was trying to choke down the fear she now felt of him.

''I want you to give up the one thing that means even more to you than I do.''

''There is nothing.''

''Oh, but there is.''

''What?''

''Your money.''

Polly blinked. "What about my money?" she asked suspiciously.

"I want you to prove your love by being willing to return all of it to Springtown. Listen to your heart, Polly. Think of the future we could have together."

"Future?" Polly's anger removed all fear. "And what will happen if I don't?"

"I'm damned to hell."

"I have no doubts that you are what you say you are. I haven't met a ghost yet that wasn't up to some kind of no good." She kicked at the air in frustration. "Just how long would we be together? Until you decided to disappear again? Or maybe until you've had time to collect the gold that you think I'd be foolish enough to put back, assuming I could even find Springtown!"

"Only you can decide what's right for yourself, and just how much I mean to you."

"You should be able to answer that without me having to do a thing," she said acidly. "After all, you're the one who always knows what I'm thinking."

"I lost the power when I fell in love with you."

"You were very good at the way you handled everything. Did you know how I sat in my room longing for you, and the hell I went through thinking everything was a damn dream? Answer me, dammit!"

"I knew."

She angrily brushed away the tears. "Lord, how I hate you for this. And what about the times you were ready to leave, and stupid me kept finding jobs for you to do so you'd stay. You must have been laughing the entire time. Are you going to deny that?"

"No."

Polly rubbed the back of her neck. "What other little things did you do that I wasn't even aware of? The poison oak! The horseback riding! Did you put that into my head?''

Polly saw his nod. She could think of nothing she wanted more than to slap his face. Then an astonishing thought suddenly occurred to her. ''You got rid of my suitors. You took me to the ball so I'd see what kind of man Malcolm was. Did you also kill him?''

''No.''

''Next thing I know you'll be telling me you're incapable of killing any man.''

''I assure you, I'm quite capable.'' He wanted to add that he'd changed since meeting her. He no longer wanted anything but for the two of them to be together.

''And Ethan. You took me to Lake Tahoe so I'd pick you instead of him! You had no intention of allowing me to marry him, did you?'' she demanded.

''You're right. I would never have allowed the wedding.''

''I can see it all so clearly now.''

Joshua smiled evilly. ''I always knew you were a smart woman.''

''You bastard! Aren't you going to say anything in your defense?''

''There's nothing to say.''

''I never knew anyone could stoop so low. You didn't make a pact with the devil. You are the devil! Well, you picked the wrong woman to fool around with. You're not getting anything of mine, including my money! Now get out of my life and never come back!''

''Is that your final word?''

''You damn well know it is! And don't bother trying to change my mind! I loathe the thought of you ever touching me again,'' she whispered.

Polly awoke and discovered she was lying on the ground. She sat up and quickly looked around. Joshua and his horse were nowhere in sight. She could clearly remember her dream, but this time she knew it was no dream. She also knew Joshua was gone forever. "Good riddance," she hissed.

With her undergarments already dry, Polly snatched up her trousers and yanked them on. "Give my money up, indeed. I'd never be that big a fool for any man!"

For the next two weeks, Polly kept going on pure energy. She even went to Mrs. Fritz's bakery for a sugar cookie, but there was a new owner. She shopped at every store, seldom buying a thing, did a lot of riding and attended social teas.

At Mrs. Cook's house, Polly and Abigail Webber had found themselves alone in the corner of the spacious sitting room.

"I'm surprised you're even talking to me," Polly said before taking a bite of cake.

"Nonsense. You did the right thing, considering your feelings. I believe you did Ethan a favor. One of the things I admired about you from the first was your straightforwardness. And besides, I know of no other woman who works in a garden wearing men's clothing."

Polly laughed gently, remembering their first meeting. "And Ethan? How is he getting along? Though I broke off the wedding, I am still very fond of him. He's a wonderful man."

"A couple of days ago, he had to go to the Graham ranch to see about some sort of legal problem. Please don't take this personally, my dear, but he came home absolutely beaming." Abigail sipped her tea. "He couldn't stop talking about the Graham girl. Anne, I believe her name is. Seems she and her father are raising horses for the army and personal sales. Did Ethan ever tell you that he planned to one day have a ranch of his own? The boy has a great affection for horses.''

''No, he never mentioned it.''

''I hope something comes of it. I do so want to see great-grandchildren before I die.''

By the third week, Polly was running out of momentum. Now that Sable had married Bidwell, there never seemed to be anyone to talk to. Loneliness was quickly settling in.

Polly spent more and more time in the library reading, trying to get interested in one book, then another. But even the books failed to hold her attention. She forgot about food, and Vera often had to hunt her down to remind her it was time to eat.

She had tried not to think about Joshua, or anything that had transpired between them. But the memories slowly returned. She missed Joshua telling her what colors looked best on her, or the compliments he would give when she least expected them. The feel of his strong arm around her waist as he taught her to ride. Grabbing her ankle and playfully knocking her to the ground.

As the little memories returned, they peeled away the armor she'd surrounded herself with, allowing other memories to flood forth when she least expected them. While gardening, she thought about how Sam had handled her like a concubine. But from the first day she and Joshua had met, he had treated her like a lady.

Everywhere she went, she was reminded of Joshua. As she rode across the land during the day, she felt vulnerable because before, she had always had Joshua to protect her. And nights were a living hell as she remembered the ecstasy of their lovemaking.

It was her bedtime when Sable stepped into the sitting room and stood watching Polly doing fine needlework by the light of a single lamp. Something had to be done. Her mistress was wasting away.

"Polly O'Neil, you're gonna ruin your eyes."

Polly laid her stitchery in her lap. "What do you want, Sable?"

"I want you to do something with yourself! You're lookin' like some scarecrow. You're gettin' too thin, and you've got dark circles under your eyes. This is worse than when you thought Mr. Joshua was dead. You don't do nothin' anymore but stay in the house. Why don't you go ridin' and get out in the sun? Or work in the garden with Bidwell like you used to? It's been nearly two months since Mr. Joshua left—"

"I've told you, I don't want to discuss that man." She picked the Berlin work back up and proceeded to run the colored wool thread through the tiny holes in the paper.

"I wish I knew were he was, 'cause I'd send Bidwell to go fetch him." Sable moved forward, and stopped in front of the armchair Polly was sitting in. "Polly, honey, I can't stand seeing you do this to yourself."

Hearing the hurt in Sable's voice was Polly's undoing. Deep, gut-wrenching sobs burst forth from her, shaking her entire body. She leaned forward and wrapped her arms around Sable's hips and pressed her head against her stomach. She could no longer hide her pain.

It was two in the morning when Sable leaned down and kissed the cheek of the sleeping woman. She pulled the covers up under Polly's chin. Polly moved her head but didn't wake up. She was too exhausted. Sable left the room and quietly closed the door behind her.

Polly awoke in the early morning hours. She wasn't surprised to see Sable had left her room. The house was quiet. She felt relieved that everyone was still asleep.

She climbed off the bed, put her robe on and walked to the window. She frowned. It was January now, and the weather was cold.

She looked down at the carriage house as she'd done so many times before. Somehow she'd expected to see candlelight coming from Joshua's window. Or what used to be Joshua's window. She closed her eyes and leaned her shoulder against the windowsill. Strange that she no longer felt stark terror at the thought of a ghost. Thinking about Springtown still made her uncomfortable, but the fear she'd known since childhood had disappeared. She realized it had been gone since she'd last talked to Joshua and let her anger take over.

She thought she saw something move past Joshua's window. She strained her eyes to get a better look, but there was no more movement. ''Joshua?'' she whispered. ''Is that you? Have you come back?'' An owl hooted and Polly jumped. Was Joshua capable of becoming an owl? No. That was ridiculous.

She turned away from the window and began pacing the floor. She'd already asked herself a hundred times if Joshua had truly loved her. That was the part that hurt the most.

The following night's sleep didn't come at all. Polly continued to pace, unaware that the rest of the household was also awake, listening to the pat of her bare feet on the floor. By not giving up her money, had she truly condemned Joshua to eternal hell?

Why couldn't Joshua have been kinder when he told her the truth? Why couldn't he have coaxed her into it as he had so many other things. At least leave her with the belief that he really had cared for her. Was that too much to ask?

Polly wanted to feel Joshua's arms around her. She wanted him to take her in his arms and tell her everything was going to be all right. She needed him with her. The loneliness was driving her mad. She knew now how much she had taken him for granted. She had thought he would always be close by. Even when she had planned to marry Ethan, it hadn't occurred to her that Joshua wouldn't still be there when she needed him.

Selfish was a perfect word for her attitude. She'd even loved him because of the physical pleasures he gave her.

For the next two weeks, it seemed to Polly that she did nothing but cry. She didn't even know if the crying was over the possibility of losing her money or if it had to do with losing Joshua. Sable managed to get her to eat soups, which Polly was convinced only turned into more tears. More than once she called Joshua's name, asking him to at least talk to her, but she couldn't reach him.

Toward the end of the second week, Polly started allowing the pieces of her scattered thoughts to fit together. She had never allowed herself to peek at just how deep her love for Joshua was. Instead she'd convinced herself she could walk away from it at any time and never look back. What a fool's paradise she'd been living in. Now she was suffering the consequences.

Have I destroyed him because I didn't return the gold? she wondered. Is he gone? What was he that he could make strange things happen?

Just the thought of spending the rest of her life without Joshua made living seem useless. And the money? What good was it? It couldn't bring her happiness. But it might possibly give her back the man she truly loved. Maybe it was all a trick, but she'd never know until she got rid of it. There were two big problems. She didn't know how to find Springtown, and she had no way of contacting Joshua. She had even tried saying that she was his for all eternity, but still nothing happened.

As the days passed, slowly Polly started to eat and sleep

more, but each night she fell asleep begging Joshua to come back to her.

"You're still too thin," Sable scolded as she helped Polly into the stagecoach headed for Sacramento. "But I think you're doin' the right thing. I'll take care of everything on this end, so you stay as long as you want at Mr. Chance and Mrs. Amanda's place. Maybe they can put some meat on your bones."

Polly smiled at her friend. "I promise I'll take care of myself."

With tears streaming down her cheeks, Sable nodded and backed away so the other passengers could board.

The driver and the man riding shotgun climbed up front. The brake was released and the reins were slapped across the team's shiny backs. A moment later all that was left was a cloud of dust. Sable turned and went back to the carriage.

"Is Miss Polly going to be all right?" Thomas asked.

"I hope so," Sable replied.

The ride was rough and jarring, but Polly was to the point of being numb after all she'd gone through during the past months. Accepting that she would never see Joshua again wasn't coming easily.

She looked out the window and watched the scenery pass by, and somehow managed to snooze off and on. At one time she said, "I love you, Joshua," and her eyes flew open, not sure whether or not she'd spoken aloud. But if she had, no one seemed to have noticed.

"We're going to all die!"

The shouting woke Polly out of a sound sleep and her eyes flew open. The short bald man sitting across from her had turned chalk white, and his eyes glistened with stark fear.

"I can see them! They're gaining on us!"

Then Polly heard the exchange of gunfire. The stage was being robbed! The bald man hurt her legs as he tried to crouch down on the floorboard to keep from being hit. The two men sitting in the center had become as stiff as statues, while the two men next to the other door had their pistols out, ready to make a fight of it.

Sheer black fright swept through Polly. Everything seemed so noisy she could hardly hear anything but more and more bullets being fired. The man across from her whimpered, "I don't want to die."

Out of the corner of her eye, she saw something move. She looked out the window. Two of the bandits rode up alongside. One of them managed to grab hold of something on the stage and pulled himself from the saddle. Polly slammed her back against the seat to avoid any contact. But when the outlaw placed his foot in the window opening to boost himself up to the top, she reached up and gave the boot a hard shove. The man lost his balance and fell to the ground.

Everything seemed to be mayhem. There were screams, and two of the men in the coach were shot. The stagecoach was traveling at a wild speed and Polly wasn't even sure they had a driver any longer. To her horror, the panicked bald man opened the door and jumped out in a desperate flight for freedom.

With the door flapping open, Polly could see the ground flying by beneath stage wheels. Again she pushed against the back of the seat, this time to keep from falling out. In desperation, she squeezed her eyes shut and covered her ears with her hands. Time seemed to stand still.

Ever so slowly, Polly realized that the stagecoach wasn't moving. She opened an eye and looked out the door. The ground was still. Carefully she removed her hands. Everything had become unnaturally quiet. She leaned forward and cautiously looked out the window. A single man was quietly sitting on his horse some distance away. The sun was behind him, making it impossible to see anything but a dark shadow, but she knew Joshua had finally come for her.

Her fear gone, Polly climbed out of the coach and walked toward the man she would now honestly be willing to die for. He'd known. He'd known all along the hell she would have to go through before she accepted the truth. Her true love was Joshua, not the money. She started running. Dear God, she'd thought she'd lost him forever.

"Oh, Joshua, you've come back! I'll give up the money! I don't want it if I can't have you."

"Polly, darlin', I never said you had to give up the money, I said you had to be willing to give it up."

"Then you'll stay with me?"

"Don't you know by now that I love you and I would never allow anything or anyone to take you from me?"

Polly's heart soared at hearing such wonderful words. She glanced back at the stagecoach. To her horror, several lifeless bodies could clearly be seen. Besides the ones on the ground, the stage driver lay across the seat, and the man riding shotgun was draped over the front.

"We have to go see if we can help anyone!"

Polly started forward, but Joshua moved his big black horse in front of her. "No, Polly, they're beyond help now."

Upon seeing so many dead, Polly wondered how she'd managed to live. Her eyes became large blue circles as she looked up at Joshua. "Am I dead?"

"Does it matter?"

"Never, as long as we're together."

Joshua laughed, a full robust laugh that carried through the air like thunder. He kicked his foot out of the stirrup, and Polly used it to climb up behind him. With her arms wrapped safely around his waist, he reined the black about and nudged him into a gallop.

The gods looked down at the couple below. Love had once again prevailed over evil. They were pleased.

* * * * *

MILLS & BOON®

Makes any time special™

**Mills & Boon publish 29 new titles
every month. Select from...**

Modern Romance™   Tender Romance™

Sensual Romance™

Medical Romance™ Historical Romance™

MAT2

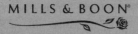

MILLS & BOON®

Historical Romance™

ROSALYN AND THE SCOUNDREL
by Anne Herries

A Regency delight!

Miss Rosalyn Eastleigh yearned for adventure beyond the narrow confines of Society life. She was irresistibly drawn to the mysterious Damian, Earl Marlowe, though he was a man who could severely damage her reputation!

CARNIVAL OF LOVE
by Helen Dickson

Maxim Purnell was a man who thrived on taking risks and Lavinia Renshaw's proposal of marriage piqued his curiosity. She intended it to be a convenient arrangement only, but what if Maxim decided to make her his wife for real?

On sale 2nd March 2001

FREE!

2 Books
and a surprise gift!

We would like to take this opportunity to thank you for reading this Mills & Boon® book by offering you the chance to take TWO more specially selected titles from the Historical Romance™ series absolutely FREE! We're also making this offer to introduce you to the benefits of the Reader Service™ —

- ★ FREE home delivery
- ★ FREE gifts and competitions
- ★ FREE monthly Newsletter
- ★ Books available before they're in the shops
- ★ Exclusive Reader Service discounts

Accepting these FREE books and gift places you under no obligation to buy; you may cancel at any time, even after receiving your free shipment. Simply complete your details below and return the entire page to the address below. *You don't even need a stamp!*

YES! Please send me 2 free Historical Romance books and a surprise gift. I understand that unless you hear from me, I will receive 4 superb new titles every month for just £2.99 each, postage and packing free. I am under no obligation to purchase any books and may cancel my subscription at any time. The free books and gift will be mine to keep in any case.

HIZEB

Ms/Mrs/Miss/Mr ....Initials................................
BLOCK CAPITALS PLEASE

Surname..

Address..

....

....Postcode ....

Send this whole page to:
UK: The Reader Service, FREEPOST CN81, Croydon, CR9 3WZ
EIRE: The Reader Service, PO Box 4546, Kilcock, County Kildare (stamp required)

Offer not valid to current Reader Service subscribers to this series. We reserve the right to refuse an application and applicants must be aged 18 years or over. Only one application per household. Terms and prices subject to change without notice. Offer expires 31st August 2001. As a result of this application, you may receive further offers from Harlequin Mills & Boon Limited and other carefully selected companies. If you would prefer not to share in this opportunity please write to The Data Manager at the address above.

Mills & Boon® is a registered trademark owned by Harlequin Mills & Boon Limited.
Historical Romance™ is being used as a trademark.